EVACUATION DAY
&
THE LOST DEED TO MANHATTAN

A NOVEL BY

JEFFREY RUBINSTEIN

D1307986

The facts

A militia during the Revolutionary War was charged with the duty to protect Manhattan. A secret alliance formed the group's core. This group raided Fort Amsterdam at the tip of the Manhattan shoreline, now known as the Battery. Publicly, it was reported that only a cannon was removed from the location. Analysis varied, but within a year, the Thirteen Colonies declared independence from the British.

Following the formation of the new nation, this militia merged into the United States Army. It is now known as the 1st Battalion, 5th Field Artillery – the country's oldest military unit.

The truth

Author's note to the Reader
The historical information contained in this novel is based on factual discoveries of past historians. All historical references and locations in this novel are real. References to the locations on Manhattan are based on the Author's observations. However, discussion of subterranean tunnels and passageways are based on reasoned and plausible historical analysis. Requests to investigate these potential tunnels and passageways were not requested by the Author on the basis of a presumed denial by the requisite authorities.

Enjoy,
Jeffrey Rubinstein

CONTENTS

August 15, 2003 - Friday

Chapter 42: DUROE LEVELS WITH MICHAEL – Friday, August 15, 2003 12:25am

Chapter 43: LATE NIGHT RUN TO HAMILTON GRANGE – Friday, August 15, 2003 1:01am

Chapter 44: SID GOES TO THE INSTITUTE – Friday, August 15, 2003 1:05am

Chapter 45: DUROE GETS THE PUMPS GOING – Friday, August 15, 2003 2:00am

Chapter 46: SID'S DISCOVERY OF THE MEANING OF 'HEARTS OF OAK' – Friday, August 15, 2003 2:01am

Chapter 47: KIDS AND DIRJKE GO TO THE GRANGE – Friday, August 15, 2003 3:00am

Chapter 48: DANNY AND BARRY ON HAMILTON TERRACE – Friday, August 15, 2003 3:31am

Chapter 49: SID AT HAMILTON'S HOUSE – Friday, August 15, 2003 3:35am

Chapter 50: CONFRONTATION AT HAMILTON'S HOUSE – Friday, August 15, 2003 3:40am

Chapter 51: SID TO THE UKRANIAN INSTITUTE – Friday, August 15, 2003 3:50am

Chapter 52: SID TORTURES VLAD – Friday, August 15, 2003 4:02am

Chapter 76: DIRJKE AND THE KIDS EXIT – Friday, August 15, 2003 7:30pm

June 7, 2008 - Sunday

Chapter 77: A NEW HEARTS OF OAK IS FORMED – Sunday, June 7, 2008 12:00pm

PROLOGUE

The old mansion had a secret. They all do. It was a classic stone structure built as a mansion for an oil titan. Now, it was home to someone else. The Ukrainian Institute had bought this mansion on 2 East 79th Street in New York, along Museum Mile.

Vlad's father, Igor, had let the young man stay home from school that day, August 11, 1954.

"Dad, what parade are we going to watch?"

"The parade for the Knights of Pythias can wait, son."

"Who are they?"

"They are just another group with power, son." Igor finished putting photos into an envelope to exchange with a contact amongst the crowd. Then he reached into the drawer on his left behind a weathered oak desk.

"I have something that I must show you. We found these when we remodeled the inside of the old building for the Ukrainian Institute a few months ago. Someday we will figure out what they mean."

Igor showed his son the object. It had the diameter of a small plate.

"So?" asked Vlad, looking up at his father.

"These are the crests of the prior owner of this house."

"So, Father, it looks like a tree with objects in the lower portion. Sometimes I have dragged my pencil over a quarter while in school. Maybe this will help us figure out the picture."

"That is a good idea, son, but turn it over."

"It has '12:25-27' etched on the reverse side."

"What do you think it means?"

"I don't know son."

"Who used to live here?"

"Augustus Van Horn Stuyvesant."

"As the director of the Institute, I have a duty to carry out the organization's true goal."

"What is that?"

"If I am successful, you will not have to find out."

Chapter 1

ENTER VLAD
Monday, August 11, 2003 10:00am

Vlad had just flipped the channel to watch TV channel NY1. The story had been running for a few days now in newspapers and press outlets. "The Mayor's press conference is to center around questions regarding a cylindrical object found in downtown Manhattan," stated the reporter on the screen.

He clicked off the TV with his remote and tossed it on the couch in his office. Then he reached into his pocket and dialed his instructed numbers into his phone.

"Mayor's office, Marjorie here."

Vlad sat in the chair behind the same desk his father had occupied at the Institute's headquarters on Museum Mile. It was paneled with dark wood about one third of the way up the wall. The remaining portion was a golf-green color that juxtaposed nicely with the red carpet. "I need to speak with the Mayor."

"He is a very busy man," answered Marjorie.

"Tell him that the man who plans to take New York back four centuries is on the phone."

"What?" asked Marjorie. Her eyes locked onto the trinkets on her desk, which included a New York City stress ball with the year 1625 on it. Chills went through her body, as she shook her head.

"Who are you? Some brand of terrorist?"

Vlad chuckled at the question. "No, a terrorist is simply lost in the struggle for his own self-promotion. I assure you, I am far more established and dangerous than that."

"One moment." Marjorie contacted her boss and connected the two men.

"Michael here," said New York's 108th mayor from behind his desk, with the speaker phone on in the northwest corner of City Hall.

"Mr. Mayor, I understand you have found something at the South Ferry Terminal construction project."

"What is your name?" The Mayor took his phone off speaker and lifted the receiver to his ear.

"You can call me Homer. I will get right to the point. You have until 4:12pm Thursday to formally surrender the island, or New York will be brought into the 1600s."

"What do you mean, Mr. Homer, or whatever?" said the Mayor, with a small tremble in his voice.

"I have told you enough. It is time for you to do your homework," answered Vlad. "You will hear from me tomorrow." The phone went *click*.

"Good work," announced the voice on the line listening in to Vlad's conversation with the Mayor.

"Thank you, Zeke."

Chapter 2

ENTER SID
Monday, August 11, 2003 11:00am

The Pentagon contains a little known and purposely silent Office of Internal Security. Sid Milliken held the chief position. This man had entered the final third of his life. However, it was his accomplishments in the first two-thirds that gave him his reputation.

His office was minimalist and barren. Sid sat behind a glass desk on a black chair. His desk consisted of a computer screen and a phone. The voice recognition software installed on his computer eliminated the need for a keypad or a mouse. The walls were white and empty. There was no identifying object that could link Sid to the office he had entered six months ago.

Reaching for the intercom, he called into the microphone, "Hoffson, I am going to New York."

"It's General Hoffson. Now Sid, I know you are an intelligence man at heart, but you have to learn at least a slight bit of military conduct. I oversee the department that houses your office."

"I know, General. It is a bureaucratic nuisance that scarcely exists in the intelligence world."

"You are no longer officially a part of that world. Got it?"

"Okay," answered Sid. "I made my lodging arrangement at my standard location. It's no different."

"Military officials have arrangements with various business fronts all over the country. We don't have the benefit of secrecy, Sid. We are forced to hide our true intent within the shadows of national security."

"Even though you were on the military side and I was part of the dark arts, I know we agree that the American media carried the image of the Soviet Empire long past its prime."

"The media is its own beast," answered Hoffson. "I can't comment."

"Still the result cannot be disputed. American's fear and vigilance toward the Soviet Empire saved American lives."

"So onto Manhattan?" asked Hoffson.

"Yeah, no doubt you read the press release as well. Like I briefed you yesterday, since 1849 there has been an official story regarding the purchase of Manhattan. It's in the Federal Government's interest to maintain that story."

"I will do what is necessary."

"Sid, that is too vague a response. The military depends on directions and orders."

"So does that intelligence world, General. I would not have lasted as long as I have in that business if I didn't do my job. I will report to you when I have or need additional information."

"You'd better," answered Hoffson. "Don't forget I outrank you. You are a member of the military now."

"May I go?" asked Sid.

"Dismissed," answered Hoffson as he slammed his phone into the holster.

Sid placed the phone back. He looked at the wristwatch he received on the day he graduated from college. In the center was the Yale crest and motto; in the shadows was a hologram that few ever noticed. He had ten minutes until his next appointment.

*   *   *

Sid was walking in front of the United States Treasury Building when his contact walked up next to him. The sun was shining over this Washington, DC sidewalk. Cars were moving in front of the entrance plaza to the building at 1500 Pennsylvania, not far from the White House.

"Good to see you old friend. Nice watch." It was identical to his. "Zeke, have you kept up your side of this?"

Zeke was a late middle aged man. He was in average shape with jet black hair and a reddish hue on his skin. He was wearing a tan summer suit on this humid day.

"Yes, well, all the arrangements have been made," answered Sid.

"So it's true the real Manhattan Project is a go," replied Zeke.

"Together we will complete something grand. Not even Mr. Alphonso Taft himself would dare dream this big."

"I know. You do your job and I will do mine." The men went their separate ways at the corner.

Chapter 3

THE PHONE CALL
Monday, August 11, 2003 3:30pm

The ringing phone was not the typical hotel wake-up sound, but the more computerized tone associated with a 21st century phone system. Collegiate School had just updated the phone system. It was not a change that Professor Dirjke had adapted to with ease.

"Martin here, how can I help you?"

"Marty, it's Michael."

Recognizing the voice, Dirjke asked, "How is my favorite mayor?"

"Good. Are you going to be at the ceremony on Wednesday?"

"It is unlike you not to engage in some pleasantries before business talk. What ceremony?"

"The ceremony at the United States Customs House. Don't tell me you are ignoring the Mayor's emails? Just because we have known each other since grade school, doesn't give you the right to ignore my emails."

"I was not ignoring your emails, Michael. I simply did not think you were this interested in me being there. After all, Native American artifacts are a little far afield, no? I thought it was a courtesy email. I mean you are a politician, now."

"Marty, I need you to be there, okay?"

"Absolutely," the professor exclaimed, turning instantly toward his computer and email account.

The find function on Dirjke's computer was one of the few that the professor could employ. It allowed him to find any email. More importantly for Dirjke, it obviated the need for him to maintain a list of contacts. Everyone's name, address, and phone number were all a find function away.

"Okay, Michael. August 13, 2003. What time should I be there? It says the ceremony starts at 11:00."

"Meet me at 9:00am at City Hall. I will leave your name with security – and arrive hungry. I will have your favorite."

"Thanks. You know the Stage Door Deli is on the way. I can…"

"Nonsense," retorted Michael. "See you then."

After the receiver met the phone, Dirjke pressed his lips together and said out loud, "Damn it. Of all the times, Danny is visiting me this week."

Still, Dirjke felt a strange thrill that his old friend had contacted him, a call that Dirjke did not anticipate. He was a man of routine. However, he laughed to himself and said, "If you are coming to New York, it's best to start at the top."

Dirjke turned his nose to his desk and went back to work preparing lesson plans for the upcoming school year.

Chapter 4

BARRY CALLS DIRJKE
Monday, August 11, 2003 5:00pm

"Argh, this damn phone has been ringing all day," Dirjke muttered out loud in his office. It was 5 o'clock. His bag was packed to go home. His desk was still covered in stacks of paper. There was a small light hovering over the center of his desk, still hot to the touch.

"Marty Dirjke here." He was standing over his desk with his phone to his ear.

"Professor, it is Barry Jasper."

"Barry, you don't need to tell me your first and last name. I know who you are," laughed Dirjke.

"Okay, it is just that you must have taught more than one Barry during your career."

"Actually, no," replied Dirjke. "I don't recall having another student named Barry. And I know you know this, but I have never had a student like you. How has your summer been?"

"It has been good. I am volunteering at the New York Historical Society. I really like it. Did you know that most of their collection isn't even on display?"

"I know. Do you know what the most interesting piece on display is?" teased Dirjke. "It is subtle. Contained within the New York Historical Society is the only version I have seen of the eagle on the United States Seal with its head turned the wrong way."

"You mean the eagle is looking at the…"

"Yup," interrupted Dirjke. "Let me know when you find it."

"Will do."

"You know, Professor, we talked all summer about having lunch together and discussing my course load for my sophomore year."

"Barry, you are at Harvard. I am a Bulldog. Surely there is someone better to counsel you."

"Well, if I get into Yale Law School, maybe we will share an alma mater," said Barry. It was enough for Dirjke to accept the invitation.

"Let's have lunch on Thursday. I will be free then."

"Awesome."

"Oh, one more thing, Barry. I got an email from the Mayor about an artifact that was found during the excavation of the new South Ferry Terminal. It doesn't seem like my cup of tea, but the Mayor asked me to attend. You should come too. Are you still with Nadine?"

"No. She is studying abroad in Australia. I am not happy that she decided to leave the country for six months. I respect her decision to see the world, but she was crushed when I said that I would not maintain a long-distance relationship for that amount of time."

"Barry, my deceased wife Samantha and I became best friends before we ever dated. It sounds like a difficult decision and maybe the right one. But what do I know?"

"That's all right. I will go by myself, or maybe rally a friend to come with me."

"Ha, because I am not sure that I want to go. A Native American artifact seems a little far afield for me."

"Really?" asked Barry. "I am eager to see any type of history."

"I will email forward the invite." Dirjke was terrible with computer language. He stared at the keyboard and continued, "I will let my nephew know you might be there. I think he was in my class one time a few years back."

"Danny, right?"

"Yeah, he is a high school senior now. He might go to college in New York. We are going to look at schools while he is visiting."

"There are lots of great schools in New York," answered Barry.

"We'll see what he ultimately decides. But I have to go. See you Thursday."

"Later on," said Barry to his old professor.

Chapter 5

THE DATE
Tuesday, August 12, 2003 2:00pm

Barry was twenty yards from finishing a lap around the Jacqueline Kennedy Onassis Reservoir. At the southwest edge, there is a natural finishing point for the run. The canopy from the trees on the west side provides a helpful shade for the finishing sprint. The path is covered in gravel that crunches under each step.

Ana watched Barry finish his run from the west side entrance on the dirt path that was 1.58 miles in circumference.

She smiled as she watched the effort he put into the last fifty yards. Barry was wiry with little muscle and few athletic gifts. His gait made that evident. His limbs were flailing in all directions. He was looking up and sucking wind as he ran. Barry's skin tanned in the sun and his hair was dark, thick, and had a slight curl.

Ana looked to her watch as he finished. "Good run, Barry, 13:35." She had just caught her breath from her own lap around the one billion gallon pool.

"Thanks. What was your time?" replied Barry, with his chest heaving so violently that he could barely get out the necessary syllables. He was wearing blue shorts with orange borders and a dark gray t-shirt.

"I ran as fast as I could to try and stay close to you."

"12:57."

Barry was impressed, but not surprised. Ana had speed. Running was not his stock and trade, but he wanted to get in shape before he started his second year at Harvard. A running date was not his ideal romantic scenario, but he would take time with Ana no matter the activity.

The pair walked from the edge of the reservoir and across the Central Park Loop with runners and bikers in

25

both directions. Every couple of steps Barry sneaked his fingertips onto Ana's shoulder. On the second and third times she looked toward his hand and smiled. They walked to one of the many rocks in Central Park and sat down.

Still half delirious and sweating, Barry said, "Ana, my old professor from high school forwarded me an email to a ceremony and a press conference on Wednesday. Do you want to come with me? Professor Dirjke is a great guy and there might be some good people watching."

"Always trying to keep your contacts for letters of recommendation in case you go to law school?"

"That is not the point," answered Barry, still breathing heavily. "Technically, he invited me. Professor Dirjke is a great teacher. He knows more about Manhattan than just about anyone. He and I spoke earlier this week."

"Well, history is not my favorite subject," answered Ana. She was wearing a similar gray tank top over a sports bra with ladies shorts that were navy blue and white. "What kind of fun would I have there?"

Barry had had a crush on her for years. She knew it and liked the attention it got her. She was also a fierce friend of Barry, who could be prone to ridicule by the cool kids. With Ana's slim athletic figure, green eyes, and light brown hair, boys listened to what she said.

"People watching, Ana. You know you like to be out and be seen. There is a ceremony downtown at the Alexander Hamilton US Customs House. Professor Dirjke told me that some construction workers building the new South Ferry Terminal found an artifact."

"What type of artifact, Barry – dinosaur bones?"

"No, well, I am not sure."

"How can you not be sure? Didn't your professor tell you? I know you, Barry, you are not that adventurous. You look before you leap."

"The professor mentioned that some Native American artifacts were found. I also checked the city's press release and it seemed to echo the same story."

"Well then, why does that sound so interesting?" asked Ana.

"I don't understand how they could have found Indian remains where they say they did," said Barry.

"Barry, if they found a spear, or beads, or arrows, who do you think they belong to?" asked Ana.

"Well, according to the press release, the location where they found the artifact is located nearby the new South Ferry Terminal, which is part of the original shoreline of Manhattan."

"Original shoreline... What on Earth are you talking about?" asked Ana, now concerned that the one-lap sprint around the reservoir had loosened a few screws in her friend. At the northern point of the reservoir, the city's buildings are framed by the park's canopy from below and the sky from above.

"I am talking about Manhattan. Believe it or not, Manhattan did not always look like it does today."

"Yes it did."

"Not so. Manhattan is probably the most modified piece of land on Earth. Even Central Park is man-made. The name Manhattan itself means 'land of many hills.' Now, think about how many large flat fields are in this park."

"Really?" Ana was no longer teasing her running partner.

"Yeah."

"Tell me about this shoreline thing."

"See they are saying that a Native American artifact was found. However, the only problem is that the area where they found the stuff was under water four hundred years ago."

"So, there is probably stuff in the reservoir in front of us. What is your point?" asked Ana.

"Well, Indians pre-date plastics and aluminum cans, which probably make up most of the underwater treasure in the reservoir."

"So what are you saying, Barry?"

"What I am saying is that I am interested to see any Indian artifact that can survive that long underwater."

"And you want to take me?" asked Ana.

"Yes."

"Okay, it's a date...I mean call my cell phone and email me the press release."

"Cool."

"All right, I am going to jog back to my parents' place. Thanks for the run, Barry. And don't forget to call me about the artifacts or whatever."

Chapter 6

THE TRAIN RIDE

Wednesday, August 13, 2003 7:00am

Danny Maxwell was on a train from Washington, DC to New York City. The trip to New York was part business and part pleasure. The car was lined with maroon carpet on all sides with blue seats.

The young man had light brown hair that he never bothered to brush. From nearly every visible angle, he looked like an athlete. From the running shoes, to the blue cargo shorts, right up to the blank oxford gray t-shirt.

The train lunged forward as it reached 30th Street Station in Philadelphia, like a slow lumbering turtle. All of a sudden, his midnight blue backpack fell square on his head and right shoulder as it startled him into consciousness.

"Whoa!" exclaimed Danny. He looked around to get his bearings.

He had two more hours before he reached his uncle's apartment on Manhattan's Upper West Side. Meanwhile, Danny's neighbors on the train were not thrilled with the commotion he was creating in the 'quiet car' of the train. To boot, his cell phone began ringing.

After digging the phone from his cargo shorts, Danny noticed it was Dirjke. He opened the phone and said, "Hey Unk, how are you?"

"Good. On your way?" asked Dirjke.

"Right on time."

"Danny, listen closely and don't repeat aloud what I say."

"Okay," answered Danny, half-confused.

"Did you know that the word 'OK' has its roots in the presidential campaign of Martin Van Buren?"

"How did that happen?"

29

"Van Buren's hometown in New York is nicknamed, Old Kinderhook. It was then shortened to OK. 'Van Buren is OK,' became the popular term of the day."

"Amazing."

"Anyway, I am meeting the Mayor and will not be able to meet you at my office."

"Wow, Unk. Look at you."

"I will find you at the 'meet and greet' after the ceremony at the US Customs House in Bowling Green Park."

"Okay," answered Danny.

"It is the city's oldest park. In the 1650s the area was a cattle market, which is ironic considering every tourist that comes to Manhattan gets a picture with the iconic Charging Bull on the northern tip of the park. The area now has the most famous cattle statue."

"No problem..." answered Danny. "Is there anything about New York that you don't know, Unk?"

"Someone always knows more," answered Dirjke. "Danny, I told my old student Barry that you will be there. If you bump into him, you'll have someone to talk with."

"Cool," answered Danny.

"All right, I just sent you the invitation on email so you know where you are going."

"Thanks Unk. Afterwards, I want to hear all about your morning."

"Deal."

"You know, your sister – my grandmother – is very concerned about you. She thinks you need to get out more. It has been nearly four years since Aunt Sam passed."

"We had a special bond, Danny."

"I know Unk, but this weekend will be good for you to get out. You can tell me about the New York sights. No one knows more than you about that island. You are also like Gilligan, because you never leave it."

"Enough jokes. I happen to keep very busy," answered Dirjke. "Wait 'til you get here and you get to feel what it is like to live like a real New Yorker."

"I'll see you soon enough to find out," finished Danny, as he closed his phone.

*   *   *

Across the train sat Sid Milliken. The commotion this young man caused with the backpack and the cell phone conversation was disturbing. Sid gave an approving nod in that direction, once Danny laid his head back onto the headrest.

Danny noticed the man's beard and Popeye-like forearms, but he closed his eyes without a second thought.

Chapter **7**

CITY HALL
Wednesday, August 13, 2003 10:00am

Dirjke walked up Broadway on his way to City Hall. As he arrived at the iron gate and metal detector quartering off the grounds, a gruff security guard who clearly knew what the inside of a gym looked like explained, "All metal, keys, and whatever else you may have on the conveyor belt."

Dirjke complied, placing all of his personal items on the belt. As he walked through, the security guard reminded him, "Glasses, sir."

Dirjke placed his glasses on the belt. After walking through the large gray rectangle, he announced, "I am here to see the Mayor."

"Marty Dir-ke?" asked the security guard.

"Close, it's pronounced *dir-j*."

"Got it, Mr. Dir-j."

Dirjke was a man of medium height. He was fit for a man of his age, but possessed little muscle strength. Dirjke was never an athlete, but he was such a nerd growing up that at a young age he had sworn off junk food and rarely ate candy.

"Okay. Well, just tell the security guard inside."

Dirjke walked over the cobblestones and up the steps. He turned the knob and entered City Hall.

It was just like he was twelve again. He was mesmerized by the French stairs as he entered. Across the rotunda was a grand marble stairway that led to the second floor.

"Marty, good to see you," Dirjke heard from across the stone hallway.

Michael was a man of medium height and a typical middle-age build. His charcoal gray suit was perfectly tailored with a white shirt and a mint green tie.

Dirjke looked toward his old friend and said, "You know, Abraham Lincoln and Ulysses Grant laid in state in this room following their deaths."

"No Marty, truly I had no idea, but come this way," as Michael slapped him on the shoulder.

The two men walked into the office and sat at two chairs surrounding a small table.

"Nova and cream cheese with onion, tomato, on a poppy seed bagel," ordered Michael, as he slid the tin puck across the table.

"You know it," answered Dirjke. He flipped the top off the black coffee and tore open the tin foil covering his breakfast sandwich.

"Do you mind if I maneuver this table toward me?"

"Not so long as you answer a few questions for me," replied Michael. "The press conference is in less than one hour. I need to know a few things before I publicly address the find. I had no idea that such an object would attract this intense of a media circus."

"It is good to be prepared. As Mayor of New York your statements are going to be seen worldwide."

"I know that Marty."

"No problem. What did those construction workers find?" asked Dirjke.

"I am not sure. That is why I called you."

"Called me? I am not a Native American specialist. In fact, I am not sure that I am interested in the topic. You know me, the American Revolution and New York City history is my game. What is going on?"

"What do you know about how Western civilization acquired possession of Manhattan in the 1600s?" asked Michael.

"Well, in truth, there is not that much to know. The story goes that the island was purchased from a Native American tribe living on the island for 60 guilders and some beads. There was also the school of thought that the

Lenape Indians did not even know what they were selling, because they did not have a European understanding of property rights."

"Marty, I did not bring you here so you could recite some folklore that I could have picked up in a social studies class at PS 253 in Brooklyn."

Dirjke was taken aback by the abrupt tone of his old friend. "Okay. Well, nothing was even known about the purchase of Manhattan, or rather how Western civilization first acquired the eventual capital of the world, until 1849."

"1849?"

"Round about then," mumbled Dirjke, as he finished the first half of his bagel. He dipped the last bite in the cream cheese that inevitably spilled out the side of the bagel. Dirjke knew that the key to any toasted bagel rested in it being toasted on the outside shell.

"Martin Van Buren, former Governor of New York, first US President of Dutch ancestry and first natural-born US President, sent John Broadhead to Holland to research the matter. After many years of research, almost ten, all Broadhead found was a letter that referenced the purchase of Manhattan. And to this day, that is where the story you scoffed at came from."

Michael took another sip of his coffee. "I think there is something you should look at."

"What is it, Michael?"

"That is the thing, Marty. I am simply not sure. Travel with me today. I will show you what I am talking about. The artifact is at the US Customs House. We can look at it before I give my statements to the press."

"But, Michael, I may not be able to tell you what you need to know," said Dirjke.

"The official story has already been released to the press. I am all for disclosure, but I am not in the business of public panic."

"What do you mean?"

"Do I really have to spell it out? Marty I have something that I want, no, need you to see. Isn't that enough?"

"Yes, sorry."

"Okay, Marty, I have some business to handle before we go to Bowling Green Park."

"No problem. I would expect nothing less from a public servant such as yourself. I have today's paper and the remaining portion of my bagel. The next hour should fly by."

"Good."

"Also, my nephew and an old student of mine will be at the ceremony. Perhaps they could be introduced to you, at the meet and greet following your statements to the press."

"Sure thing, Marty. Sorry if I seem a little strange. After all, if the Mayor doesn't protect Manhattan, who will?"

"Listen, spending one of the dog days of August with you is an unexpected treat. Just hope I can help."

"We'll find out," answered Michael.

Dirjke nodded in general agreement. He left the Mayor to his work.

Chapter 8

DIRJKE AND THE MAYOR SEE STICK
Wednesday, August 13, 2003 11:00am

Traveling with the Mayor of New York was always a scene in the media capital of the world. The two men exited the car that chauffeured them to the edge of Battery Park. Dirjke placed himself within the buffer zone of Michael's handlers. He tried to fit in.

It was a sunny day. From underneath the canopy of trees in Battery Park, Dirjke could see the harbor. He breathed in the salty air as he turned to his friend.

"I would have thought that your promise of a press conference would have limited the reporters and microphones in your way."

"I know, Marty. This story has escalated since the discovery on Monday. I thought people would stay in their offices and read the transcript. What could be so interesting?"

The two men walked past Bowling Green subway station. Dirjke looked up at a massive stone structure built in a classical Roman style, with ornate etchings along all the edges. The US Customs House was part of the City Beautiful Movement in the 1890s. The sky behind it was a deep blue.

"That part of the building is called the Museum of the Native American," observed Dirjke.

"I know you don't travel frequently to the southern tip, downtown Manhattan. Not all of us have our lives within an eight block radius."

"Home, work, gym, and groceries. What can I say," retorted Dirjke with a smile.

As the two men made their way through the building, in mid thought, Michael said, "I am really glad that you are here."

36

"That is great, but what am I here for? I mean there is an entire museum on the other side of this building for the specific purpose of Native American artifacts. What am I going to add?"

"If I knew that, you wouldn't be here, Dirjke. Be patient."

The men made another turn toward a room which was under heavy lock and key. They entered a tiny room in the deep recesses of this old structure. Michael entered the code into the key pad and opened the door. Dirjke followed his friend into this strange room.

"Amazing."

"Yeah, it is pretty cool. This room was never remodeled during the most recent renovation. Therefore, this room does not exist on any of the current building plans."

Dirjke was turning his head in all directions to take in his surroundings. Then he saw the artifact and gasped in excitement. His hands were flexed behind his neck, as he bit his lip.

"So?" asked Michael. "What do you think? It has the number 1626 carved into it."

"That was not in the press release. You only said it was estimated to be four hundred years old."

"Have you observed any other markings on this piece?"

"No," answered Michael. "But tell me what is going through your mind. You are the expert." Dirjke continued to look at the object without replying.

After about five seconds, to extract some information from Dirjke's brain, Michael said, "From the research I did, in and around the New York County Supreme Courthouse, I know that the Seal of New York says 1664 on it. I know it from the cast iron seal in 60 Centre Street on the floor as you enter the building."

"That date is not correct."

"What do you mean?" asked Michael. Dirjke had not lifted his eyes from the cylindrical wood object.

"The current Seal of New York City is not dated 1664," responded Dirjke again without looking up from the object.

"Then why does that piece of wood say 1626?" asked Michael.

"I think that's why you asked me here."

"But you know I was in front of the Brooklyn-Battery Tunnel as well. There is a gigantic City Seal that says 1664. I had my eyes on it for ten minutes, during someone's terrible speech."

Dirjke began, "It's an interesting story. In 1975, on the heels of the bicentennial anniversary of the signing of the Declaration of Independence, the City Council changed the date on the seal. It passed unanimously and Mayor Abraham Beame ratified it. So in essence, New York celebrated its 300th and 350th birthdays only eleven years apart. There are still a few instances where the Seal was not changed. Apparently, that includes the New York County, Supreme Court and the Brooklyn-Battery Tunnel. My guess is that no one wanted to spend the money to change it. Every now and then I see a New York Seal with 1664 on it."

Michael's eyes lit up. "I can't believe that what you are telling me is true."

Dirjke added, "There is also a 1664 Seal at the restaurant at Pershing Square across from Grand Central Terminal and a school on 50th and the West Side."

"What does 1664 represent, anyway?" asked Michael.

"It represents the date that the English took the island from the Dutch. Manhattan was surrendered by the Dutch West India Company without a British shot fired. Amazing," added Dirjke.

"Amazing?" asked Michael, a little confused.

38

"Manhattan has never been conquered by the force of war. Even Washington fled New York very early in the war. It was the biggest stronghold the British held. After the Revolutionary War, a parade was held to celebrate the departure of the final British soldier from Manhattan."

"Then why was the 1664 date changed on the City Seal? In the 1970s of all times – it makes no sense. Where are you going with the explanation?" asked Michael.

"It isn't really that they changed the date on the Seal of New York. It was the year they changed it to. That is what makes no sense."

"Let me guess, the current seal says 1626?" asked Michael as he gestured toward the stick with 1626 engraved onto it.

"Nope, try again," smiled Dirjke. But before it could go any farther he said, "You're one year off. It says 1625"

"Why would it say 1625? Is that when New York State was founded?" asked Michael.

"No, New York State was technically founded in 1624 on Governors Island."

"So why 1625, then?" asked Michael.

"No one is entirely sure. The date is largely arbitrary. Henry Hudson discovered New York in 1609. The first European settlements started in 1613. The first charter was in 1653. The seal itself was not established until 1686. It is widely believed that it was simply a publicity stunt to have a continual celebration for the United States' 200th birthday. Also, it was an affirmation of Manhattan's existence, which included Dutch rule over the island."

"I guess that makes New York older than Boston," answered Michael.

"Yes, 1630 is the date that Boston was founded. Anytime New York beats Boston it is a good thing," said Dirjke with a chuckle.

The professor continued to study the piece. Eventually, with Michael's nod of approval, Dirjke picked up and studied the piece up close. He noticed that it was lighter than he expected, but did not notice any other carvings besides 1626. After a few minutes, Dirjke put the small log down and asked, "Where is the other stuff?"

"No other stuff. I just wanted to know what I have on my hands before this goes public."

"Where did you find it?"

"In one of the deepest sections of the excavation of the new South Ferry Terminal. No more front five cars," answered Michael.

"It is one of the oldest subway stations."

"Yes, it has moved from quaint to decrepit in the past ten years. The *schreel* from the wheels on the curved metal tracks pained the ears. It is not the signal tourists need, since it is the most used subway station to get to the Statue of Liberty."

"How deep?" asked Dirjke.

"It was in one of the deepest points in the excavation."

Dirjke's eyes widened. "Michael this is the location of Fort Amsterdam during the Revolutionary War, and a couple hundred yards from where we are at the US Customs House was the original Manhattan shoreline. And you said it was deep in the excavation."

"Yeah," answered Michael.

"The growth and expansion of Manhattan's shoreline was basically due to landfill material. This had to have been at the bottom of all that. That is why Broad Street is the widest street in Lower Manhattan."

"But why does it say 1626?" asked Michael.

"Not sure. Maybe the Deed to Manhattan is in here," laughed Dirjke.

Upon picking it up a second time, Dirjke noticed that it was light, to the point of hollow. Dirjke knocked on the piece. "If this thing is hollow, something is inside of it."

He continued to study it and noticed a uniform hairline fracture around the cylinder. The entire piece was covered in a strange finish that seemed to seal the joint.

"Michael, can I try to open it?"

"Is that really a good idea? It is probably shut for a reason."

"Exactly," stated Dirjke. "That's why we need to open it. You have all these people talking about this object. Why wait to find out what is inside along with the rest of the public?"

"I guess that is true. Before you told me about all this Deed stuff, I was not sure what to do with this. I am glad I called you. Imagine if I gave an object related to the Deed to Manhattan to the Federal Government," admitted Michael.

"Well, that is an unnerving comment considering you have to speak with the press in moments." Michael nodded with his head for Dirjke to proceed further.

Dirjke took off his glasses and used the endpoint of the stems to score the adhesive, which held the two pieces of wood together. Slowly the adhesive was removed and Dirjke opened the box. With Michael peering over his shoulder the two men found a small note on parchment that was clearly very old.

Dirjke opened the dry brown paper. Dirjke said, "It is a note that appears to say,

11-25-1783

One Deed Left. I Pray Whereby you will find it.

7-11"

"What could that mean?" asked Michael.

"I am accustomed to studying and piecing together facts from my office hundreds of years after their find. Now, we are in the theater itself."

"This is insane, Marty. What am I going to tell the press? There is already an unusual amount of interest in this artifact to begin with. Now, I can't even provide any concrete answers. Moreover, we just found a strange note gift-wrapped in a package that says 1626. I will speak to the press, but Marty I need you to study the note and the piece of wood. Although I can't deny its existence, we can keep its contents to ourselves."

"Agreed."

"However, I won't be able to keep this quiet for long. Various groups are going to want to see this piece. Marty. I need you to stay ahead of the curve and give me some idea of what this all means."

"Okay."

"I am going to speak to the press, but don't leave here without letting me know what more you think about this."

"Understood," stated Dirjke, realizing that he was talking to the Mayor of New York, not merely a friend in this situation.

"Good. I am on my way to the press conference."

Dirjke studied the note and the wooden stick that housed it for a few minutes, but he shook his head in dismay when no answer seemed to rise to his mind. Then, before he even realized the time that had passed, his cell phone buzzed. It was Danny texting him that the press conference was over.

Dirjke took the note and put it in the front pocket of his button down shirt and put the stick in his bag covered by the day's newspaper.

Chapter 9

PRESS CONFERENCE
Wednesday, August 13, 2003 12:00pm

Barry and Ana got above ground at the escalator leading out of Bowling Green Station. She was wearing a light colored sundress and stylish sandals. Barry was wearing shorts and sneakers with a beat up short-sleeve plaid button down.

Ana looked up and said, "I like the buildings downtown; they have a more iconic look than the monuments to glass in midtown."

"Look," said Barry, "there is the Charging Bull that all the tourists take their picture with."

"Cool," answered Ana. "I mean, they just look like fun buildings."

"Don't get me started. We are here to see Professor Dirjke and maybe meet the Mayor. But I must say, there is a plaque about two hundred yards away, commemorating the location of the second executive mansion."

"Wow. I never thought about it. I guess it took a few years to build the White House."

"You have no idea," answered Barry. Then as he was looking toward the bull he saw Dirjke's nephew.

Danny was looking at the backside of the Charging Bull. He laughed to himself when he saw which areas were the most worn down. He was under dressed for the occasion in shorts and a wrinkled green collared shirt.

"Danny," called Barry from the other side of Bowling Green. Danny turned around as he heard his voice. This caught Ana's attention and she nudged Barry.

"Who is that?" asked Ana.

"That is Danny. He's Professor Dirjke's nephew. I met him a few times, years ago, when he was in ninth grade."

"He is in good shape," noticed Ana.

"Yeah, he is a good guy. He's only concerned about sports and movies, but a good guy."

"C'mon Barry. You sound judgmental and jealous. You met him years ago. No telling how he is all grown up," teased Ana.

"Ha, all grown up? I think he is a high school senior by now." His tone made him realize that Ana was right. Barry knew enough to know not to engage further in discussion with Ana on this topic.

As Danny approached them, he said, "Hey Danny. Good to see you. What grade are you in?"

"Starting my senior year."

"Nice, you must be thinking about schools," replied Barry, before introducing Ana to Danny.

He shook her hand. There was a slight smile between them. She gave him a full handshake, not one of those fingers-only half handshakes that some girls offer. Her summer dress accentuated her slim figure, as a slight breeze moved through her long hair.

"Have you two seen my uncle?" asked Danny in Barry's direction.

"Not yet, but it was really nice of him to invite me," said Barry.

"Have you ever met my uncle?" asked Danny, trying to engage Ana.

"No, but Barry raves about him. How are you related again?"

"Professor Dirjke is my great-uncle. My grandmother is his sister."

"I took two classes with Dirjke. *Revolutionary Way History* and *New York City History*; they were amazing classes," said Barry.

"You know how he is then, Barry."

"What brings you to New York this August weekday, Danny?" asked Ana.

"My uncle and I are going to look at some schools in the area. Where do you go to school?"

"I go to Georgetown."

"I live outside DC, in Maryland. Do you play a sport?" asked Danny.

"Soccer," answered Ana.

"Me too. I'm trying to decide between playing soccer and fencing."

"Interesting," Ana said with a smile and a slight tilt of her head. "My father played…"

However, before those two could engage in further conversation, Barry located the Mayor mingling among the reporters and passersby.

"Ana, look. There is the Mayor," said Barry.

"Wow," exclaimed Ana. "Seeing him without the help of a TV is amazing." As a native New Yorker, she knew better than to gawk at celebrity. This is not Los Angeles. Robert De Niro and even Jackie Onassis moved to and lived in New York, because celebrities can hide in plain sight.

The comment caught Danny's attention. He looked around, but did not see his uncle. Then he saw Dirjke proceeding down the stairs at the Alexander Hamilton US Customs House and toward Bowling Green Park.

Dirjke met up with the Mayor and the two exchanged a quick conversation. Dirjke looked around and saw his nephew. As he proceeded toward Danny, he noticed that he was standing with his old student, Barry, and a girl.

He walked toward the group. Danny saw his favorite uncle and gave him a warm hug.

"Hello Unk."

"How was your train ride?" answered Dirjke.

"Okay. I was up early in order to get here in time," replied Danny.

"Hey Barry, how are you? How is Cambridge, Mass?" asked Dirjke, delighted to see his old student at the ceremony. Mentioning Cambridge spared Dirjke from saying his least favorite word. *Haaarrrrvard.*

"I'm good Professor. Thanks for inviting me. I must say, the artifact sounds very interesting. The press release described a medium-sized cylinder with some carvings on it. But I must say the location of the find is probably the best part, right? I mean can you imagine a Native American artifact that is nearly four hundred years old."

"He has been going on about this for two days and, by the way, I'm Ana."

"Sorry," admitted Barry. "The press release says that the object was found underground, where they are building the new South Ferry Terminal."

"Did you guys enjoy the press conference and the Mayor's statements?" asked Dirjke.

"Yeah," said the group almost all at once.

"But, he seemed sort of distracted," added Ana.

"Have you seen the object?" asked Danny.

"Yes...I mean no!" Dirjke was a horrible liar, but he tried to change the subject. "What are you kids going to do today?"

"Well, Ana and I just bumped into Danny...I am not sure what Ana and I have planned for the rest of the day."

"We were thinking about relaxing in Central Park and catching a movie since it is so hot out today," said Ana.

At that moment, the Mayor walked over and greeted everyone in the group. He was on the verge of sweating due to the August heat combined with his suit.

"You kids know that Marty is one of my oldest friends from elementary school. You didn't forget anything did you Marty?"

"No," stated Dirjke. "But that reminds me. I am going back to my office. I have some work to do."

"Me too," said Michael. "I am already getting calls from various groups that want to see the official photos of the artifact. Also, there is a military official that my chief of staff scheduled for an appointment later this afternoon."

"I will come uptown with you Unk. I want to check out Columbia's campus."

"The Hamilton Deli is up there. We'll have lunch before I get to work. That reminds me Barry," stated Dirjke. "I think I will have to take a rain check on our lunch plans. I think this artifact will be keeping me busy tomorrow, most likely."

"I understand," said Barry, slouching in disappointment.

Dirjke sensed it and said, "If Danny doesn't mind, maybe we can all have dinner tonight."

"Really?" asked Barry.

Danny smiled and said, "Sure as long as you bring Ana with you."

"I'm game," answered Ana.

"All right then, Barry. I will call you later this afternoon."

"It was great meeting you all. Marty, be in touch," said Michael. He turned away from the group and met his handlers to be escorted back to City Hall.

"You guys have fun in Central Park," said Danny.

"Let's catch the 1/9," suggested Dirjke.

"See you this evening and thanks for inviting me," finished Barry.

Danny and Dirjke began walking up Broadway. "Thanks for understanding," said Dirjke.

"No problem," answered Danny. "You inviting Barry gives me another opportunity to see that girl, Ana. Barry can tag along with us as long as he wants."

Dirjke smiled at his great-nephew and grabbed the back of his neck as they made their way up New York's Canyon of Heroes.

"You know your grandmother and my sister do not want you competing in college athletics. College is for the purpose of a good time."

"Unk, I love the competition."

"I know, but as you grow up you will find competition in other forms more stimulating."

"Yes, but for now, I have to do what I want most."

"I understand, but let me tell you the Dirjke family version of 'the ole' college try."

"Really, Unk, what is that?"

"Do what you love and have a lot of fun in college. The only caveat is that you have those same four years to find a profession that will support you once you graduate. With a college degree, you are expected to be financially independent. I will help you in any way, but you have four years to accomplish this task. College in New York might be perfect for you."

"We'll see," answered Danny, as the pair made a left off Broadway and onto Rector Street, along the southern edge of Trinity Church. The gilded cross on the top of the steeple made a shadow through the cemetery, which was the tallest point in Manhattan until 1890.

Chapter 10

SID WITH MAYOR
Wednesday, August 13, 2003 3:15pm

The Mayor was seated behind his desk reading reports and clicking through the pages on his computer screen. His desk was clear, with the exception of office essentials. He received a call from his receptionist that a gentleman from the military was waiting outside his office.

"Let him in Marjorie."

Sid walked into the Mayor's office with all the confidence in the world. He was dressed in casual pants and a midnight blue collared shirt with the emblem of the Department of Defense sewed onto the left breast. His skin was tanned and his eyes were small blue slits due to age.

"Sid Milliken, here. Thanks for seeing me at such short notice."

"I must say, I expected someone with a uniform."

"I hold a special office Mr. Mayor, which lets me dress in these civilian clothes." He pointed to the emblem on his shirt.

"No problem," answered Michael. "What can I do for you?"

"This artifact found at the South Ferry Terminal. Is it possible I can see it?"

"Not really."

"Mr. Mayor, perhaps I did not fully explain myself. I have security clearance and military credentials. I am..."

"Mr. Milliken it is out of my hands. The object has been turned over to the US Customs House tentatively for further analysis. At this point, I can only offer the official photo."

"That would be excellent."

Michael rummaged amongst some files in a drawer behind his desk. He located a plain brown envelope, from which he carefully extracted a color photo.

"Okay. Well here is the official photo of the object. As you can see, it says '1626' on it," said Michael. "In this post-9/11 world, I know that the military wants stats and facts."

Sid looked at the photo with astonishment and responded to the Mayor without looking up.

"Exactly. To be frank, we are not interested in your analysis. That is what the military is for – analysis and action. That said, Mr. Mayor, what do you make of it?" Sid lifted his head and gave the Mayor his attention.

"Not sure," said Michael. "Perhaps we will need to change the City's seal," as he pointed to the flag in his office.

"Curious," stated Sid.

"Indeed," agreed Michael with the hope of ushering Sid out of his office. "But what is more curious is the fact that you are even here at all. Really? Why is the military concerned with this object? Perhaps I have a right to know that, as the holder of this office. As you know, New York is more than the United States' largest city, or the financial capital of the world."

"I know," stated Sid.

"No, you did not let me finish…it is the capital of the world."

"1626," said Sid. "How many things could have happened on Manhattan in 1626?"

"I am not sure. That is why I have people studying the object."

"I am no historian, but 1626 must relate to one of the earliest dates that Europeans arrived on Manhattan."

Michael let out a nervous laugh. "According to folklore, Manhattan was purchased from a group of Indians for beads and mirrors, maybe some guilders."

"Is that really the type of reports you are receiving?" asked Sid. "What would the West want in return? Proof of purchase of the island, a piece of paper reflecting the transaction. I think you can see why the military is interested in this object."

"No, I am still not sure what the military could need with a historical object. Name me one important piece of land that was not claimed by warfare."

"Don't be so obtuse," answered Sid. Michael turned his head in astonishment. "Since the removal of the dollar from the gold standard, money is based on the faith that people have in it. If that doesn't provide a platform to manipulate the frailties of the masses, what else will? Would a document of this type be valid today, or better yet, could a third party even disprove its validity? What would happen to world financial markets if the owner of the financial capital, no the 'capital of the world' to use your words, was unknown?"

"Really, if that is the case, why is so much taxpayer money spent on defense in the form of guns, tanks, and planes?" asked Michael.

"You are missing the point. A claim of right is all an army needs to invade new lands. What if this Deed to Manhattan – if it exists – fell into the wrong hands?" Sid paused, composing himself.

"Then, those tanks and guns would become the hottest commodity on Wall Street," stated Michael.

"Ha, exactly," answered Sid.

"Well, I am sure that Chinese banks, the nation's biggest creditor, would no doubt applaud proof that the United States actually owned its most valuable parcel of real estate."

"Precisely, which is why I must see this object."

"Mr. Milliken, you will have an opportunity to see it soon enough. Just give me a few days."

"Mr. Mayor, I would like to see it now."

"You know, I must admit I am little concerned that you want to see the object more than offer security for its protection. You will see the object in due course."

Sid's face flashed with an expression of controlled anger before returning to his stoic cloak.

"Well, I was sent here to inquire as to this object. I guess my work here is done then. Mr. Mayor I will leave you to your work."

"Thank you," Michael said, as he turned to his computer screen.

Chapter 11

DINNER WITH THE KIDS
Wednesday, August 13, 2003 7:15pm
Dirjke met up with Barry, Ana, and Danny. The foursome arrived at Talia's on 92nd Street. The dining room had dark wood up a portion of the wall with a mustard color on the remaining wall. It was a typical Upper West Side restaurant. The tables were arranged tightly together with a white paper table cover. There was a fair crowd of people for a Wednesday night.

The group was escorted to a table along the west wall. Ana and Barry sat with a view of the entire restaurant. Danny and Dirjke sat facing them.

"This place just opened. I am curious to taste the food," began Dirjke.

"Unk, tell us about your day. What is the deal with that artifact?" asked Danny.

"Did you see the artifact?" asked Barry.

"Yeah, because the Mayor never commented with specifics at the press conference," added Danny.

"Well, I know the latest press release is going to show the year carved in the cylinder is 1626."

Barry's eyes widened as he asked, "Is the legend real?"

"Oh boy," exclaimed Ana, quite sure that her dear friend had steered the conversation in the wrong direction.

"What legend?" asked Dirjke. "What do you mean? I never delivered a lesson with any memorable issues over the purchase of Manhattan."

"The Legend of the Lost Deed to Manhattan..."

"What do you mean, Barry?" said Dirjke, as the waiter delivered the group's appetizers.

The people adjacent to Danny and Ana were having dessert and finishing their cocktails. One of the women looked visibly drunk. Another man was talking way too loud. Next to Barry and Dirjke a couple was exchanging basic information about each other's past. They were on a first date.

Danny and Ana dug into their spinach and apple salads.

"I know of no such legend."

"I know President Van Buren sent someone to Holland to locate the Deed, but he only found a letter referencing the purchase. I don't know. Maybe there is no legend, but I had always thought that if the document was not in Holland, it must be here on Manhattan, where the transaction took place," stated Barry.

"Interesting," replied Dirjke. "I never really thought much about it. I always thought it was a straight forward event."

"Even though Director-General Peter Minuit, of the Dutch West India Company, was fired after the purchase of Manhattan, no one could actually lose the document. It doesn't make sense. They would need the document during the early existence of the settlement to prove that the company's entitlement to the land was valid," finished Barry. He felt like the teacher for a second.

"I don't know much about this stuff," interjected Ana, "but Barry made some worthwhile points. Why do you historians assume that the Deed could only be in Holland? The deal took place on Manhattan."

"Also, the value of Manhattan to commerce has never been disputed. The island was targeted by a company, for its economic value, as an asset," added Barry.

Dirjke asked, "Well, given what you know, where would you look for it? Where would you start, Barry?"

"If it were me, I would start by reviewing the city's oldest maps," explained Barry. "First of all, this way, you could include all maps dated in and around 1626, so you could exhaust at least one avenue before you look somewhere else."

"What maps do you know of from the 1600s?" asked Danny.

"1614, Adriaen Block, was the first person to discover that Manhattan was actually an island. He created a map naming the area New Netherlands."

"That sounds like a fair point," said Danny with a glance to his uncle.

"Barry, so what if the Deed to Manhattan exists? I mean, do you think my parents will still own their apartment on the Upper West Side?" said Ana, half sarcastically. "You are now monopolizing the conversation with arcane historical artifacts."

"Yeah, why don't you guys start your appetizers," suggested Danny.

Dirjke recognized his faux pas and admitted, "You're right. I have not even started my salad. Ana, we met for the first time today. Tell me a little about yourself."

"There is not really that much to tell. My name is Ana McNamara. I grew up in Manhattan and my family has lived on this island since the Civil War. My great-grandfathers came to New York in the 1850s as young men, because of the potato famine. Originally, they lived in Hell's Kitchen. The men fought for the Union in the Civil War. As Barry tells me, 'because they were first generation immigrants, they did not have the money to buy their way out of the draft.'"

"It is true. A few hundred dollars would buy any potential Union soldier out of the draft," interjected Barry, as he shoveled a forkful of Caesar salad into his mouth.

"About me – I am going to be a sophomore at Georgetown. I started out as a pre-med major, but I think I am going to get a degree in English," finished Ana.

"Major in what you like," said Dirjke. "It was the reason I focused on history at Yale."

The group received their entrees. As with any group, the table became near silent, but after a few bites and before the waiter came back, Dirjke broke out, as if in mid-thought, "Still if the Deed to Manhattan was in existence, aside from eggheads like Barry and me, who would want it?"

Danny said, "If the Deed has not been found and you found something with a marking with the year of Manhattan's purchase, chances are it was a secret for a reason – or the Deed is inside of it."

"Danny, what if there was a note inside the artifact with the 1626 carved into it?" asked Dirjke.

"For real? That is amazing!" blurted Barry.

"He said 'what if' Barry. Stay in your seat," said Ana. There was a strange silence at the table, because Dirjke had yet to respond.

"Let's not discuss it here. But if you want, follow me after dinner." Dirjke gestured with his hands and his eyes that he did not want their answer or any excitement over the invitation.

Ana said in a low tone, "Don't worry, the police would not believe this story if you told it to them."

Dirjke laughed and said, "Yeah, tell something like this to an officer and he would probably respond, 'Do you want to buy the Brooklyn Bridge too?'"

Seconds later the waiter arrived to check on their meals.

Chapter 12

BACK TO THE OFFICE
Wednesday, August 13, 2003 8:30pm

Without further discussion about the note and the stick, the group followed Dirjke back to Collegiate School on 78th Street and Broadway. The school's main building consisted of a one-story granite façade with the school's name etched in it. The levels above were made of ordinary reddish-gray bricks.

He led the group into his office located within Room 42. The place had been Dirjke's office for years. He was very neat, but there were books stacked ceiling to floor with New York City and Revolutionary War history.

They each sat at the round table in Dirjke's office. Dirjke went to his desk to get the note and brought it for viewing.

11-25-1783

One Deed Left. I Pray Whereby you will find it.

7-11

Barry, Ana, and Danny each looked at the small piece of paper.

"This is amazing!" said Barry as he tried to read the handwriting on the parchment.

"Barry, thanks for commenting on the obvious. Well, from here 'one Deed left' is an obvious reference to the Deed to Manhattan, right?" asked Ana.

"What makes you think so?" asked Danny.

"The 'D' in Deed is capitalized," replied Ana. "It is being used as a noun and not a verb. Being an English student can be very useful," smiled Ana. Her smile was captivating, especially for Barry, who had known her for years.

"It is a primitive form of encryption, where the answer hides in plain sight. I have even heard that some artists do the same," added Barry.

Danny, having noticed the '11-25-1783' numbers, followed Ana's lead and asked, "Unk, can I use your computer?"

"Sure," answered Dirjke, surprised by the urgency of the youngsters. Barry continued to analyze the information contained in the note. At that moment, Dirjke rushed to one book in the vast collection in his office.

"The numbers at the top of the parchment refer to Evacuation Day," said Barry.

"How can you even know that?" asked Ana.

Dirjke said, "Keep going. Maybe the Internet can provide more answers," said Dirjke.

"What is Evacuation Day?" asked Ana. "I have never even heard of it."

"Evacuation Day celebrates the removal of the last British soldier from Manhattan at the end of the Revolutionary War. It used to be a larger celebration, because people were alive to remember a time when the British occupied Manhattan. Then Thanksgiving was created in 1863 by President Lincoln to soothe the tension between North and South. After World War I, Evacuation Day lost favor almost entirely with the American people."

"Thanksgiving, honoring our relationship with the Indians, which never really existed, instead of celebrating a victory during the brief negative period in our longstanding relationship with the British. Sounds like this history stuff is just made up by people and their whims," stated Ana.

"Actually, history is written by the winner," responded Danny with a smile.

"I know, that's sometimes the problem. The idea that I couldn't work or vote less than a hundred years ago scares the hell out of me."

"That is what makes Manhattan special. It was bought and not conquered. So technically, we treated the native population with respect," countered Dirjke. "Equal rights are rooted in the transfer of Manhattan."

"But not for women," finished Ana.

"Back to Evacuation Day," stated Danny.

"Washington made his triumphant return to Manhattan, which had been a bastion of British support, so making your presence felt was a must. He technically held the first ticker tape parade. There was not a bigger event in New York until Washington's Inauguration." Dirjke then put his nose back into his book.

"What are you looking up, Professor?" asked Barry.

"I am trying to decode the '7-11' reference on the note."

"You mean '7-11' references a person and not a convenience store," teased Ana.

There were about twenty seconds where no one talked. The kids each looked at Dirjke with his glasses half way down the bridge of his nose waiting for an answer.

"'7-11' is military coding for General George Washington," said Dirjke, as he looked at one of his old notebooks on Revolutionary War History. "See, George Washington was not only our greatest military commander, he was active in intelligence matters against the British."

"Culper Ring?" asked Barry.

"Exactly," answered Dirjke.

"What are you guys talking about?" asked Ana.

"The Culper Ring was this country's first intelligence apparatus, which was renewed as the Office of Strategic Services during World War II and renamed again as the Central Intelligence Agency. That is the current public face of the intelligence world. Back then,

59

Washington was active in both intelligence and counter-intelligence activities to deceive the British forces," added Dirjke.

"But that does not answer the question," said Danny. "Get to the point."

"A numerical substitution code was developed by Major Benjamin Tallmadge. Washington was given the number 7-11," stated Dirjke.

"Wow," said Barry. "We have a note from Washington referencing the Deed to Manhattan."

Danny searched the Internet to confirm Barry's theory on the date on the note. Sure enough, November 25, 1783 was Evacuation Day.

Dirjke began to assess the information at hand. "Could Washington have learned the location of the Deed to Manhattan?"

"What church could Washington have prayed in?" asked Ana.

"But that still doesn't tell us where the Deed is. I mean there could have been any number of churches in Manhattan in the 1780s and how many could still be around today?" added Danny.

"At that time, both the Governor of New York and the President prayed in the same church in Lower Manhattan, St. Paul's Chapel. People forget that New York was the country's first capital," continued Dirjke.

"The next time that happened, Martin Van Buren was Commander in Chief," added Barry.

"Huh?" asked Dirjke.

"The point being that Van Buren was both a Governor of New York and President of the United States."

"So maybe the Deed is at St. Paul's Chapel. Where and why?" asked Ana.

"Well, the Deed must be in an accessible spot, right?" asked Danny. "I am amazed that so much was actually happening during the first Evacuation Day celebration. In addition to the party, there were steps being taken to protect the Union and New York's future prosperity."

"Hold on," answered Dirjke, trying to field one question at a time. "I mean, assuming we are reading this right, it could be at St. Paul's Chapel. I know it is one of the oldest buildings in Manhattan. Federal Hall, the location of the country's first inauguration, was just down the street, on Wall Street."

"But it doesn't say who the note is to," stated Barry.

"Maybe it is to whoever found the stick?" responded Danny. "A first clue to whoever found it. If the note is from Washington, we can't question his intelligence," with a smile at the end to show that he recognized his own pun.

The comment made Ana laugh for a second.

"Has anyone been to St. Paul's Chapel?" asked Danny to the other New Yorkers in the room.

"No."

Dirjke then said aloud, "Strange that this country's first natural-born citizen-president, former Governor of New York and a Dutchman, would be the first to undertake this effort in 1832 and not release an answer until 1849."

"And as of today, not come up with the real story," added Barry.

The idea of researching this over the coming years seemed exhilarating to Dirjke, then suddenly shaking him out of his thoughts was his nephew's voice.

"Let's go there tomorrow and stake out the place. It will be like *Ocean's 11*."

"I like the idea, Danny," said Barry.

"Me three," said Ana.

"No. I don't think this is such a good idea. I am going to call the Mayor in the morning. No one does anything until I speak with him. I will get in contact with you guys," stated Dirjke.

"Who is going to let me know?" asked Ana.

"Sorry, Ana I did not mean to exclude, it's just that I don't have your number. Besides, do you really want to get involved with this?"

"Professor, I am a New Yorker. I was born on this island. I am a part of this, like it or not."

"No problem Ana. I just wanted..."

"I understand," responded Ana, cutting off Dirjke and defusing the situation.

Dirjke said, "Okay, well, I will talk to you all tomorrow."

Chapter 13

SID GOES TO CUSTOMS HOUSE
Thursday, August 14, 2003 8:00am

It was early the next morning when Sid took the 1/9 train from Times Square Station to South Ferry Station. Times Square was a mixture of tourists looking up at the lights and professionals looking to get to work on time. Sid went underground to the entrance on 42nd Street, between 7th Avenue and Broadway.

It was a twenty-five minute ride. As the cars pulled into the station Sid was struck by the terrible *schreeeeck* the front five cars made around the tight circle. A metal grate extended to eliminate the gap created by the straight train car against the curved platform. Then the train doors opened.

The station was at least 10 degrees hotter than the outside August temperature. The mosaic tiles that spelled 'South Ferry Station' were covered with soot and various tiles were missing. The station looked every bit of a hundred years old.

"It's about time the city remodeled this station," commented Sid to the family next to him. The old station had a roundabout turn at the end of the 1/9 at South Ferry Station and only half the train had access to the platform.

"I know," replied the patriarch of the family in a southern tone. "We couldn't understand the speakers in our train car. By the time we realized what we had to do, it was too late. I can't have my daughters walking between the train cars while the train is moving. So this is our second attempt to get to South Ferry Station."

"Fall down six times, get up seven," said Sid in a polite manner to end the conversation with agreement.

Sid could feel the excitement through his body. After a lifetime within the intelligence community, the nature of right and wrong simply did not exist for him. For

Sid, the wholesale drug dealer was no different than a commodities trader: people trading paper for what they want.

Sid laughed at people who lauded the United States' debt to other countries. China loans the United States $100 billion in pieces of paper and in return we manufacture tanks, fighter jets, and bombs. It's a good trade for the United States considering the fact that the debt becomes unenforceable once the debtor has $100 billion dollars' worth of whatever the latest military weaponry permits.

It was a weakness the United States' enemies would soon exploit.

Sid walked up the stone steps to the entrance of the Alexander Hamilton US Customs Building. On each side of the external stairway were two hulking statues of classical Roman figures. The trim around the building was filled with meticulous bas-reliefs on its surface.

Sid flashed his credentials to the security.

"Sid Milliken, Department of Defense. Do you know how I can locate, or is there anyone to talk to, about the artifact?" he asked the guard in front of him.

"Artifact, you mean that piece of wood found at the construction site of the South Ferry Terminal?"

"Yes," answered Sid. "You see, I would like to get a picture for the archives..." as Sid waved his hand in a manner to elicit the officer's name.

"Ralph," answered the figure.

"Where is it?" asked Sid.

"I am not supposed to tell you, sir," answered Ralph.

"Tell me?" Sid reached for his credentials. "Look at this."

"Sir, I'm under orders."

"Whose orders?"

"The Mayor of New York."

"Haven't you taken enough social studies classes, or seen enough action movies, to know that Federal authority trumps local mandate."

"I have orders to the contrary that I intend to carry out," said Ralph as he unlocked his holster and put his right hand on his gun. Sid's eyes darted to the movement of Ralph's hand. He took a step back to give the man some space.

"I am not looking for a confrontation," responded Sid.

"Sir, no one is allowed in this room. That's all I know," said Ralph. Sid could see perspiration starting to form above the man's eyebrows.

"Good day, Ralph," answered Sid, as he stepped away. Sid made his way out of the building.

He walked to Bowling Green Park. He sat at one of the benches that surround the fountain which shoots water about twenty feet in the air. The perimeter of the pool was lined with red flowers and shaded with a canopy of trees. The water crashing back into the fountain provided a faint background noise for the people enjoying this.

There was a family with a crude, almost cartoonish, map of Manhattan. Their daughter was reading from the map to her parents that, "the fountain is for the representation of the first public water well at this very location in Manhattan." The girl's father was holding another map on his lap with his wife leaning over.

"See, the problem, honey is that we are down by all these crooked streets and Times Square's over there," announced the women in a British accent.

"I guess you're right, let's see if we can figure out the subway."

Sid needed to speak to the Mayor again.

Chapter 14

SID AND THE MAYOR MEET AGAIN
Thursday, August 14, 2003 9:18am

Sid moved past the security at City Hall and found his way to the receptionist in front of Michael's office. "I need to see the Mayor. This is Sid Milliken," stated Sid in a hurried voice. It had been a purposeful walk for him from Bowling Green Park to City Hall. The August heat caused the man to sweat.

"What can I tell him it's about?" asked the young lady.

"The US Customs House," answered Sid. This ambiguous response left the young receptionist confused.

"Mr. Mayor, Mr. Milliken is here regarding the US Customs House."

Ordinarily, someone cannot simply walk in and see the Mayor, but Sid was a military man; they walked between the raindrops.

Michael met Sid at the threshold of his office.

"Sid, what can I do for you on two consecutive days?" The men shook hands for a second time.

"Mr. Mayor, I went to see the stick at the US Customs House. Why can't I see it?"

"Well, for one reason, it's being studied by experts at the moment..."

"Mr. Mayor, as a matter of national security, I need to see the artifact."

"Mr. Milliken, if this is a matter of national security, as Mayor perhaps I should know why?"

"Mayor, I am not willing to tell you that," answered Sid.

"Well, I am not willing to allow you to view the artifact."

The intercom to Michael's office rang.

"Mr. Mayor, Professor Dirjke is here."

"I intend to make the artifact available to the public next week. If your office files the proper paperwork, perhaps you can view the item privately, but for now, there is nothing further to discuss."

"Thank you, Mr. Mayor," answered Sid.

Chapter 15

DIRJKE TELLS MAYOR
Thursday, August 14, 2003 10:00am

The Mayor's office was subdued. It was the largest office in City Hall, but it was modest compared to the offices of New York CEOs. The office was painted in official New York City eggshell white. Michael's office was immaculate and paperless.

Michael was dressed in a summer suit. The tan outline was complimented by a light blue shirt and navy blue tie. The brown leather shoes made for a very dapper look.

Dirjke was wearing olive pants with a blue polo shirt. His hair was thinning, but for a man his age it was a full head of hair. Michael greeted him just inside his office.

"Did you see the guy who just walked out of my office? Bullying military-man, 'national security'. We could invade Cuba under the guise of national security," said Michael.

"That's already been done, old friend," replied Dirjke, as he put his hand on Michael's shoulder.

As Dirjke walked to the chairs facing the Mayor's desk, he could no longer contain himself.

He turned and said, "Michael, I deciphered the note."

"Really? Where is the Deed?"

"Well, all signs point to St. Paul's Chapel, a little south of here."

"How so?" asked Michael.

"It is a long story and really it is only a theory."

"A theory?"

"Yeah, the note alludes to the fact that the Deed might be at St. Paul's Chapel. When was the last time you went to church?" asked Dirjke.

"St. Paul's," exclaimed Michael. "Did you know that the President George Washington has a special pew in that church?" answered the Mayor. "The church is across the street from the World Trade Center Site."

"I know it is really amazing. Washington protected the Deed to Manhattan."

"Because of its proximity to the World Trade Center site, at any given time there are probably more tourists in there than parishioners. Do you really think the Deed is in the church?" asked Michael.

"Tough to say. As Ana said last night, almost four hundred years later and all we found was another letter referencing a Deed. Either way, in the interest of Manhattan, we can't stop now."

The Mayor turned his head to ask, "You discussed this with whom?"

"A couple of kids, young adults actually – my nephew, a student of mine, and a girlfriend of his."

"Are you kidding me?" asked Michael. "You entrusted the information I gave you to a bunch of kids. I have some crazy military guy named Sid Milliken questioning me over this stick and you are telling children!"

"Young adults and they are quite capable. One is a former student of mine who goes to school in Cambridge, Massachusetts. The other is my nephew and the third is a crafty young woman named Ana."

Then a wave of fear rushed over Dirjke. As a high school professor and because of his nature, Dirjke had few enemies, if any.

"Did you say Sid Milliken?" asked Dirjke.

"Yes," answered Michael.

"Michael, do you know who Sid Milliken is? He is the foremost mind in the intelligence world. In some circles, he is known as the man who brought down the

Soviet Empire. If he is even on this island, we have cause for concern."

"Why? Maybe he can help. What makes you think otherwise?" asked Michael.

"You remember my piece following 9/11, which alleged an even larger connection for New York to that date than radical religious terrorists."

"Okay," answered Michael, waiting for Dirjke to continue. It took Dirjke a second to realize that Michael did not remember the story.

"The article had a lot to say. But the rub was that I argued that the destruction of the World Trade Center was not the only event in New York's history on September 11th." Michael shook his head in astonishment.

"Refresh my memory Marty. What was another important event to take place in New York on September 11th?"

"An Englishman for the Dutch West India Company sailed his ship, the *Half Moon*, under what would become the Verrazano Bridge and into New York Harbor for the first time."

"I know. I am there the first Sunday in November each year for the New York City Marathon," said Michael. "Just explain it to me."

"Henry Hudson sailed into what would become New York Harbor on September 11, 1609. And I make the point that Manhattan was rocked to the core on that day, but it was not destroyed. And we should still celebrate Manhattan's discovery, the very same date. That was roundly criticized by certain factions in various media outlets."

"So? Isn't history written so that people like you can argue about it like they are baseball players?" replied Michael, with a smile showing that he was only half joking.

"Exactly, only this time someone stifled the point. The ability to analyze and question was neutered. For heaven's sake, I was making the argument that if we don't celebrate Hudson's voyage, then the terrorists win."

"So you think Sid Milliken is responsible for this?" asked Michael.

"Yeah," stated Dirjke with his eyes widening. "Did you know that construction broke ground on the Pentagon on September 11, 1941?"

"Really, do you mean it?" asked the Mayor.

"I'll go you one better," announced Dirjke. "In the center courtyard of the Pentagon, there is a café named, Ground Zero. Know why that is? Because during the Cold War military officials were certain that the Soviet Union had a nuclear missile aimed at the courtyard."

Michael raised his eyebrows, as he placed his elbows on his desk.

"Then think about it. Both places are attacked and have a distinct connection to that date. One is okay to discuss and one isn't. This is what this guy Sid Milliken does. That is just our most recent run in. He has vexed me my entire life. Remember the time…"

"Okay. Okay. So you don't like the guy. Why can't he help?"

"Michael, this is the Deed to Manhattan we are talking about. This island was one of the first settlements on this continent. We cannot count on someone else to help. How do we know who he is truly working for or what his intentions, if successful, are? I'm sorry Michael, but we are stuck with this job."

"Are you telling me you want to search for the lost Deed to Manhattan?" asked Michael. "Come on, this guy Sid works for the military and Federal Government."

"I am a New Yorker. Given the choice between the two, you are the Mayor of New York. You have one official choice, but I know you better than that Michael. You place your duty to your office ahead of Federal authority."

Michael looked at Dirjke, puzzled by the analysis.

"No different than the young men in the 1860s from the South that left West Point Military Academy to fight for their State and the Confederacy. New Yorkers are one of the last people in this country that still place their city ahead of all else, including the State. We steer the ship," finished Dirjke.

"How are we going to get into the church without making a scene?" asked Michael. A wave of relief spread through Dirjke that his lesson had worked. "As Mayor, I can't just walk in there and look around. What about you, Dirjke. Why don't you go to the church?"

"I'll need Danny, Barry, and Ana to help. This is not a one-man job."

"C'mon Marty," exclaimed Michael.

"They can help, you can brief them."

"But why should I let some kids into this mess?"

"Michael, this is the Deed to Manhattan we are talking about. This is not a job for bureaucrats. The city does not have a clandestine department – we can fill that niche."

"I can't believe the position you are putting me in. Okay, but I am going to have to see these kids before I tell them anything. I will give them a chance to convince me," answered Michael, from behind his desk. "Tell them to be here at two o'clock. Also, where are the stick and the note?"

"In my office," answered Dirjke.

"Well, tell one of your crackerjack apprentices to get it and bring it here for safe keeping. Also, I have another thing to tell you. I received a strange call yesterday that is appearing less and less strange," said Michael in a guarded tone.

"What do you mean?"

"I mean that some crack pot called yesterday and told me he was going to bring New York into the 1600s."

"Now, you have got to be kidding me," replied Dirjke, returning Michael's astonishment that he had entrusted secrets to a bunch of young kids. "What's his name?"

"Homer," answered Michael.

"This is nuts. Who knew that the excavation in the Battery was going to renew a legend long lost to history?" asked Dirjke.

"Enough romantics – get me those kids and the artifacts."

Chapter 16

SID GOES TO OFFICE
Thursday, August 14, 2003 11:00am
Sid walked right through the security at the old New York school. Military credentials have that effect. He told the security guards he was here to see Professor Dirjke. Knowing Dirjke, the security guards assumed that he would be working in his office. It was a non-hurdle, just as Sid anticipated.

Sid made his way to Office 42. He knew it was likely to be empty with Dirjke speaking with the Mayor. But he knocked on the door anyway. After a few seconds, he pushed on the door to determine if the deadbolt was in use.

"Damn, that means I am going to have to do this twice." Sid took his keys out of his pocket. He flipped them in hand to find a standard key issued to all CIA field agents. The end of the key is removable. Titanium wires at the end of the model key maneuver to fit the conformities of the lock.

Sid started with the easy doorknob lock first. He got it unlocked so quick that he thought a plastic ID card might have done the job just as well. He inserted the key into the deadbolt and began to maneuver it around. Sid's nose was nearly six inches from the deadbolt when he said to himself, "These Yale locks always give me the most trouble."

Seconds later some kids began to walk along the hallway. They were looking toward each other with one threatening to throw a soccer ball at the other. Sid sensed the pressure rising. Only from a great distance could he be mistaken for Dirjke. At the next instant, with a deep breath and his eyes closed visualizing the inside of the lock, he heard that familiar click. His eyes opened and he exhaled. His face was turned away from the approaching boys.

Sid let himself into Dirjke's office and closed the door behind him. All he saw were books floor to ceiling and a computer that was probably purchased during the first Clinton administration. Then, on the table in his office, Sid located the stick and note underneath it.

Sid left the old school and returned to his rooming house in Hell's Kitchen.

*   *   *

The walk to Collegiate School was not far from the apartment. Dirjke lived on Riverside Drive and 83rd Street. A view of the water was his constant reminder that he lived on an island.

Danny arrived at the threshold of Dirjke's office. He put the key in the lock, but the door was already open. He pressed his face against the door as he opened it. Once he did not see any one through the four-inch sliver, he swung the door open and stepped into the office. He looked around for something, but before the door could shut he stuck his foot out. After a few more seconds, Danny let the door close behind him.

Danny rummaged over the papers and piles on Dirjke's desk. He could not see the stick and the note on Dirjke's desk. He ran his hand though his hair and finished by grabbing his own neck. He shook his head and reached into his pocket with his other hand.

Danny opened his cell phone and called Barry.

After the first ring, he picked up, "Barry, meet me at City Hall and call Ana."

"All right, I will be there in an hour."

"The sooner the better," demanded Danny.

"What's the matter?" asked Barry.

"Just meet me there with Ana."

"Barry, I am not trying to tell you what to do, but I am not going to tell you what is going on by phone. Okay?" said Danny.

"Did you call your uncle?"

"Barry, I can't explain it to you now, but no, I haven't. If this situation is as serious as it seems, Dirjke's cell phone being tapped is not out of the question."

"I understand. See you at City Hall."

The pair hung up.

Chapter 17

ZEKE CALLS VLAD
Thursday, August 14, 2003 12:00pm

"We're going. Call the Mayor and alert him to his newest problem."

"Okay," answered Vlad. He looked around his office at the Ukrainian Institute and leaned back in his chair.

"Yes," finished the voice on the other end of the line, Zeke. He was comfortable in his penthouse on the West Side. On 70th Street between Columbus and Broadway, built in the 1920s as a meeting place for the Knights of Phythias, the building's current posture was that of luxury condominium. The structure still demonstrated elements of both art deco and Egyptian design, from the previous owner.

Zeke's family's old money had owned the penthouse since the building's transformation. Zeke was an elderly man with jet black hair and a cut jaw line. As a businessman, he had ridiculous success. This was going to be his latest and largest transaction.

"It's time to flip the switch. There are others searching around. No doubt they will be formidable. Especially with the new information that has reached into public discourse. The discovery of an object with the date 1626 means nothing on a Thursday, but by Friday, everyone in the world will know that is the year the island was purchased."

"Understood," answered Vlad.

"If all you are interested in is that stick, this should be enough to negotiate its transfer," stated Zeke. "I have a larger purpose, my friend. The Deed to Manhattan will provide the true One World Order centered on commerce and without divides of land borders and religion that have stifled human progress."

"We think alike," answered Vlad. "We're doing the right thing. New York needs a new shepherd."

"Exactly. A board of overseers, enlightened men to lead this planet from its true capital. We, my group, have every intention of ruling Manhattan, just by a more elaborate proposal."

"You remember our deal?" asked Vlad.

"You do as you are told. It will result in much more than that," replied Zeke. "Vlad, for what you are willing to do for me, you and your people will prosper financially. You are here in America. Have some of America's most intoxicating drug, unlimited money. You'll have the power to help and promote whatever causes you determine worthy. You will rise to the level of world humanitarian and philanthropist."

Chapter 18

KIDS BRIEFED BY MAYOR
Thursday, August 14, 2003 2:10pm

As the two walked along the cobblestones to City Hall, Barry looked back down Broadway's Canyon of Heroes. He saw St. Paul's Chapel. It was a brown and beige building with a tall steeple that would be impressive on nearly any other street in the world. But this was downtown Manhattan. The building looked distinguished, but like a gray-brown box.

"See that brown building over there."

"Yes," answered Ana.

"If we play our cards right, that's where we are headed."

"Wow. Well, let's just focus on the business we have in this building," said Ana, as she pointed to City Hall.

"Did you know that the statue of Justice on top of City Hall is not blindfolded?"

"Are you okay? Who on Earth knows that? Can you please just focus on what is in front of us? You know, it is not how much you know, but how you apply it."

"Give me one example?" demanded Barry.

"That pitcher for the Yankees at the end of games," answered Ana.

"Mariano Rivera," answered Barry. "You remembered from that game we went to in 2000."

"It was a Subway Series Game, c'mon. And yeah him, you said he only has one pitch and no one can hit it." As the pair entered the building, Barry could not look away from the staircase.

"It looks like the Mayor's office is this way," pointed Ana. "C'mon," as she grabbed his arm. The pair walked down the hall with open doors on both sides. The terrazzo floor was speckled with a natural white with dark edges along the walls. They met up with Danny outside the Mayor's office.

"Hey you two," said Danny.

"Hi, Danny," answered Ana, glad to see him.

"Danny, did you get the stick from the professor's office?" asked Barry.

"Well, that's what I need to tell everyone about. See, the stick and the note – they weren't there."

"What?" exclaimed Barry and Ana in unison.

"Yeah, it's not there. The Mayor and Dirjke don't know yet. Let me do the talking first. We have at least the time it takes for someone to decipher the note and most people aren't Dirjke or you, Barry."

"Okay. Well you can see St. Paul's from the front door of City Hall. So let's just convince the Mayor and go to St. Paul's," added Barry.

"That should be easy," added Ana.

The group made their way to the area outside the Mayor's office.

"The Mayor will see you now," said the administrative assistant in a southern drawl. Her name badge read, Georgia.

The group walked into the Mayor's office and took seats at the medium-sized conference table. Ana could not help but notice the City's Seal on the wall, which stated the wrong year, 1664. Dirjke was sitting at the table in a relaxed manner.

The group respectfully greeted the Mayor.

"It was only yesterday that we first met – today is a new day. Dirjke told me that you might be ready for an assignment. Before we get started, where is the stick and the note?" asked Michael.

"Mr. Mayor, I regret to report that the stick and the note were not in my uncle's office."

"I can't believe that. Are you sure you looked everywhere?"

"Yeah, Danny. How can we be sure that you did not just miss it?"

"Unk, the door to your office was not locked."

"What?" asked Michael.

"I saw you lock it when we left last night. Both locks."

"True and I never usually lock the top lock."

"I guess the good news is that for the thief to be a threat, he would need an encyclopedic knowledge of New York and Revolutionary War History," said Danny.

"Only someone who could decipher the note was a true threat," finished Ana.

"They have a point," added Dirjke.

"Look, as you might understand, we have a potentially serious situation on our hands. Now, Dirjke and I have known each other a long time. He trusts you. So, I have little choice, but to trust you. I don't want you to tell this to anyone else. But what I have to know right now, is why I should trust 'the Hardy Boys' and 'Nancy Drew' to protect Manhattan?" asked Michael.

The group went silent for a second. "Mr. Mayor, I have lived on this island my entire life. My parents know of no other existence than this island. If someone is plotting to take this island, I have a duty as a native-born New Yorker to protect it," stated Ana.

"The point makes sense," said Dirjke. "Remember there is a clause in the US Constitution which carves out a special protection that the United States Commander-in-Chief is a natural-born US citizen. Without knowing it, Ana, you are evoking that clause."

"Well, every president since Jackson, who was the last non-American-born president," finished Barry.

Michael was more impressed with Ana's answer. He let her know with a nod of acceptance.

"I know I am not a native New Yorker, but my uncle is involved in this and I want to participate," said Danny.

"Well, this is not an after-school activity, boy. We are talking about the Deed to Manhattan," replied Michael.

"Loyalty," stated Danny.

"What?" asked Michael.

"This is about loyalty. Mr. Mayor, my loyalty to my uncle is unwavering. I will do what I can to help," answered Danny.

"You know the problem with that, right? Your kinship with Dirjke could compromise the larger purpose."

"Yes, but that's a weakness that I will not allow an enemy to exploit," responded Danny.

"Mr. Mayor, with all due respect, Dirjke is not my uncle, but I still care about him. I am susceptible to the same attack, and that's not fair. You would not have even contacted Dirjke if you didn't trust him," stated Barry.

"Yeah, Mr. Mayor, I barely know the kid, but still, Danny belongs with us," finished Ana.

"With all due respect, Michael, he needs to stay with us," explained Dirjke. "Where is my great-nephew going to go. My apartment? It's not safe there."

"Fine," answered Michael. "I need you focused on the matter at hand, not Danny's safety."

"What about me?"

"You are included," answered Michael with a smile. "After all, according to Dirjke, you are one of the most knowledgeable people on the island about this stuff."

"Thank you, Mr. Mayor, you won't regret this. I am going to do my best and this is such a wonderful opportunity..."

"Enough, Barry, the Mayor did not give you an internship. We are on a clandestine mission to save this island," said Ana.

"That might be a slight overstatement, Ana. We, I mean – you guys – have got to figure out a non-attention catching way to find out whatever it is we are supposed to find in St. Paul's Chapel. Understood?"

"Yes," answered the group.

"I can't believe what I'm asking you kids to do."

"Are you coming with us Professor?" asked Barry.

"Well, we know that Sid knows I'm involved, he must be the one that stole the stick and the note from my office. My presence might endanger the mission," answered Dirjke. "Remember, do not draw attention to yourselves."

"Yeah, you don't have to tell us twice. Taking something from St. Paul's Chapel must be like robbing a casino. There is no way we'll get out the door," stated Danny.

"Well, get to work," added the Mayor. "Report back here when you are done."

Danny, Barry, and Ana each proceeded out of the room. Their journey to St. Paul's Chapel had begun.

Chapter 19

GO TO ST. PAUL'S
Thursday, August 14, 2003 3:15pm

It was a warm midafternoon in Manhattan. The group made their way out the back of City Hall. Barry pointed to the statue at the end of the path to the east and toward the Brooklyn Bridge and said, "Horace Greely was the founder of the *New York Tribune* and ran for president in 1872," as the group looked at a hulking sculpture that depicts Greeley sitting and perusing the newspaper.

"He is the only presidential candidate to die before the electoral votes were counted, which didn't matter…"

"Which didn't matter because he has nothing to do with the task at hand," stated Danny in a mildly annoyed and interrupting tone.

"Well it did not matter, because he lost in a landslide to Ulysses S. Grant, who is buried on Manhattan."

"C'mon Barry, we have got to focus," answered Ana. "The closest route to St. Paul's Chapel is this way." The group walked down Broadway and past the Woolworth Building. It was an ornate structure that was once the tallest building in the world.

"I can't believe there is a sign preventing tourists from seeing the lobby," said Barry. The sidewalk was packed with people moving in both directions. As a buffer from the sidewalk to the street, vendors sold everything from water, to clothing and handbags.

Barry was ahead of Danny and Ana. She smiled at Danny and said, "Enough, now. How are we going to do this?"

As the group got closer to Vesey Street, Danny said, "I know where we are. My uncle talks about the Stage Door Deli in Midtown; he is not downtown often but when he is here, he always goes to the Stage Door Deli. It's on the far corner. This church has two entrances. Also, there is a cemetery that surrounds the church building. Let's casually meet at one of the benches in twenty minutes and discuss," suggested Danny.

"All right, that sounds like a plan. Ana, you are going to come with me?"

"Barry, are you trying to tell me what to do?"

"No. It is just that I might need your help," answered Barry.

"My help, Barry. You are the salutatorian on this island as to its history. I am not sure how I will help, but it makes no difference to me. We will all be in the same place in twenty minutes," responded Ana.

As the group split up, Danny walked through the gate mid-block on Vesey Street and into the cemetery that surrounded the church. He looked at the sign on the gate that read 'Oldest building in continuous use in Manhattan.'

He took a moment and looked around the grounds to allow Barry and Ana a head start into the building. All around him was the hustle of commerce. Construction workers, civil servants, bankers, doctors, lawyers, traders, and business executives were all walking past each other.

The cemetery showed its age with headstones tilted in all directions. The yard itself was well manicured with stone paths leading to the significant grave sites.

As he entered the church, Danny saw Washington's pew on the north wall of the room. Ana and Barry had already found the same location.

Washington's pew in St. Paul's Chapel was a small rectangle that was quartered off from the rest of the church. The plaque in St. Paul's said that Washington prayed here following his inauguration at Federal Hall on Wall Street. Above the pew was a large painting of the Seal of the United States of America.

Barry studied the painting for some nuance that might provide a further clue. It seemed like a dead end to him. For an extremely early rendering of the Seal, it

85

appeared to have the same basic elements as every United States Seal. There was a bald eagle with its wings outstretched with the standard thirteen arrows in one talon and an olive branch in the other.

As he studied the piece, Barry remembered from his time in Dirjke's class that the eagle is always looking to the talon that holds the olive branch. The United States looks to peace, before war, thought Barry. It was just the type of symbol within a symbol that Barry enjoyed. Meanwhile, Ana left Barry's side to read some of the verbiage surrounding the pew.

Danny proceeded into St. Paul's Chapel and saw Ana and Barry when the lights in the church went out.

Barry heard the tourist next to him in an English accent say, "Looks like the electric in this old building needs work."

From his frame of reference, it was not a coincidence. Barry and Ana looked up and then back at each other. They clasped hands and walked toward the lighted opening that they knew Danny would be entering through.

"They've come for it," whispered Ana as the two made their way to the west entrance of the church. They moved between the stunned groups and families looking up.

The pair locked eyes with Danny and proceeded outside to a bench in the cemetery.

"What the hell is going on?" asked Danny.

"This is getting dangerous. First someone steals the stick and the note. Now the lights go out in the building where we believe the next clue is," said Barry.

"I agree Ana. I mean we are a rag tag group with marching orders to be discrete. The guy who stole the stuff from my uncle's office has figured out the note and cut the power to the entire church," exclaimed Danny.

"Not the entire church. Danny look," said Barry. They were awestruck. From buildings and subways people were spilling out of every crevice of the city and onto the street like ants after someone steps on their nest.

"It looks like the power was cut to the whole city," answered Ana.

Barry continued, "The painting. We need to get the painting."

"How Barry? We are clearly outclassed. I mean the guy who stole the note obviously cut the power to the entire city. Not to mention the fact that he probably deciphered the note," answered Danny.

"But now is our only chance. We can't just turn back and tell the Mayor that Barry thinks it has something to do with the painting of the US Seal over Washington's pew. What good would that do us?" answered Ana.

"She is right. We need a few moments with the painting. Maybe there is something written on the back," said Barry.

"What makes you think there is something on the back of the painting, Barry? It's a picture of the Seal of the United States. By definition it has to postdate the date on the note. You are leading yourself down a dead end."

"The United States Seal itself was adopted in 1782. Evacuation Day was in 1783. The Seal could have been here when Washington prayed here."

"Yeah, but it says that the painting wasn't commissioned until 1785," snapped Ana.

"Really?" asked Barry, somewhat convinced by Ana's point. "If you look close enough, the bird looks more like a turkey than an eagle."

"So what?" asked Danny.

"Well, the turkey is the result of Ben Franklin's influence on the country's seal."

"Stop telling me things that are tangential to the matter at hand," demanded Danny.

"Evacuation Day was in 1783," responded Barry, with his head dipping slightly.

"So the painting is not old enough to have been here when Washington was in New York on Evacuation Day," stated Danny. "What's our next option?"

"I don't know," answered Barry.

"I do," announced Ana. "You boys are missing the point. The note says that the 'Deed is whereby Washington prays'. Unless, Barry can tell me I'm wrong, this was the only church on Manhattan at this time."

"It was. Most of Manhattan was burned to the ground, except this church because of its northern location on the island. St. Paul's Chapel is approximately one mile from the southern tip of Manhattan. It's about two-thirds of the distance traveled by those individuals and sports teams that were given Canyon of Heroes parades."

"Look, there is no mistaking that Washington prayed here. And the Seal of the United States predates Evacuation Day in 1783," added Ana.

Seeing that in their faces, to sell her point Ana told the boys, "Let's put it this way. I have a stronger belief that Washington laid eyes on that painting than I do the fact that he actually ever sat in that chair they have there."

Barry let out a nervous laugh.

"So, what now?" asked Danny.

"It's possible that Washington left a message behind or around the painting," suggested Barry. "Look, there's a note that says on Evacuation Day, Washington prays close to where we will find it."

"The lights went out before I got a good look at the painting and I did not even get close enough to see the chair. All right, well even if the painting is what we are after, how are we supposed to get access to it?" asked Danny.

"True," followed Barry. "I mean we can't just walk in there and tell the priest that we need to take a look at the first ever Seal of the United States."

"No. I think we can. Look around. This entire city is without power, from what we can tell. I have a plan. Are you ready for this, boys?"

"What is it?" asked Barry.

The trio huddled and listened to Ana's idea.

Chapter 20

JACK DUROE ENTERS
Thursday, August 14, 2003 4:18pm

The power just went out at the power plant on 14th Street and the East River on Manhattan. Jack was situated within one of the many identical buildings within the complex.

"Of all the days, my first day," said Jack, out loud to himself. "Am I really expected to know and implement the emergency procedures on my first day? Now the lights are off in my windowless office."

He fumbled his way along the edge of the wall toward his locker at the other end of the room. At the power plant, a hard hat and flashlight were standard equipment.

"Much better," said Jack to himself as he clicked on the flashlight and sat in his chair.

He started with the table of contents to find the proper section of the manual he needed to follow.

"The manual says that I'm supposed to go to this other office to coordinate the necessary emergency pumps. Reading these drawings should be a lot of fun."

He gathered what he needed and walked outside.

Overhead were wires and transformers. The path was made of small stones which led to numerous buildings and transformers, each quartered off by a chain link fence. Usually, the place buzzed with noise.

After winding his way through the power plant, flashlight in hand, he arrived in the pump room within the old facility. There was a gigantic board on the wall on one side of the small room. The buttons and bulbs and screens were all blank. Then he noticed a pen on the floor in front of the other exit door in the pump room.

Jack walked to the door that led to an emergency exit. He pushed the door open. He was drenched in sunlight. He placed his hand over his eyes to protect them from the glare. Then he looked down and about five feet from the fence, about twenty yards from where he was standing, a man was lying on the ground.

He rushed down the stairs to the motionless body. His time as a soldier in the army had toughened his stomach for what he thought he was going to witness. But, on arrival, he was confused. "No blood, no wounds," thought Jack. He grabbed the man's wrist. No pulse.

He looked around for an explanation.

As a city employee, he was not going to waste another city employee's time during the blackout to call 911 for a man that was already dead. He would report it in due course. He looked around for some sign of foul play and saw nothing.

"There is no way this guy committed suicide, but how did he die? And who killed him?"

Jack walked back to the empty office looking left and right to figure out what had happened. As he entered the small room, he looked around with his flashlight. He found a five hundred-page emergency contingency plan for the power plant.

Chapter 21

SID'S LOCATION DURING BLACKOUT
Thursday, August 14, 2003 4:21pm

Sid was in his rooming house in Hell's Kitchen when the lights went out. The room Sid stayed in had windows that faced the courtyard. It provided natural light.

When he heard numerous screams from inside the building and then the buzz of people from the sidewalk, and the sound of car horns, he knew the blackout was not merely confined to his room. Sid gathered his things and left.

The full implications hit him as he walked onto 46th Street between 9th and 10th avenues in front of Hartley House. The people in their brownstone apartments were sticking their heads out their windows. As Sid approached the corner of 9th Avenue, people were spilling out of the various business fronts to see what was happening. Everyone was looking at the screen on their cell phones. Cars and pedestrians were gridlocked south of 9th Avenue.

Unlike most people's initial reaction of fear to the day's events, an air of confidence washed over him. He looked around and smiled to himself.

Chapter 22

VLAD TALKS TO MAYOR
Thursday, August 14, 2003 4:15pm

About twenty minutes after the kids left his office, the lights in Michael's office went out. He walked into the hallway. All he saw was chaos. Some people were on their cell phones. Others were looking around trying to decide what was happening. Due to the large windows at City Hall, the room was a dark gray with shadows, not a pitch black. However, without power, the computers on everyone's desk were brought to a standstill.

Then a young staffer who was interning during his second summer at law school said, "The lights are down all over the city! We are looking at another 9/11."

"Come here," he shouted to the young man. "You have no data. The single fact you know is that the power is out. Keep your head," scolded Michael.

"Understood," answered the young man. "I guess I got too caught up in the moment."

"You need something to do. Go get me Marty Dirjke. He is in one of the offices on this hall. Find him."

"Marty Dirjke, got it," answered the staffer. Michael went back to his office. It was a corner office that had windows on two sides of the room.

Minutes later the young staffer came to the threshold of Michael's office with Dirjke right behind him. Dirjke continued into Michael's office and sat at the chair in front of his desk.

"You have a call," announced the secretary.

"Who is it?" asked Michael.

"Someone named Homer."

"Okay, put him through, and close the door behind you," directed Michael.

"I have a call from a man named Homer. This is that crackpot I mentioned to you. Guess I know what he meant by 1600s," said Michael.

"What is really going on?" asked Dirjke.

"I'm not sure. I told you about the odd call I got and you told me about Sid Milliken. Now, the note and the stick have been stolen and the power to the entire city is out. Whatever is going on, we are clearly behind the curve. I am tired of trying to react to the day's events."

"Okay, here comes your call." She had a phone between her shoulder and her ear, while she attempted to type text messages to her family.

"Mr. Mayor. It's good to once again have your attention," mocked the Ukrainian accent on the other end of the line.

"What do you want?" asked Michael.

"I already told you. My wants are simple, Mr. Mayor. I want the object found at the South Ferry Terminal," demanded Vlad.

"Well, you see Mr. Homer we are a little preoccupied on this August afternoon. In case you are not in New York, or watching TV, there is a massive blackout going on here."

"Mayor, perhaps you should take a second and focus on the collateral effects of the blackout rather than chasing after the Deed." There was a momentary pause on the line.

"The entire eastern seaboard is without power Mr. Mayor. Surely you know what is at stake with the power out in New York," teased Vlad.

"What is your game, Homer?" Michael asked.

"I have already told you. The artifact you found yesterday is all I want," stated Vlad in a heavier than usual accent.

"Well, I already told you that we are all booked up today Mr. Homer. Call back again another time," responded Michael.

"Sir, I am the one who caused the blackout," answered Vlad.

"What could you want with the artifact found yesterday," responded Michael.

"Mayor, I am not going to fence with you on this issue. The way I see it, your administration has two options. One, allow the blackout to run its course, which will result in massive looting, arson, and robbery. The world will, for once, see the true fear that has coursed through the veins of New Yorkers since 9/11."

"You are wrong," answered Michael.

"Second, you can choose to give me the artifact, which will eliminate this crisis, but if you want to allow the city to languish in the dark – feel free. The financial markets and the country in general will lose how many billions of dollars per day? Surely there are incentives to give me what I want."

"So what, even if you are right?"

"Mayor, I don't understand why you are not thanking me. Your associates who must be out looking for the Deed will be helped by this circumstance."

"All right, talk," answered Michael. "Why should I accept these terms?"

"The reasons are several. First, I can end the blackout sooner than your technicians can figure out what I did. Second, if I am capable of this, I have the means to cause mass destruction. Consider a mere blackout with some looting, like in the 1970s, a warning shot."

"I get the picture."

"You have two hours until I call again. By then I expect you to have made arrangements to have the artifact delivered to me. You think you can uncover this mystery in the span of a couple hours. What you don't know is that forces have been searching for the Deed for decades. But I am telling you this, you have two hours."

"Two hours? What does that mean?" exclaimed Michael.

"Give me the object you found and I will at least give you another hint," stated Vlad.

The phone went *click* as Michael continued to hold the phone to his ear.

"I know what to do…I am calling Sid."

"What?" asked Dirjke.

"We tell Sid that this 'Homer' guy is demanding that we give him the stick and the note," stated Michael.

"We blackmail Sid with the only information he has. Not a bad idea. Mr. Mayor," complimented Dirjke.

"I will call Sid. I want you to stay in the room while I speak to him. I want you to know everything that is said between us. But let him think you are in the field."

"Okay," responded Dirjke. "Michael, the stick and the note must have piqued interest in the Deed to Manhattan. Frankly, I did not know that others were looking for it. Then last night my student, Barry, asked me whether the legend is real. How could something hide in plain sight for so long?"

Chapter 23

KIDS EXECUTE PLAN TO SEE PAINTING
Thursday, August 14, 2003 4:20pm
Like an offense in football breaking from the huddle, the group went into action. With Ana lagging behind them, Barry and Danny followed the winding path through the St. Paul's Cemetery. The headstones were tilted in all directions and worn to the point that the names were illegible. It was a tiny field surrounded by business and commerce.

The two boys entered the church and sought out the nearest priest. The stained glass windows allowed in a substantial portion of artificial light. The tourists in the church were unsure of what to do. Everyone was looking around for an answer.

"We are going to go to hell for this," stated Danny.

"Relax. I have known Ana a long time. She is good at this stuff, which is why I wanted her with me earlier. Just stick to the plan. The worst they can say is no," said Barry. The boys approached the priest.

Danny began, "Excuse me Father, but with this blackout, don't you think that you should consider moving some of the paintings that are hanging on the walls?"

It caught the priest's attention and before he could think any further Barry added, "No one can be sure as to the scope of the blackout, or how long the power will be out."

"You raise a good point gentleman, but we don't have enough room to move all of the valuable art to the basement. It is just going to have to stay where it is and we'll just have to have faith in the people."

At that instant, Ana walked by and said, "Father have you considered moving some of St. Paul's most valuable pieces into the lower level or a secure room. I was at Trinity Church on Broadway and Wall Street. They have already begun their Electrical Emergency Contingency Plan. What can I do to help these boys? Which of these pieces have you told them to move first?"

"Well, I am not sure where to start," answered the priest. "But St. Paul's is a branch of Trinity Church, so we can follow their lead."

"Yeah, you don't want to be out done by big brother now, do ya?" asked Ana.

Danny took advantage of the priest's indecision. "Fortunately, most of the works in here are too big to move. I think we can get by with only moving the paintings down to the basement."

"Okay. Start with the United States Seal and then move the Seal of New York," agreed the priest. The group entered the pew and each took the picture by the large gold-colored frame. They took the painting off the wall and carried it through the small swinging door to exit Washington's prayer space.

With the priest leading them by flashlight, Barry and Danny carried the picture through the church and down the steps by the west entrance.

"There are no emergency lights?" asked Barry, as he got to the first step.

"No," answered the priest. "It is one of the collateral effects associated with being a church and the oldest building in Manhattan that the building is grandfathered into most legislation and exempted from most laws."

"No lights, great," stated Barry. "Should have realized that."

Danny carried the tail end of the painting down the narrow staircase. Ana stood on the higher side of the painting and looked for some writing or a document. As Danny looked back at her, she signaled with a look on her face that she had had no luck.

The priest opened the door and Danny and Barry carried the painting into the room.

"Okay, one more to go," said the priest.

Ana said, "Maybe this gentleman should stay with the painting while this other boy and I get the Seal of New York State."

After reading the worried look on Ana's face, Barry added onto it and said, "Yeah, you two get the other painting. I will keep watch here and this way, Father, you won't have to open the door again."

"Lord knows, the painting of the Seal of United States is too heavy for one person to carry down the stairs," announced Danny.

"Okay, you stay here and keep guard," answered the priest in the direction of Ana.

"It is twenty-o-three. Father, surely a woman can do some heavy lifting. I will help this other young man carry the Seal of New York State."

"Let's go," Ana said, as the priest and Danny followed her up the stairs.

Barry was alone with the painting.

He reached into his pocket and took out his cell phone to use as a primitive flashlight.

Barry flipped open his cell phone and waived it like a wand over the back of the painting. He methodically went back and forth like the grass checkers on a baseball outfield. He also rubbed his hand against the paper on the back, in the event that there was an envelope or note behind the backing. Then on the bottom corner he saw some numbers:

21181457621921424

He typed the numbers into his cell phone. As he finished inputting the last two digits, he could hear the priest, Ana, and Danny coming down the stairs. Barry gathered himself. He stood up straight and put his phone in his pants pocket.

"How did it go?" asked Barry.

"Not to sound sexist, but we could have used your help. This young woman struggled a little with the painting. We had to keep stopping to let her catch her breath, or to re-grip the painting," said Danny. Ana was not afraid to use her status as a woman as both a shield and a sword, at the same time.

"Well thank you," said the priest in the direction of Ana. "I am just happy to have the job done."

"No, thank you," said Barry, as the priest ushered the kids out of the small room and locked the door.

When the group got to the top of the stairs, Barry and Danny introduced themselves to Ana and the priest thanked the young adults for their help. The group left St. Paul's Chapel and met a few blocks south at Liberty Plaza in front of the Brown Brothers Harriman building.

"That was one well-executed plan," said Danny.

"We really worked well as a group. That was actually very exciting," said Ana.

"Good idea to buy some more alone time with the painting," said Barry.

"Did you find anything?" asked Ana.

"Sort of...I found some writing that amounted to a series of numbers. I have no idea what it means," Barry showed off the numbers inside his cell phone.

"What do those numbers have to do with anything?" said Danny discouraged.

"It could mean anything, or nothing at all," stated Ana.

"At least we know the painting is safe," added Barry.

"Safe from what?" asked Danny. "Our belief that the painting of the Seal of the United States is connected to the Deed to Manhattan was only a hunch. I am skeptical that we actually accomplished anything."

Before the discussion between the two boys devolved any further Ana interceded, "Look guys, we did the best we could. As it is, we exceeded our mandate, protected the object we thought was relevant to the search, and got a long series of numbers on the back of the painting."

At that moment, Danny said, "Look we did the best we could."

"I think I have to agree with you," replied Barry.

"Fine, we need to find the professor and the Mayor," said Ana.

Chapter 24

MAYOR AND DIRJKE GO TO COMMAND CENTER

Thursday, August 14, 2003 4:30pm

As the two men arrived at the AT&T building and walked into the Mayor's command center, Michael was fuming. The building was framed by large clay-color granite panels that lined the windowless structure that was at least forty stories. The building looked like a fortress among the other skyscrapers in Lower Manhattan.

"'Need to talk.' Damn right we need to talk. I am the mayor and I am presiding over the first blackout in New York since the 1970s. Last time this happened, there was looting all over the city," stated Michael.

Dirjke replied, "Michael, let me cut to the chase. Your administration and this entire island are in danger and not for the reasons you think. Your press release has renewed a legend that was long believed to be dead. Your press release has set off the legend of the sale of Manhattan.

"What you have to understand is that this night, tonight, your responsibilities as Mayor of New York will conflict with certain notions you have as a United States citizen."

"What are you talking about?"

"Michael, if someone from our Federal Government or anyone else for that matter wants the Deed to New York, are you going to give it to them?"

"No," answered Michael. "The Mayor cannot simply turn over the Deed to Manhattan, if it was even found. His duty is to Manhattan Island, New York.

"Old friend, I think I just made my point. You cannot surrender this island to anyone."

"Fine, Dirjke. I have to admit that. The Deed to Manhattan supersedes all; whether State or Federal."

"Thank you," answered Dirjke relieved.

"And the blackout?" asked Michael.

"Too broad an operation to be carried out by Sid – the guy is a surgeon. He would never be this clumsy," stated Dirjke.

"Who is this Sid Milliken character?" asked Michael.

"Sid is the best of the best. His business is intelligence," answered Dirjke

"So, why is that a threat to us?" asked Michael.

"In 1775, a small band of New York militiamen led by George Washington invaded Fort Amsterdam and stole a cannon. Less than a year later we declared our independence from Britain."

"Really?" asked Michael.

"The militiamen got the Deed to Manhattan, or information pertaining to it. With the Deed to Manhattan, the Continental Army basically surrendered the city. The skirmishes that Washington led in this area were never about independence: they were about the Deed. Once the British knew they would never find it, New York was all but burned to the ground in the fire of September 1776, just two months after the Declaration of Independence was signed."

"Not too shabby, Mr. Dirjke," answered Michael.

"Yes, Michael, the lens that judges history is only as good as the facts available. Knowing that Washington made decisions with knowledge of the Deed to Manhattan changes everything."

"But the real question is, how do you know this Sid character is involved?"

"It's an old story. Sid is a member of Skull and Bones."

103

"What?" asked Michael. "Wait, Marty, you are not going to give some nonsense about how Yale and Illuminati are trying to take over the world. This is a blackout and the Deed to Manhattan we are talking about. I don't have the time – this city doesn't have the time – for you to dig up tired conspiracy theories."

"Michael, I am going to tell you a few things that even you don't know about me."

"Are you telling me you are in Skull and Bones?" interrupted Michael.

"No, just listen. I am not in Skull and Bones, just like nearly every other person in the world. But I was a pledge, I was tapped for Skull and Bones. However, I quit before the initiation."

"So, you are not part of their little club? Why does it matter?"

"Michael, the organization is built on a secret alliance. I am a potential compromise to that secret. When they tap your left shoulder in late April the question is: 'Skull and Bones accept or reject?' It isn't: 'Do you want to try this out?'"

The point made sense to Michael. But he needed to know, "How does this relate to Sid?"

"Sid was a year older than me. I was his replacement of sorts."

"Replacement?" quizzed Michael.

"Yes, you see Skull and Bones needs to continually have certain people in certain positions of power. Sid had always planned to enter the intelligence world and sculpt the present. He had designs on my ability of historical analysis to carry out this long-term plan. It was a partnership that he expected to last decades. Instead, I changed my mind. It has made me his sworn enemy to this day."

"You really think Sid has watched and studied your career? Marty, this is preposterous."

"He always has plausible deniability, I will give him that. But do you remember my piece on Hudson's discovery of Manhattan?" asked Dirjke.

"Not really, to be honest with you old friend," answered Michael.

"In the months following 9/11 I wrote what I thought was an uplifting piece on how Manhattan was discovered by Englishman, Henry Hudson on September 11, 1609 and that in essence Manhattan, New York, this nation had a rediscovery, a new Pearl Harbor in 2001."

"So?" asked Michael.

"Certain Internet sites and cable news outlets attacked my comments over Hudson's discovery of the island on this same day. That type of subtle attack is Sid's trademark," continued Dirjke. "Here, we have a similar scenario. You put out a press release relating to the 1600s being this island's Western genesis – now Sid Milliken wants to see the object."

"Yeah," answered Michael tensely.

"Do you know why you have everybody and their brother asking you about that press release? All one has to do is look at an old map of Manhattan. If you compare the stick's location with a map from the 1600s, it is clear that the South Ferry Terminal was underwater."

"You're not telling me anything I don't already know," said Michael. "I mean the Deed to Manhattan is nearly priceless to a private collector..."

"That's what you think this is about?" replied Dirjke. "The Deed to Manhattan is the last great treasure hunt. Think about it. The story hides for us all to see. Dutchmen gave Indians sixty guilders and some beads. What did the Dutch West India Company – the world's first corporation – get? A 'make yourself comfortable here' talk from the chief of the Lenape tribe? No. They got a piece of paper that the Dutch West India Company drafted. The world's first corporation: with the world's first corporate lawyers. Now, we have known since President Van Buren that the Deed was not in Holland, but we did not know until your press release that the first clue as to where the Deed is located on Manhattan."

Michael was astounded.

"Imagine the Deed to Manhattan in your hands. Others would have to disprove its validity as a legal document today. And let me tell you, you can get two lawyers to disagree on anything."

"I have learned that in my short time occupying this office, lawyers can disagree over the sunrise," he told Dirjke.

"What if the document fell into the wrong hands? Could it be used as a pretext to invade New York? What would happen if an emerging world power or a terrorist group – under a claim of right – started attacking Manhattan and its people? Lastly, what would happen to US financial markets if we did not own Wall Street?"

"I am calling the Pentagon. Maybe they will have something to offer to this mess," stated Michael.

"Go ahead," dared Dirjke to the Mayor of New York. "Do you see it? Who do you think they are going to assign? Are they going to fly someone in from DC? No, they are going to put you in touch with Sid Milliken."

Chapter 25

HOFFSON AND MAYOR
Thursday, August 14, 2003 5:00pm

The blackout got the Pentagon humming. A potential military act either had to be handled or summarily dismissed. For the American people, General Hoffson was on the case.

"Hoffson, a call from the Mayor of the City of New York," stated the other end of the intercom.

"Put him through," answered the old military man. He was a lifer at the Pentagon. He had been there since the Nixon administration. He had worn the same flat top haircut that long too. The colors and bars on his uniform were impressive. However, his office was on one of the internal rings of the Pentagon. It was windowless and without pictures on the walls. Hoffson's discipline to military code bordered on religious.

"General Hoffson, this is the Mayor of New York. I would like to know what your military intentions are."

"Mr. Mayor, we have no military intentions. All of our reports indicate that this is an infrastructure issue, not a military attack."

"Really?" asked Michael. "Because I have received a military threat."

"What is it?" asked Hoffson.

"Someone is claiming to have caused the blackout," stated Michael.

"Then what are his demands?" asked Hoffson. "The hallmark of a terrorist event is the transaction that the terrorist seeks. Only children destroy things for destruction's sake."

"He wants an artifact found downtown," said Michael.

"What could he want with that?" asked Hoffson.

"My hunch is that he thinks it will lead to the Deed to Manhattan."

Hoffson chuckled from the other end of the line. "Really, this is what you are worried about? I suggest you make sure the property damage and looting are kept to a minimum."

"What about the threat I just told you about?" asked Michael, redirecting the conversation.

"If this is really your biggest concern – which I suggest that it shouldn't be – you have authority to call Sid Milliken. Mr. Mayor, your United States military is already on the case, Sid Milliken is in the vicinity. He called me regarding an artifact found on the island. If you are really that concerned you can call him," advised Hoffson.

"Call him? He already came to my office twice to question me."

"Well, there you go. All set," answered Hoffson.

"Okay," said Michael. "I will contact Mr. Milliken."

"Good," answered Hoffson.

Michael hung up the phone. Dirjke stood there and waited for him to speak first.

"All right, old friend – it is up to you and your associates. It is your responsibility to protect this island from all threats – whether foreign or Federal."

"Understood," answered Dirjke.

Chapter 26

SID AT BAR

Thursday, August 14, 2003 5:15pm

Sid traveled east on 46th Street and away from his rooming house on 9th Avenue. He noticed an air of confusion as he looked south on 9th Avenue. People were staring at their cell phones. Battery radios were the hot commodity today.

"How am I going to get home without the Long Island railroad," announced a middle-aged woman on the sidewalk.

"My son was meeting me in midtown this afternoon. Now he is probably stuck in the R train under the East River." Sid was not concerned with these issues.

Far in the distance he could see the lime green land bridge over 9th Avenue that allowed buses to enter into the Port Authority Bus Terminal.

As he walked down 9th Avenue, between 45th and 46th streets, he saw a man dressed in black encouraging people to come inside and relax.

Sid entered the Bar Restaurant. It had a glass front that allowed a lot of natural light on this clear hot August day. There was a long bar along one of the walls and booths along the other side. TVs were everywhere and blank.

Sid sat at one of the circular booths. After a few minutes and about half way through his Jack Daniels and Diet Coke, he heard a battery radio resting on the bar broadcast a story about an 'Electrical Emergency Contingency Plan' and how St. Paul's Chapel – in Lower Manhattan – had safely concealed the Seal of New York and the Seal of the United States.

Sid got a call from an unlisted number. "Sid Milliken," announced the intelligence veteran.

"Sid, this is the Mayor of New York. Are you in a place where you can listen to me?"

"Yeah," answered Sid. "People are milling around the bar. There is enough background noise to hide your voice."

"Sid, I need your help. I received a crackpot threat a few days ago that I did not prepare for. I am playing catch-up while dealing with this blackout, a terrorist threat, and a city-wide emergency."

"Is that why the Mayor is ordering old paintings in churches to be removed from their walls? News outlets are already reporting it. It is just the type of feel good story that news outlets relay during these types of events to reassure the public."

"Now, to get right to the point, that stick and the note you took, there is someone demanding it."

"Stole a stick?" answered Sid. "I'm afraid you have your facts mixed up."

"Enough Sid, you came twice looking for it and the only way you could have known where to look for it was by hearing Dirjke's name through my intercom," countered Michael.

"That still doesn't prove anything," stated Sid.

"I spoke with General Hoffson who told me you came to New York, because of the artifacts."

"Mr. Mayor, I am a member of the United States military, so my superior has to know my whereabouts."

"You are not denying what you did. So enough with this, I know you are going to tell me that you were acting within your authority via the Pentagon. So, here is another national security concern for you to chew on," stated Michael.

"I am listening," answered Sid.

"The person who is claiming to have caused the blackout wants the stick and the note," said Michael.

"Who?"

"Someone named Homer."

"What can I do to help?"

"Sid, in a few hours a man will call you regarding a meeting. I want you to meet this person and give him the stick and the note."

"Is the Mayor of New York negotiating with terrorists?"

"No. This is an intelligence matter. We have a spy attempting to extract information under the cover of a blackout. I am the one who is in charge."

"Am I actually supposed to give him the stick and the note?" quizzed Sid.

"Yes," answered Michael. "The information it possesses is not of lasting importance."

"What does that mean?" asked Sid.

"This operation is compartmentalized. You don't need any further information. Sid, when this person calls, you will meet him. Give him the stick and the note. Got it?"

"Sure thing," answered Sid. He snapped his phone shut. He looked around the bar at the people using this event as an excuse to party. He picked up his glass one last time and took in the remaining ice cubes from his drink.

Chapter 27

DUROE LEARNS THE TASK BEFORE HIM
Thursday, August 14, 2003 5:57pm

Jack Duroe had two books under his nose. A flashlight was duct taped into position above his head. Beads of sweat were developing over his forehead in a warm un-air-conditioned and windowless room. He was in the pump room of the old facility on 14th Street and the East River.

Jack received various messages and he had access to the latest reports. He knew the scope of the blackout. This was more than just his problem.

He had reported the dead body to the proper channels at Con Edison. He did not know how promptly it would be addressed today. He kept going back to it in his mind. How did he die?

Jack got up from his makeshift desk in the pump room. He walked outside and down the four steps to the stone path. He was drenched in sunlight and had to shade eyes to allow them to adjust. The gravel crunched under Duroe's feet with each step.

After a few more yards, he returned to where he found the dead body. It was a gravel path with large transformers on each side. A twelve-foot chain link fence protected the passersby.

Jack noticed electrified cable about fifteen feet above his head. Then he saw a flexible copper cable that was shaped like cane.

Jack's mouth fell open. "He killed him when he shook his hand. He electrified him via the live cable. The electricity passed through him and onto the victim."

Jack was crouched down and read the man's name and department. "Why murder this man?"

Chapter 28

KIDS AT COMMAND CENTER
Thursday, August 14, 2003 6:00pm
The group proceeded to the AT&T building on Worth Street and Lafayette Street. It is one of the few buildings in New York that did not have any windows. The Verizon Building on the West Side in the 50s is one of the few buildings without windows. As a result of a trade between economic interests and national security, the City Government Emergency Headquarters was relocated to this fortress of a building in Lower Manhattan in the past eighteen months.

As they went to the front of the building, they walked through the door and were met by Dirjke. The group exchanged hellos, but before any news could be relayed, Dirjke brought them into the Mayor's command center. The group nodded to each other as they sat around a large conference room table in the fortress that was the City Emergency Command Center.

"Bad news first. The Mayor and I believe Sid Milliken stole that stick and note from my office."

Danny asked, "But he works for the Federal Government, right?"

"Sid is dangerous because what he would do with the Deed is open to question. He is an intelligence expert, but he lacks a moral code. There is nothing to support the idea that Sid would actually deliver the document to Federal authority."

"Did Sid cause the blackout?" asked Barry.

"I am not sure, but it is unlikely. Sid would never be this clumsy. The guy is a surgeon in the field," answered Dirjke.

"Did you uncover anything at St. Paul's?" asked the Mayor.

"We found some numbers on the back of a painting."

The room fell silent.

"What are the numbers?" asked the Mayor.

Barry recited the numbers for the group.

"21181457621921424."

Michael went to the dry board and began to write.

"Let me do this," said Dirjke. "Good handwriting on a chalkboard is distinct from writing on a desk. Those are things only teachers know."

"How are we ever going to crack this code?" asked Barry.

"It is obviously a coded message of some sort and the power went out in New York City as you were uncovering it. Good job. Most people would have lost their focus," said Michael to the group. "But how are we going to figure out what this means?" asked Michael in Dirjke's direction.

"It's a Caesar Cipher," answered Dirjke. "It is a simple but effective form of encryption. It is a type of substitution cipher in which the plain text is replaced by another number, which is located at another point in the alphabet."

"How do you know that?" asked Ana.

"It has to be. It is one of the only forms of encryption available during that time. The real problem is figuring out the shift," answered Dirjke.

"The numbers on the page represent letters, but plus or minus a certain number. So 'A' in a minus one shift is 26," figured out Ana.

"Precisely," stated Barry. "But that is not the only challenge. After the letter 'J' the numbers are two digits."

"I got it," answered Danny.

114

"Good," answered Dirjke. "Now if we start logically maybe we can each take five letters of the alphabet. Maybe we can have this thing answered in a short while."

Danny replied, "No. When I say 'I got it' I mean I already figured it out," announced Danny.

"Got what?" asked Michael.

"Its 576," said Danny. "I know the shift on the cipher."

"What does that mean? How on Earth can you already know the shift?" asked Barry.

"I watched *Wheel of Fortune* a million times growing up with my Grandma Rita."

Dirjke's mind went to his older sister. "She is a puzzle addict. She even took the time to calculate the stitches in the sweaters she knits."

"So tell me, how does *Wheel of Fortune* help you solve a code from Washington?" asked Ana.

"I learned many years ago that R-S-T-L-N-E are the most used letters in the alphabet. Also, R-S-T are consecutive in the alphabet. The 5-7-6 represents R-T-S. The 'T' and the 'S' are flipped," announced Danny.

Dirjke started writing out the alphabet and the corresponding numbers.

"The shift is 13," added Dirjke, having done the calculations in his head. Barry worked on decoding the remaining numbers on the board. After a few combinations, and about twenty minutes, the cipher became clear:

HEARTS OF OAK

Danny, Ana, and the Mayor waited for Barry and Dirjke to explain the meaning.

"This is truly amazing…" added Dirjke. "Washington leaving office after two terms was not the greatest abdication of power that he displayed."

Michael asked, "What do you mean?"

"Washington knew where the Deed to Manhattan was during the American Revolution. Following the British surrender of Manhattan, a loyalist stronghold during the Revolution, the war was symbolically over. New York was the crown jewel of the colonies. The note from Washington within the stick reveals this fact."

"Hearts of Oak. What does that mean?" asked Ana. "How does that relate to Washington and Evacuation Day?"

"Hearts of Oak was the militia charged with the duty to protect Manhattan during the Revolutionary War," stated Dirjke.

"So Hearts of Oak knows where the Deed to Manhattan is?" asked Danny. "But who are they?"

Dirjke replied, "The Hearts of Oak was a core group from the Corsicans, a militia, whose mission was to protect Manhattan. They used to perform their drills at St. Paul's Chapel. They raided Fort Amsterdam about six months prior to the signing of the Declaration of Independence. They claimed to have just stolen a cannon, but I think now we can surmise that they somehow got something more."

"You mean once the colonies knew they owned Manhattan they declared independence from the Crown," suggested Michael.

"That is what it appears to be," said Dirjke.

"So, Hearts of Oak has the Deed. Are we supposed to infiltrate this group?" asked Ana.

"Maybe the group will come to us, since we found this clue at St. Paul's," stated Danny.

"No, the group doesn't exist anymore," answered Dirjke.

"I am afraid that we are stuck with looking to its past members for answers," added Barry.

"Washington held the Deed to Manhattan, or at least information as to its location, throughout the

Revolutionary War and relayed it to the Hearts of Oak on Evacuation Day in 1783. Amazing," said Barry.

"Who could have been in this group?" asked Danny.

"Alexander Hamilton," answered Barry.

"Why? What proof do you have?" asked the Mayor.

"Once you view all subsequent history through the lens and implications of an actual, in existence, Deed to Manhattan, things are not as they seem," stated Barry.

"What are you talking about?" asked Ana.

"The duel between Hamilton and Aaron Burr was over the Deed to Manhattan," stated Barry.

"What do you mean?" asked Dirjke. "Even I am not sure I can go along on this one. The duel is a straight forward historical event."

"No, Burr served in the same regiment as Benedict Arnold and achieved success in an expedition to Quebec and earned a place within Washington's staff in Manhattan. However, supposedly he quit after two weeks to go back into the field. History is clear that Washington did not care for Burr," stated Barry.

"I do recall something similar following the Revolutionary War, whereby Burr applied for access to the National Archives for the purpose of writing a definitive history of the fight for independence, but was denied by President Washington," added Dirjke.

"So you think our sitting vice-president in 1804 shot Hamilton over the Deed to Manhattan? That is nuts!" added Ana.

"No, seriously, Burr was constantly on the outside, looking in, with respect to intelligence activities in the Revolutionary War. He likely knew that Hamilton was a member of the Hearts of Oak and orchestrated the raiding of Fort Amsterdam immediately prior to the signing of the Declaration of Independence," stated Barry.

117

"Barry, perhaps we should consider the fact that Hamilton was a military leader during the Revolutionary War. He led the Hearts of Oak in battles at White Plains and Trenton."

Danny had commandeered one of the few viable laptop computers in the command center. He was in the corner of the room with his nose at the screen in the Mayor's emergency office. Due to the generator in the basement of the building, they possessed electric power. The Internet connection was slow, but viable.

"Barry might be right," added Danny, the statement was a show of support that gave Barry some confidence. "Burr killed Hamilton, while he was running for Governor of New York. We just moved a painting from the New York State Governor's pew in St. Paul's along with the first Seal of the United States."

"You mean that Hamilton chose death over disclosure of the Deed to Manhattan?" asked the Mayor, addressing Barry.

"Yes. Burr had an idea that Hearts of Oak had something big and he wanted in. But that didn't happen."

"So he killed Hamilton?"

"Exactly," exclaimed Barry. "Alexander Hamilton is the man. He is the most forgotten of the Founding Fathers. He is juxtaposed with Thomas Jefferson, but the real truth is that he was Washington's consigliore. We should investigate his grave."

"Why go to Hamilton's grave and is it even on Manhattan?" asked the Mayor.

"Look, I have to disagree with Barry." The whole room looked at Dirjke with surprise. "He is right that we need to go to Hamilton's grave, but I am going to remain a skeptic as to whether Aaron Burr was even smart enough to know the legend of the Deed to Manhattan."

"Marty, was Hamilton a member of the Hearts of Oak?" asked the Mayor.

118

"Yes, but…"

"On to the matter at hand," stated Michael, as he turned his head toward Danny, Barry, and Ana.

"Hamilton is buried on Manhattan at Trinity Church. It is not far from here, regardless of whether we are right, or not," added Ana. "I vote that we investigate."

"How in God's name do you know that?" asked Barry. "I don't ever remember mentioning Hamilton's grave to you."

"My father went to Columbia. He took me through the church and cemetery and he pointed out King's College's most famous student when we went to the Yankee's ticker tape parade in 1996."

"Michael, Hamilton was killed abruptly and it is possible that his comrades placed something in his grave that amounts to a clue, whether they know it or not," added Dirjke.

"It will give us one final chance to interrogate Hamilton, at a minimum," added Danny.

"All right. Enough. I will permit you guys to go to Hamilton's grave to 'investigate' as Ana said, but I don't want you guys making a scene. If police arrive, saying that 'the Mayor gave you permission' is not going to cut it," explained Michael.

"We'll take care of it," said Barry.

"You'd better," answered Michael. "Do you know the gamble I am taking? I need the Deed to Manhattan found."

Chapter 29

SID GOES TO ST. PAUL'S
Thursday, August 14, 2003 7:00pm
Sid found a bicycle shop on 9th Avenue and 47th Street and
bought a black mountain bike. He even told the sales clerk
to remove all of the reflectors from the bike, because his
son was also a competitive rider. The sales clerk, happy to
make a sale, did not think twice. Sid paid in cash. He
bought a lock and chain. He also got some food designed to
replace electrolytes and provide carbohydrates, as well as a
rope and the best knife he could find in a bike shop.

Sid rode the bike west on 46th Street to the Hudson
River. He walked the bike on the land bridge above the
West Side Highway. People were flocking onto boats and
ferries to get back to New Jersey.

"I mean there is simply no way to get out of
Manhattan today," stated the woman into her phone. "I am
going to stay with some friends of friends." She was
heading in the opposite direction to Sid.

"Where are you headed, sir?" asked the woman next
to Sid in the slow lanes of traffic that developed on the
overpass.

"Downtown," answered Sid. "Yourself?"

"I am going to work. I work on one of the local
cruises around Manhattan. My boss is going to make a
fortune today. The tips should be good too."

"Good luck," answered Sid, as he made his way to
the bike path along the West Side Highway. It was
congested, but navigable at a medium pace.

After a forty-minute bike ride down the highway,
Sid arrived on Vesey Street. He walked his bike along the
north border of the World Trade Center site. He locked his
bike to the fence surrounding St. Paul's Chapel. The fence
reminded him of a joke his father had once told him: 'Son,

you know why there is a fence around this cemetery? Because people are dying to get in here.'

Sid entered through the gate on Vesey Street with the sign reading: Oldest building in continuous use in Manhattan. He knew he was in the right place.

He found the priest and inquired as to the location of the painting that had been taken off the wall.

"Father, I am Sid Milliken from the Office of Internal Security. I understand that as part of an Emergency Contingency Plan you moved some paintings?" as Sid showed the priest his credentials.

"The paintings were moved downstairs. Some kids volunteered to help," said the priest.

"Can I simply verify the location of the paintings? I mean just to know that they are still here..." He knew it was a little weak, but he needed to get a moment with the painting.

"Mr. Milliken, please, the matter has been taken care of by two boys and a nice girl," said the priest.

"I understand," answered Sid, with a bow of his head to demonstrate deference.

Sid left St. Paul's Chapel and walked down the Canyon of Heroes. Along the route, he could not help but notice some of the notable historical events that were listed on the various sidewalk planks. Ticker tape parades were common following World War I. There were placards for all types of events on the sidewalk on Broadway. However, after Dallas 1963 and the Kennedy assassination, ticker tape parades were reserved solely for sports championships.

As Sid walked down Broadway, he noticed the Brown Brothers Harriman Building and sat down at one of the benches in front of Liberty Plaza. Sid looked around and was amazed by the compassionate and helpful nature of Manhattan's residents. People were coping with and enjoying their foray into the 16th century.

Then he saw a guy selling historical maps of Manhattan. It was a slender young man who had strategically placed himself close, but not too near, the World Trade Center site. Sid recognized the man's genius. This type of micro-capitalism impressed Sid. He approached the entrepreneur.

"How are you doing this hot blackout afternoon?" asked Sid.

"Business is good. I took a class at Columbia on early American finance in New York and created this locations map. There are some really cool landmarks down here," he said, as the he made another sale. "Tourists are at a loss for things to do with their kids once they finally get to Lower Manhattan."

"And the South Ferry Subway station leaves something to be desired."

"True. I sell a self-guided walking tour. Go at your own pace... Get your Lower Manhattan map here," the young boy yelled as if he were selling programs at Yankee Stadium. "It is going to be a long hot walk back to the hotel if you don't have this map – your kids will love it...I have them in Spanish, French, Dutch, and German."

Sid was sold a map. Also, he liked this young kid. "How much time do you have left at Columbia?" asked Sid.

"I finished the course last year. I am studying for my SATs."

"You are still in high school?" inquired Sid.

"Yup, I lived nearby and snuck into the class for a semester. That's what I meant when I said 'took'," answered the boy, too preoccupied with making money to submit to Sid's interview.

Sid was impressed. The CIA has an interest in sculpting the history of Manhattan. Some venture capital thrown to this hard worker would make him rich, without him even knowing why. College isn't cheap and this guy seemed to have learned enough already.

"What is your business's name?" asked Sid.

The sole proprietor had already made his sale and moved on. "Check the bottom of the map, sir..."

The map was rudimentary, but it was good for Sid to see all the names on one board. After a few minutes, Sid made sense of the map.

Based on the map, at the end of Wall Street there was a church that housed a cemetery, which is where some banker killed himself in the stock crash of 1987.

Sid walked down Trinity Place. The street runs along the west side of Trinity Church. Sid made a left uphill and onto Rector Street, in front of Champ's Deli.

It was there that he noticed a plaque half way up the block. It commemorated the birth site of King's College, currently known as Columbia University.

He looked around from the plaque commemorating King's College's founding to imagine what it might be like to study here nearly 250 years ago. There, behind the very plaque commemorating the birth of King's College, was the large obelisk that some banker had impaled himself on.

He was standing in front of Hamilton's grave.

Chapter 30

DISCUSSION AT COMMAND CENTER
Thursday, August 14, 2003 7:30pm

"Okay. It looks like we'd better get a move on this," announced Barry, from inside the City Emergency Command Center. The room was along the perimeter of the command center. There were about twenty city employees in cubicles each delegated a city department and function.

"Don't try and boss me around," answered Ana, teasing Barry. Ana was a young woman who used all her facilities. She was as crafty as she was smart – a formidable combination.

"Yeah, but we should get some tools, flashlights, a Swiss Army knife, and some tape. I will ask the Mayor when he gets back," said Barry.

"And money..." announced Ana.

The group took a look at her as though she had crossed a line. "What? It's a real request. When does money not come in handy? Don't worry I will keep all my receipts so that nearly four hundred years later there is no doubt whether I purchased something, or not."

Danny laughed at the comment and the rest of the room smiled at her dry sense of humor.

"I am going with you this time," said Dirjke. "I can't stay holed up in here any longer."

At that moment, Michael walked back into the room. "We have a problem."

"What is it?" asked Dirjke.

"There have been news reports about some good Samaritans who – albeit with a priest's permission – moved some art work in St. Paul's Chapel," announced the Mayor.

"No doubt, Sid has heard the news story," answered Dirjke.

"So," questioned Barry. "It seems harmless enough."

"That may be to you, but Sid is too smart not to catch something like that. You may have outsmarted the priest and successfully used your surroundings to get a look at the cipher, but Sid is on another level. You guys have been playing spy all afternoon. This is Sid's way of life," said Dirjke.

"I don't get it. Why can't this Sid character be trusted, or can't we just work with him to find the Deed or whatever we are eventually after?" asked Ana.

"I have to get involved. There could be clues out there that Barry, Ana, and Danny miss. Mayor, you called me to get to the bottom of this. I can't just sit on the sideline and have these youngsters be my eyes and ears and report back to me. Sid is out there, checking every lead and any location old enough to plausibly have a clue."

"You said it yourself, you being involved is not a good idea," responded Michael.

"That has changed now. I cannot in good conscience allow Sid to define this event. The birth certificate of this island must not become another pawn for some cabal. Sid is not going to give up the Deed, if he gets his hands on it," answered Dirjke.

"How do you know that?" asked the Mayor.

"He already stole the note and the stick," announced Dirjke. "Clearly, he cannot be trusted. But that is also the reason I must go along this time. If Sid is in the vicinity, he is less likely to act if he knows you guys are with me."

"Okay, you've sold me," announced Michael. "Go out there and find what we're looking for. I don't have time to deal with and assess the personal politics of this situation. The only thing I am sure of is this: when the lights go back on, either someone in this room has the Deed to Manhattan, or it is still tucked away in whatever part of the city has been its secret resting place."

"Okay," said Dirjke.

"I have to deal with the other crisis New York is dealing with, the one the rest of the country is watching unfold on their TVs."

"I understand."

"Dirjke, I don't have time for historical analysis without action. Do you want me to call the President, the Commander in Chief, and tell him that the Mayor of New York is chasing the Deed to Manhattan, during a blackout? I guess, the question is: do you want to get me relieved of my office, or are you going to find the Deed to Manhattan?"

"Understood," said Dirjke, just short of giving the Mayor an official military salute.

"Mayor, you have a phone call," announced one of the staffers in the command center.

*   *   *

"Mr. Mayor it is nearly 7:30. I hope you have the information I desire," intoned Vlad. The time had gone by too fast for the Mayor, but as he looked toward his wristwatch, he noticed it was exactly 7:30pm. With the exception of a single light over his desk, the office at the Ukrainian Institute was dark and without air-conditioning.

"I will have someone deliver the artifacts, as we discussed," answered Michael. "Name your location."

"The only international location on Manhattan." He could impersonate a Ukrainian accent and not be caught via voice recognition.

"You think you are playing a cute game with me, but I know where that is. You got a deal," answered Michael. He slammed down the phone.

"Well done," stated Zeke listening in on the call. "Now go to the United Nations complex. Stand along the water and wait for your American counterpart."

126

"How do you know who they are going to send? How will he find me?"

"Leave that to them. I know precisely who they are going to send. The best. He will obtain what you want and distract everyone from our true intent."

Chapter 31

DUROE FIGURES IT OUT

Thursday, August 14, 2003 8:45pm

Duroe looked up from the manual he was reading in complete terror. The rest of the room was dark. His eyes had not adjusted from the light under his nose, making the ceiling view within this room especially dark. The walls were lined with blank screens and buttons.

His instincts told him that the entire Eastern Seaboard and parts of the Midwest cannot go dark without someone daring enough to capitalize. At that instant, he knew the city's weakness – the connection between the dead body and the blackout.

He was still looking up in the room and now placed his palms over his eyes.

Duroe did not have time to swim the ordinary channels, but they were the only ones available. He picked up his phone and dialed 311.

Eventually, he would connect with the Mayor's office.

Chapter 32

KIDS, DIRJKE GO TO HAMILTON'S GRAVE
Thursday, August 14, 2003 9:00pm

After compiling all their stuff, the foursome had set off on their journey to Hamilton's grave. Darkness had begun to take hold over Lower Manhattan.

They walked down Broadway, as Barry commented, "Not as many people as I expected."

"It is nearly nine o'clock. People are heading to the residential areas of the island," replied Ana.

"Yeah, I bet the east and west sides are teaming with people," said Dirjke. The group approached the cemetery that surrounded the church.

The first structure representative of Trinity Church did not face Wall Street. Initially, the church faced the North River, now called the Hudson River, on the natural shoreline. Only for the past one hundred and fifty years, had Trinity Church faced Wall Street.

As they walked that perimeter of Trinity Church Danny commented, "Look at this stone wall that holds back the dirt in the cemetery. It is an interesting red clay color."

"But, the squares appear to be in no set order," followed Barry.

"Well it doesn't take a geologist to deduce that the stone wall holds back earth and dirt around each grave," added Ana.

"It also provides an easy means to fashion a tunnel," finished Dirjke.

"Okay, you guys wait here. Let me take a look at Hamilton's grave..." said Dirjke.

"How are you going to do that?" asked Barry.

"Is that really a good idea," asked Ana. "This guy Sid is probably waiting and watching for us to approach Hamilton's grave."

"What do you have in mind?" asked Danny before his uncle could stumble out a response.

"The way I see it, Sid is definitely watching us, so we should split up," answered Ana. "We need to go under the grave...Professor, Barry, you two go through the black metal door on the side of the built up wall. Danny and I will scout the scene."

The group of men looked around and agreed it made sense.

Dirjke and Barry proceeded through the open door under the land bridge on Trinity Street. However, a twenty-first-century padlock on this old door was now left open. The battery had run out of juice. The door was black against the auburn-colored stone. There was a black cross riveted onto the door, which looked out of place.

"Let's go in here," suggested Dirjke. The door knob amounted to a steel metal circle. Dirjke twisted it and opened the door.

The room was a maze of pipes and tanks, with stairs that led upward. They looked around the room to find something that might take them closer to Hamilton's grave.

"Look, there are some wood panels in the corner, Professor, behind one of these water tanks."

"You might be right. It doesn't have the rough stone that encases the rest of the room."

"Over here, Professor," called Barry. With three loud stomps he had broken through the wood panels.

"Look, beneath the wood panels are steps," exclaimed Barry.

"Amazing... It is a well-designed staircase. So steep that it only requires a hole in the floor the shoulder width of a grown man."

Barry stepped down the steep steps and almost banged his head on the stone floor. "C'mon..." went Barry's echo.

Dirjke made his way down the steps. He announced, "I can't believe this. In my many years of historical study, I never went on an actual treasure hunt."

Barry and Dirjke walked down the narrow tunnel that began at the bottom of the stairs. The tunnel possessed a salty musky smell with moss and mildew growing in the grout between bricks of Manhattan Schist.

"We are definitely walking in the direction of Hamilton's grave," stated Dirjke after a few steps through the tunnel. "Someone must have built the room to protect and hide the entrance to the tunnel."

"Makes sense," agreed Barry.

Barry turned on the flashlight he had picked up at the command center. He flashed it in all directions to get his bearings. There was a narrow tunnel that seemed to have no end.

"What are we looking for Professor?"

"Not sure," admitted Dirjke. "But there has to be something. We'll just keep going forward."

"I can't believe there's a tunnel in the cemetery at Trinity Church," said Barry. It was narrow and approximately six feet tall. The smell was putrid.

They walked about twenty feet, before they made a right turn. Then as they made the final turn, the tunnel ended. But the end of the tunnel was wider than the rest of the hallway, large enough for two people to stand. As Dirjke and Barry walked to the end of the tunnel and into the small room, they saw a strange logo and crest.

"Look over there…" said Barry. On the ceiling of the room was a crest carved from stone that was severely weathered due to almost two hundred years near the salty New York Harbor.

"Can you make it out?" asked Barry.

"Nope, but I have just the idea." Dirjke got out a piece of paper and pencil, his chosen supplies from the command center.

"What are you doing?" asked Barry.

"What's the matter? You never ran your pencil over a quarter when you were bored in second grade? You must be a bigger nerd than me," responded Dirjke with a smile.

After Dirjke had finished his stencil work, he held it under Barry's flashlight.

"In this light, I can't tell what it is," said Barry.

"Me neither," admitted Dirjke. "It looks like there is some sort of tree with thirteen 'somethings' on the branches."

"This symbol is strange for this setting. Maybe there is something behind it. The symbol is embedded within another larger brick." Barry got out a knife and began to score the perimeter of the disk. The mortar was so old that it wore away in no time.

"Here I am recording history and you, Barry, are actually uncovering it."

As Barry made the final rotations on the disk, he was careful to prevent the object from falling and breaking on the ground. The whiff of air was dank.

"What are you going to do now?" asked Dirjke.

"Do you want to put your hand in Alexander Hamilton's grave or should I?" The statement shocked Dirjke.

"I will do it," said Dirjke. The older man walked towards the opening. Barry angled the beam from his flashlight to the circular space in the brick. With a little trepidation, he made his hand into a fist. He closed his eyes as he reached into the space.

He reached his fingertips to the top of the space, moved his hand around inside the brick, and felt around the sides. "There are some papers," exclaimed Dirjke.

Barry felt a huge sigh of relief.

"After all, it was only fitting that Hamilton would have the Deed, as the leader of the Hearts of Oak, the militia charged with the duty to protect Manhattan," said Barry. "He died for that Deed."

"Don't be so quick," replied Dirjke.

"At the time of the event, it caused a furor. In 1804, Burr was the sitting vice-president. Even in my wildest dreams, I could not contemplate that the current vice-president, Dick Cheney, would shoot someone while in office."

"Let's think about the Deed to Manhattan."

As Dirjke took the papers out from the brick above his head, Barry walked over to peruse them. They were severely weathered and a dark tan color. The pages were slick with moisture. The ink had bled through to the reverse side of the pages.

"It has been two hundred years, since Hamilton was shot in 1804 and that someone has read this document, Barry. Look at this parchment. It isn't even old enough to be the Deed to Manhattan."

"How many other deeds to land in North America have you seen, Professor?"

"You are looking at a man who has seen many old documents, including the Deed to Staten Island and the Deed for a portion of the land that comprises Rhode Island."

As Dirjke opened the papers, he could not believe what they were holding in their hands. He shined the flashlight onto the top of the paper. It was in delicate shape and had turned to a light brown color.

"These are the religious incorporation documents for St. Mark's Church," said Dirjke.

"You have got to be kidding me," exclaimed Barry.

"C'mon Barry, you can't really tell me that you thought the Deed to Manhattan was in here, did you?" asked Dirjke, laughing at Barry's innocent tone.

"Well, I thought that because Hamilton was the leader of the Hearts of Oak, he took the Deed with him, to his grave. What better place to keep it?"

"That's true, but it's more complicated than that," stated Dirjke. "There is something to the Hearts of Oak. Why name your organization that? If you were naming a company, or a militia that is charged with the right, nay the privilege of protecting Manhattan during the Revolutionary War, you, Barry, would choose something meaningful. There is something that we are missing, some larger overall clue that would have actually told us to come to Hamilton's grave."

"I guess, but what are we going to do with these documents?"

"I'm not sure right now." But Dirjke was concerned about the level to which this entire scenario had escalated. "You are missing the point. What you have to understand is that everyone – like it or not – everyone has a position as to what to do with the Deed to Manhattan. This is the seminal object that divides New York from the Federal Government. Where is your loyalty?"

"As you know, when the Civil War broke out, this country's first two generations of men were loyal to their states over the Federal Government. Of course, that largely changed following the Civil War, but for New Yorkers it's still not a question. Native New Yorkers place this city above all else."

"I know, but there is the argument for keeping the Deed from falling into the wrong hands. Barry, are our hands the wrong hands? What I am asking you now, Barry, as a fellow historian, is whose hands would you put your faith in?"

"Dirjke, I was born and raised on this island. I am a native New Yorker. With all due respect, Professor Dirjke, you are merely a New Yorker. Only native New Yorkers are born and grow up on this island."

"The way I see it, we are here to protect Manhattan, like the Hearts of Oak before us. We will do what we must," finished Dirjke.

"Let's get to the surface and take a fresh look at these documents," said Barry.

"Okay. Here…I want you to take the stone disk and the parchment. I have a hunch Sid is nearby."

Chapter 33

SID OVERLOOKS HAMILTON SCENE
Thursday, August 14, 2003 9:15pm

Sid was comfortable in his location. He had found a spot near the tomb. As it got darker, less people were walking the sidewalks and streets of this, the least residential area of Manhattan.

He looked toward the grave. Its signature element was an obelisk at the center of the tomb. It was a single stone piece, gray and worn by the weather. Sid noticed a young boy and a girl near Hamilton's grave. They caught his attention because the youngsters were actually touching one of the four stone objects that surrounded Hamilton's tomb.

Sid decided not to approach the young kids, but he was done sitting on those metal steps. As he stepped over the metal railing onto the ground, Sid walked to the metal gate along the west property line of Trinity Church. He was approximately ten feet above street level looking towards the World Trade Center site.

Then he noticed an old black door was open. He saw another young man and Dirjke step out.

Dirjke looked left then right. He stepped out onto Trinity Street. He went north toward the World Trade Center site and the young man turned left. As Dirjke walked up Trinity Street, the young man took a seat a Liberty Plaza Park.

Sid double-stepped it along the stone path another ten yards to the steps leading to the Cherub Gate. He kept Dirjke in sight. He had to calm himself, as he followed Dirjke north up Trinity Place. Sid crossed Thames Street and was about thirty yards away from Dirjke.

Dirjke was sitting on a bench in Liberty Plaza. He looked around to gather his bearings. His right leg was crossed over his left with his hair slightly moving due to the breeze. Then, walking toward Dirjke was the likeness of a man he had not seen for many years.

"Marty Dirjke, I am surprised that our paths have not crossed prior to today."

"Good to see that you have not changed much in all this time."

"Thank you," answered Sid.

"Still meddling in other's affairs."

"Well, you know, it is what it is, Marty."

"What do you want?" asked Dirjke.

"I have a job to do," answered Sid. "Not all of us wimp out and teach."

"Teaching is anything but wimping out. Working with kids all day is about the single best thing you can do to make this world a better place."

"What? You don't think that I have made this world better? Safer?"

"I know you think you made the world a better place Sid and I am not looking to alter your impression of your own accomplishments, but I too have made this world a better place."

"Teaching some hormonal teens about history, really?" stated Sid. "You know what power is Marty. Look around you. See the Brown Brothers Harriman Building over there."

"Yes, it is one of the oldest investment banks in New York with business in all aspects of industry and finance."

"When the investment company was merged to form its current iteration, it was even noted by *Time* magazine that of the company's sixteen founding partners, eleven were graduates from Yale, but even more telling is the fact that ten of those founding partners were members of the Skull and Bones."

"That's great, Sid. Then you must also know that the company was accused of financing the Nazi war machine in the buildup to World War II. So be careful when you consider whether you have made the world better."

"Whatever. More to the point is that after all this time you and I are now true adversaries."

"You must be kidding. You have continually meddled in my academic affairs. I know you are the one that torpedoed my recent article about Hudson entering New York Harbor on September 11, 1609."

"Marty, what are you talking about?" asked Sid.

"You made sure that my Hudson connection to 9/11 was permanently discredited. You know it. What office do you officially hold, anyway?"

"Office of Internal Security, Department of Defense. I was brought into the Pentagon shortly after the events of 9/11. The American military was caught off guard on 9/11 and I was tapped as the only man who could best help the military obtain an upper hand."

"Sid, I know you think that you are doing something positive, but you are wrong. You can't tamper with the truth and expect it not to have lasting implications and results."

"Truth is simply based on the light shed onto a situation. If that can be tampered with, so be it."

"You are an Eli, you know this, Sid. Yale's motto acknowledges that the truth is shaped by the perspective, or the light shone on any set of facts. *Lux Et Veritas* 'light and truth.'"

"So," asked Sid.

"And you have lived this as your own personal motto.

"I have seen too much in this life to believe that there exists a single truth. Truth depends largely on the point of perception."

"Let's talk about your latest transgression against my exploits," returned Dirjke.

"I heard your name in the Mayor's office. How easy can you make something?"

"Do you even know what you are looking for?" asked Dirjke.

"This island's birth certificate," answered Sid.

"And what does Sid Milliken plan to do with this document, if it exists, and you are the first to find it?" asked Dirjke.

"Officially, I intend to burn the document on sight."

"Burn it? What?" asked Dirjke.

"Marty, I am going to explain things to you that you don't know. You are a quitter remember? Skull and Bones has been looking for the Deed to Manhattan for nearly one hundred years?"

"Is that so?" asked Dirjke.

"Yeah, President Van Buren, the first natural-born president, Dutch man, and the only president to order an investigation into the Deed's location – we robbed his grave decades ago in search of it."

"Why are you telling me this?"

"Because I am still pissed that you quit. I want you to know the kind of information you missed out on by choosing history over the dark arts. Anyway, following the end of World War II, one of the German historians who we granted citizenship to told us of a secret Nazi search for the Deed to Manhattan as an attack on the United States."

"So you think Skull and Bones' search for the Deed to Manhattan is credible because Nazis were also searching for it? Again, be careful with whom your group aligns itself. Based on what you are telling me, I made the right decision."

"Look, I know how to peaceably handle this situation. There is no need to pit New York against its Federal Government and risk the other implications of the Deed to Manhattan being put through mass interpretation. Can't we agree on that?"

"Secrets are costly to those who want them kept that way," answered Dirjke.

"Yes, the covert influence to be wielded with the Deed to Manhattan is far reaching. Officially the Deed to Manhattan will be burned on sight."

"Why burn it? Why not give the document to the National Archives, or deliver it personally to the Commander in Chief?" asked Dirjke.

"Not a chance. I am not going to allow the press to potentially manipulate and impute actual validity into the document. What effect do you think that will have on US markets? The Deed to Manhattan will never reach public discussion."

"You are twisted," answered Dirjke. "Now, should I assume that you caused this blackout, since Skull and Bones is robbing people's graves for the Deed?"

"I did not cause it. And I doubt the Mayor purposely turned the lights off. It appears to be a benign event," said Sid.

"Don't bullshit me, Sid," answered Dirjke.

"For real," said Sid, "I don't know what this is about."

Dirjke stood up to end the conversation.

"Sid, I wish I could say that it was good seeing you."

"Mutual, ole chum. See you around."

Chapter 34

GROUP MEETS UP
Thursday, August 14, 2003 9:30pm
On Wall Street, the group met at the steps of Federal Hall underneath the iconic statue of George Washington. The likeness of Washington oversees the site of America's economic core. It was the location of the first inauguration, first Congress and the center of financial activity in New York, if not the country and the world.

Danny and Ana were sitting on the east side of the steps with a view down Broad Street and the New York Stock Exchange. The road is made of small stones with a line of granite along the center as a dividing line. "Do you know why this is called Broad Street?" asked Danny.

"Because of the 'broads'. I noticed John Street not far away from here. Maybe this was the red light district in the 1600s and 1700s," teased Ana. "They still tolerate prostitution in Amsterdam."

"True, but do you know why the street is so wide?" asked Danny.

"Fine, no," answered Ana.

"Well, this street is called Broad Street, because it used to be a creek that led into Manhattan. It's bizarre to think about it."

"What happened to it?" asked Ana.

"It was filled in with landfill and waste, but the original settlement, the part that was burned to the ground during the American Revolution by the British, straddles what is now the filled in river called Broad Street. Actually, the expansion of Manhattan from all sides has been the result of landfill."

"I guess that is why Front Street by the South Street Seaport isn't on the water," said Ana. "Remember, I was born on this island. I am a native New Yorker."

"How do you like Georgetown?"

"It's great. The social scene's not what I expected, but I guess I'm there for an education."

"Not meeting any boys, huh?" detected Danny.

"No, I meet plenty. It's just that I have become adept at turning down meatheads with an Adonis complex. A fake tan, hair gel, and big muscles are not my style."

Barry walked to the steps of Federal Hall and sat down above the pair creating the point on the triangle. He told them in a low voice, "Dirjke and I found the incorporation documents for St. Mark's Church."

"What does that mean?" asked Danny.

"Not sure," admitted Barry.

"Where is the professor?" asked Ana.

"I think he got held up," answered Barry.

"I hope not literally," responded Danny.

"I think Sid wanted to talk to him," answered Barry.

"We better go help him out," announced Ana.

"No, Sid knows he is a civilian and it's not as if he can kidnap or murder a grown man in public on a day like today. One holler and you will be surrounded by officers," answered Danny.

As they looked down Broad Street, the New York Stock Exchange was on their right. It was armed to the gills with security and the American flag was canvassing the pillars that form the front façade. The statue at the top titled *Integrity Protecting the Work of Man* was a dazzling piece.

"Can you believe that none of the police authorities knows about the threat to national security that is happening right now?" asked Barry.

"I never thought this city's first great challenge after 9/11 would be a blackout," stated Danny.

"Or that we would be in the thick of it," finished Ana. "What is the deal between Dirjke and Sid? Do they know each other?" inquired Ana.

"I'm not completely sure," answered Danny. "I know it's somehow connected to Dirjke's article

142

mentioning that Hudson entered New York Harbor on September 11, 1609. That story was summarily quashed."

"Yeah, Sid just wants information. Not blood. From what I can tell, this guy can exploit someone's largest weakness with the smallest intelligence," added Barry.

"Here's an apple, Barry," said Ana. "I bought a few when Danny and I walked to Federal Hall." It was a deep red. Barry smiled.

"Only you would think to buy an apple as a snack on a day like today," smiled Barry, as he took that first bite.

"There he is," said Danny, happy to see his uncle.

As they looked, they saw Dirjke walking east on Wall Street opposite the location of Trinity Church.

The group spent the next fifteen minutes looking at the old parchment. They possessed the high ground on the steps; there was no danger that someone was looking over their shoulder.

"What are we going to do?" asked Danny.

"The incorporation documents for St. Mark's Church in the Bowery seem to provide no concrete direction to go in," stated Barry.

"I am at a dead end," said Dirjke. "I mean in hindsight we were lucky to find anything in Hamilton's grave, much less something helpful to the search for the Deed."

"That's right," answered Ana. "The documents you guys found could relate to an entirely different set of clues that Hamilton left behind for another entirely separate treasure hunt."

Her dry delivery of the facts did not amuse Dirjke or Barry.

"I am going to have to disagree with that," announced Danny. "We've already been to two churches today. Why not go for the hat trick?"

143

"The idea seems like a reasonable next step, but I need more. What should we do when we get there?" asked Dirjke.

"I think we should present the documents to the priest," said Ana.

"That is the most ridiculous thing I have ever heard," exclaimed Barry.

"We have worked too hard to give these documents to a church that doesn't even miss them." Danny seemed to agree nodding his head.

"That is the same attitude that makes Sid dangerous with the Deed to Manhattan," said Dirjke. "Maybe she has a point. Isn't the whole idea of this Deed thing that no one can decide what to do with it, Manhattan versus the Federal Government, the Federal Government against a foreign sovereign, or a terrorist group? Washington and Hamilton were two people smart enough to anticipate this conflict."

"What's your point?" asked Barry.

"His point is that maybe if someone were to show some integrity, and take the obvious route, how could this hurt our chances of eventually getting the Deed, if it still exists?" suggested Ana.

"Also, if my memory serves me correctly, in one of the long rants by my father about Hamilton, he always mentioned that Hamilton was his favorite attorney, as well."

"Ana is correct," added Dirjke. "Hamilton did draft the incorporation documents for St. Mark's Church. I know that much."

"I know that St. Mark's was founded as the first church in New York that did not fall within the auspice of Trinity Church," added Barry.

"How is that important, Barry?" asked Danny.

"It's important because Trinity Church and St. Paul's are governed by the Church of England," stated Barry. "Remember it was the raid on Fort Amsterdam at the tip of Manhattan that led to the Declaration of Independence from the British."

"Either way, we need to continue on this journey. Who is to say that we are collecting the clues in the right order? And as Ana says, maybe this relates to another grand treasure hunt in some alternate universe, but our job is to do what is right, here and now," responded Dirjke.

"We are going to St. Mark's," announced Dirjke, like a teacher leading his students through a field trip.

Chapter 35

SID SEES VLAD
Thursday, August 14, 2003 10:00pm

It was a difficult bike ride up the East Side for Sid. Cars were everywhere and people were still milling round. He looked to the east and across the East River into Queens and Brooklyn. People were sitting on their cars and talking with other around them. Traffic was at a standstill.

As he arrived at 42nd Street, Sid got off his bike to walk. Sid was standing along the water with his hands on the railing. He was looking over the East River from the United Nations complex.

The place was an interesting hybrid of competing interests that sat between 42nd and 48th streets in Manhattan. It is the only part of Manhattan that is not considered part of New York. It's International Territory.

After a few minutes, a man approached him. Vlad was dressed in blue pants and a short-sleeve button down shirt. His hair was thinning and blonde. Vlad had pale white skin and a prominent nose. His small pot belly and large ears made him look especially ordinary.

"Call me Homer," stated the gentlemen in a Russian tone. Vlad could not help letting out a smile as he looked at Sid.

"I trust that you have what I am in need of."

"Indeed. But you don't get something for nothing. Are you really this interested in the Deed to Manhattan? You must have a larger purpose than this."

"That is for me to know and you to find out when I want you to – when it is too late to stop."

"Really?" asked Sid. "I notice that your accent is Ukrainian. Perhaps you should speak with your principals about me."

Vlad laughed, "You and the Mayor are protecting this island as best you can. But in the end, it won't matter."

"Good luck," answered Sid. Vlad walked away from Sid having obtained what he wanted. As soon as Vlad was beyond sight, Sid looked at the digital screen that was tracking the movement of the stick and the note.

Chapter 36

AT ST. MARK'S CHURCH
Thursday, August 14, 2003 10:55pm

It was a long two-and-a-half mile walk to St. Mark's Church on the Bowery. Barry was crestfallen. "I don't know why we are doing this."

"Barry," pleaded Ana.

"No, he is known as the Father of our Country because he was willing to walk away from his power, including the Deed to Manhattan. Washington gave the Deed to Manhattan to the militia charged with the task of protecting this island and it is now the oldest regiment in the army. That is the definition of Evacuation Day. I mean after giving away the Deed to Manhattan, walking away from the presidency after only two terms sounds easy."

"Barry, isn't it part of the Constitution that the President can only serve two terms?" asked Danny.

"Yes, but it took World War II and a president of Dutch ancestry to violate Washington's term precedent and create the need for the Twenty-Second Amendment – Franklin Roosevelt."

"Enough Barry, this is a good idea. It's the first good idea we have had. We've had lucky ideas and historical ideas. Let's do the right thing," said Ana.

"What do you mean – Evacuation Day?" pressed Danny.

"Evacuation Day was a classic move in deception. It was New York's largest celebration to date: the removal of the last British soldier from Manhattan soil, ostensibly ending their occupation of the island. Meanwhile, this country's Founding Fathers, including Hamilton and Washington, were securing the Deed to Manhattan," stated Dirjke.

"Also, did you know that in the main hall of the Bronx County Courthouse there is a mural of Evacuation

Day?" added Barry. "The real noteworthy aspect of the mural was that the Seal of the City said 1664. Do you remember, Ana, when we went to the Bronx County Courthouse during a rain delay at a Yankee game?"

"Yes, we were looking for a pay phone. Remember those days?" asked Ana with a laugh.

"The painting was pre-1974," said Dirjke.

"So? You mean the Seal was changed after the Federal Government denied a loan to New York City?" asked Barry.

"Tough to say, the Seal was changed in 1974, but the budget crisis of New York in the following years taints the analysis."

"Professor, do you think the reason Hamilton and Washington were able to convince the Federal Government to assume the considerable debts of the original thirteen colonies was due to the collateral they possessed in the form of the Deed to Manhattan?" hypothesized Barry.

"Perhaps, if I thought about it, Barry, but let's focus on what we are all doing. Ana had a good idea. My meeting with Sid has changed some of my thinking."

"We have to remember that we are competing against a spy," stated Danny.

"Yes, returning the documents to St. Mark's creates an untraceable cover story."

"Huh?" asked Barry.

"If we can hide our evidence, we can end this race. Then dedicate time to locating the Deed on my schedule, not Sid's," said Dirjke.

The group walked up Broadway and made a right onto Astor Place toward St. Mark's Church. On one of the brownstones, the group walked past a college kid playing his guitar with two attractive young ladies intently listening. On another portion of the sidewalk, a couple had taken out their lawn chairs and were playing Crazy Eights with their two young children.

As the group arrived at the church, they were struck by how many people chose to hang out in front of the building. "I can't believe how well this city is handling the blackout," announced Danny.

"Really, is that so surprising for New York?"

"There are so many thousands of people that can't evacuate the city," smiled Danny in Ana's direction.

"Yeah, that's true," answered Dirjke. "I remember the previous blackouts in 1965 and 1977. It was chaos. There was looting, larceny, and arson. It was dangerous. It's encouraging in this post 9/11 world to see such camaraderie between New Yorkers."

As they made their way to the front entrance of St. Mark's Church, Dirjke noticed two Native American statues titled *Aspiration* and *Inspiration* on either side of the entrance.

"Look at these sculptures," said Danny.

"I noticed it, too. Churches are not my area of expertise, but I will agree that it is unusual for an American church to celebrate Native American culture."

"The fact that it is strange for a church to have these native-type statues makes me think we might be in the right place," stated Danny.

They made their way to the priest that was in charge. He was along the side yard, speaking with neighborhood families. Dirjke slowly approached the priest.

"Father, I am Marty Dirjke, a professor at Collegiate School on the Upper West Side. Through the course of today, we located some documents that pertain to your church."

"My church, what do you mean?" asked the priest. "I can't believe that I am being presented with this issue today of all days. What have you found, or what do you think you have found?" asked the priest.

"We located the incorporation documents for St. Mark's Church," said Dirjke.

"Located?" queried the priest.

"Yes Father, the documents that created your church," repeated Dirjke.

"Yes," interjected Ana, letting the priest know that she intended to be included. Dirjke looked back at her with an annoyed grimace on his face.

"Follow me," said the priest. He placed his hand on the back of his own neck. He clicked on his flashlight and led the group through the yard to the side of the church. The steps were very precarious in the dark combined with the moss that had grown on the bricks, making them very slick on a humid August night. They entered the pitch-black church. The priest waving his flashlight on the stained glass windows on the inside of the church created scary shadows and images, as they made their way to the back of the room.

The priest opened a door toward the back of the church. He made two or three steps before he turned to enter his office. Barry, Danny, and Ana were behind Dirjke and had positioned themselves close enough to the priest to allow inclusion. The group went into the priest's office in the back of the church. As the priest sat behind his desk, the group was relegated to a sofa on the sidewall. Dirjke sat at the lone chair positioned in front of the desk.

Before Dirjke could begin to stammer out an explanation, the priest began to speak. "Now, tell me again what you think you found."

"What we have is the incorporation documents to St. Mark's Church," said Dirjke.

"Really? And where did you get these documents?" asked the priest.

"Father, with all due respect, assuming you don't have the document, the only other place to get it is from the lawyer who drafted the papers," explained Dirjke.

"That does not answer my question. I asked where," answered the priest.

"I am not sure that I can tell you that," responded Dirjke.

"Professor Dirjke, I am a man of the Church. What you tell me is privileged, by law. Consider this a confession," stated the priest.

"Father, I have never really been the religious type. I can't even recall the last time I went to church."

"Enough, just tell me, where you got this document. Was it in some attic in a brownstone? And why are you here, today, during the city's first blackout in a generation?" asked the priest.

"To be honest, we obtained the documents from Alexander Hamilton," said Dirjke.

"He's been dead a long time," answered the priest. "How did you know where to look?"

"With all due respect, Father, that is what made it very easy to find him," stated Dirjke. He was not willing to admit certain things to the priest, regardless of the confidential reassurances he had given him.

"Who do you represent?"

"Hearts of Oak," answered Dirjke. It was a terrible lie from a terrible liar, but it was what the priest wanted to hear.

"Hearts of Oak?" answered the priest to his surprise.

"Yes," answered Dirjke.

"Hearts of Oak. Does that include the sofa?"

"Indeed," answered Dirjke.

"I understand, but really if you could shed some light on this," responded the priest.

"Father, this is really all I know. Why do you keep asking me questions when all I am trying to do is give you this document?"

"Well, there is one secret associated with the top job here at St. Mark's Church on the Bowery, just as there are typically secrets passed down between presidents and other heads of state."

Barry had begun to nudge Ana's knee. Her idea to give the document to their rightful owner had worked. She felt vindicated. Dirjke tried to calm his nerves, as the priest stood up.

"Indoctrination as priest at St. Mark's has one caveat, one secret – with no explanation or foundation."

"What is it?" blurted out Barry, unable to control himself. The statement caused Ana and Danny to slouch down on the sofa.

"Easy," answered the priest, as he stepped toward the back wall in his office. He pulled open a hinged oil painting within his office. It was a classic safe. "See, these documents have been in our possession since the church's inception. Our only information is that they belong to the Hearts of Oak. And until today no one had ever mentioned that name to us."

"What do they say?" asked Ana.

"That's the thing. We don't know. To be honest I have not spent any time trying to decode it, but others before me have been driven nearly mad trying to figure it out – without success."

Then the priest placed the large piece of parchment paper into Dirjke's hands.

"This is the Hearts of Oak's next challenge," announced the priest.

Chapter 37

VLAD OPENS POSTER ROLL
Thursday, August 14, 2003 11:00pm

Vlad made his way back from the United Nations and returned to the Ukrainian Institute. He walked up the wide spiral staircase into his office overlooking Central Park. The fourth floor was just above the tree line. He walked into his office, closed the door, and sat behind his desk.

His attention was focused on the stick. He shook it a few times and could feel the note floating around the inside of the wooden cylinder.

"Foolish New Yorkers, they would never know what they bargained away," thought Vlad.

Vlad could feel a rush of anticipation wash over him as he separated the two halves of the stick. He opened the note and read its contents.

11-25-1783

One Deed Left. I Pray Whereby you will find it.

7-11

Vlad had no idea what this phrase meant. He picked up his cell phone to call his contact.

"Zeke, I have what we need," explained Vlad. "It's not the final object, but a definite clue."

"Now we have to accelerate this plan. After four hundred years, and with these artifacts, even these Americans will figure this out," stated Zeke. "We will be there when they do."

"Vlad you must warn the Mayor as to why they must hand over the Deed."

"I still have the disposable cell phone you gave me. That is no problem."

154

"Understood, twelve hours, right?" asked Vlad.

"Yes from 4:11 p.m., August 14, 2003." That was start time of the blackout in Manhattan.

"Got it," answered Vlad. "How are we going to use this new clue?"

"Describe the man you met."

"He was older and fit, with a beard."

"Good, everything is proceeding as planned. I will have him meet you again. He will find you when the time is right."

"Can he really be trusted?" asked Vlad.

"He gave you the stick and the note. Vlad, if you want what we agreed to, you are going to have to do this my way. If the Institute had what it takes to find the Deed, we would have never met."

"Understood," answered Vlad.

* * *

It was a quick bicycle ride for Sid across 42nd Street to 6th Avenue. He was sitting on a bench under the tree-lined canopy of Bryant Park. In the 1980s the park was closed for renovations. The result is that the entire renovated park was built on top of the New York Public Library's archives.

Sid looked at his device to track the stick and the note. It had remained motionless for the past ten minutes. "That's where my new friend must be located," said Sid aloud as he looked around at the New Yorkers managing the blackout.

Chapter 38

DIRJKE AND KIDS GO TO COMMAND CENTER
Thursday, August 14, 2003 11:35pm

The group walked out of St. Mark's Church. They started down Third Avenue. The bars were still packed with people. Others had vacated their walkups and were relaxing on the sidewalk in lawn chairs or on blankets. Candles and flashlights were everywhere. There was a buzz among the people, but violence was at a minimum.

"What are we going to do now?" asked Danny. Dirjke was holding a folded piece of parchment.

Barry was bursting. "One minute we're returning the only clue we have to the Deed to Manhattan in the form of the incorporation documents for St. Mark's Church. The next, we have a piece of parchment with over one hundred numbers on it."

Ana felt like a real member of the group. Her quick thinking had landed them alone with the first seal of the United States and now her idea had brought them something else. "Where to now, Professor?"

"We are going to the command center to talk to the Mayor," answered Dirjke. It was a slow walk back downtown. The group moved through the streets of Little Italy and Chinatown toward the City Command Center on Broadway and Duane Street. Once at the building, they walked the steps to the third floor.

The group arrived at the Mayor's Official Emergency Office. Michael leaned back in his chair and asked, "What did you get at Hamilton's grave?"

Dirjke relayed the story and the executive decision they made to go to St. Mark's. To round out the story Dirjke said, "All we got was this piece of paper."

Michael's eyes widened to the size of quarters. "Don't get that look. It's not the final piece of the puzzle," said Dirjke.

"It is a puzzle," added Barry.

Dirjke unfolded the parchment and pushed it across Michael's desk.

"The series of numbers is staggering. What is this?" asked Michael.

"It's an Arnold Cipher," answered Dirjke.

"Caesar Cipher, Arnold Cipher, geez," added Ana.

"How is the code hidden within this type of cipher?" queried Danny.

"The code is a hidden series of three numbers separated by periods. The numbers correspond to a word on a certain page, on a certain line, and the word number on that line," stated Dirjke.

"Figuring out what the code book is, that's the challenge," said Barry. "We don't know which book it is."

"How do we get past this hurdle, Dirjke?" asked the Mayor.

"Barry is correct. The code book is the secret to the code," said Dirjke.

"How are we ever going to figure out what the code book is?" asked Ana.

"That's a good question," said Barry.

"I have a couple of ideas," said Dirjke.

"Good, because I don't have the first idea," answered the Mayor.

"It's called an Arnold Cipher because Benedict Arnold used it to communicate with the British while he committed treason. For those communications he used either the *Commentaries on the Laws of England* by William Blackstone or Nathan Bailey's *Dictionary*," stated Dirjke.

"Unk, I don't really think it's likely that this message is coded with a code from a treasonous spy," interrupted Danny. "I'm not a historian, but I know what Benedict Arnold's name means on the playground – not good."

"He's right," said Barry, agreeing with Danny. "But before you just jump down my throat Ana, I believe that I know the code book," anticipating Ana's usual reaction to his ideas.

"How?" asked Dirjke. "What do you know?"

"Remember the '7-11' on the note inside the stick?" asked Barry in the direction of the group's attentive ears.

"Yeah," they answered.

"That code name for Washington was developed by Benjamin Tallmadge. He employed an Arnold Code for his work with the Culper Ring," explained Barry. "The Culper Ring was our first intelligence apparatus."

"Do you know the name of the code book or not?" asked Ana.

"Entick's *Dictionary*, that is the code book we need," said Barry.

"No problem," said Dirjke. "I see your point. Use the code book that our country's first intelligence unit used. Now, where the hell are we going to go to find this damn book?" asked Dirjke.

"Google Books," answered Danny. He was sitting at the desk in the room with his nose to the screen searching for a PDF display of the old dictionary.

"We have Internet service in my office, but it's connected to landlines. And the computers only run on batteries, so our time is limited," said Michael.

"What makes you think it's on the Internet?" asked Dirjke.

"It's the best hope we have," said Ana, as she looked over Danny's shoulder. Danny, remembering the days before cable Internet, heard the familiar buzzing sound, and then he was online.

"Don't you guys thank me all at once," said Barry, to Danny and Ana. He was hoping for more of a reaction from Ana. Worse, she was already looking over Danny's shoulder to decode the message.

"We will know how smart you are in a few minutes," Michael observed to Barry.

"I am not sure what my theory will accomplish."

Ana had her hand on Danny's back. The Mayor, standing with his arms crossed, looked less than pleased with the entire situation.

Chapter 39

VLAD AND MAYOR TALK
Thursday, August 14, 2003 11:22am

Vlad contacted the Mayor, as he had promised following their earlier conversation. He was standing behind his desk. The air in the Institute was getting warm and stale. Vlad's forehead was shiny with oil, because the generator could only be used for necessities.

"Mr. Mayor, good to speak with you again," taunted Vlad.

"Homer, did things go smoothly?" asked Michael.

"Not as smoothly as I thought," answered Vlad.

"Well, I am not sorry to hear that," said Michael. "But I held up my end of the bargain. You have the stick that you wanted, right? It's time to turn the lights back on."

"I don't think so."

"Now, we had a deal."

"Now, here is your next challenge. It took you four hundred years to even realize that the Deed to Manhattan is located here. I cannot allow another four hundred years to pass for you to actually find the document."

"What do you mean?" asked Michael.

"Motivation," answered Vlad. "Mr. Mayor, you have exactly five hours until Manhattan is flooded with water."

"How?" asked the Mayor.

"I am telling you when. Isn't that enough? The how is for me to watch and enjoy," replied Vlad.

"Flooded with water?" asked Michael. His thoughts went to the idea of a tidal wave crashing over Manhattan, on the night that the city's population swelled due to the lack of transportation off the island.

"Yes," answered Vlad. "Manhattan will be filled with water. Know this: the blackout provides you with the easiest means to give me the Deed without anyone knowing

– no media coverage. Give me the document and this will all end."

"Why would I ever do that?" asked Michael.

"Because my intent is not to kill Manhattan's people, it is to rule Manhattan."

"Then why flood the island?"

"You know I work hard to speak English. I try to use the right words to tell you what I intend to do, but you don't see their meaning. You have a misplaced belief that I am a monster bent on mass murder."

The phone went *click.*

Chapter 40

MAYOR TALKS TO HOFFSON
Thursday, August 15, 2003 11:45pm

The Mayor was rattled by his conversation with Vlad. With his elbows on his desk, he rested his face in his hands for a few seconds. Then he took in a deep breath and carried on.

Michael looked into a list of numbers for emergencies that required military attention in a drawer behind his desk. It was a folder that he received from his predecessor that he hoped he would never have to open. Mac Hoffson's name came up.

"Mac Hoffson, here," answered the grizzled military veteran. The military always knew who was calling. Sometimes Hoffson told the person their own name. It usually startled the listener, which is the attack Hoffson planned.

"Mr. Mayor, I must say I am pleased at the manner in which the city is handling the blackout."

"I agree," answered Michael.

"So why is the Mayor calling me again?" asked Hoffson.

"I am now calling for a few other reasons," answered Michael, "potentially military reasons."

"What could you need the military for?" asked Hoffson.

"Well, I am not sure yet. General Hoffson, in order to do my job, I can't tell you the whole story. But I might require military intervention," warned Michael. "I don't have time to play politics with military officials."

"That's not how this works," answered Hoffson. "I need to know what your concern is."

"There is a threat to flood the city," answered Michael.

"Flood the city?"

"Yeah, we don't know the means or methods of detonation, but we know the result."

"Huh?" asked Hoffson.

"General, I don't have the time, to explain the story, but there is a potential threat to the island. The Mayor of New York needs military support," stated Michael.

"Mr. Mayor, we have already had this conversation. Contact Sid Milliken. He can help with your infrastructure problem. Does the military have to do everything?"

*   *   *

Michael dialed Sid's number.

"Mr. Mayor. I did not expect your call," said Sid.

"Well, you'd better get used to my voice. We have a problem."

"What is it?"

"I received another threat from Homer."

"Really, what did he say?"

"Sid, he threatened to flood Manhattan."

"Flood the city. How is he going to do that?"

"Exactly – and without the power on, it makes no sense," said Michael.

"Well, what does he want?"

"He wants the Deed to Manhattan," answered Michael. "Looks like I need you. This city needs you."

"I will do what I must," answered Sid.

"Not so quick my new friend. Your job is to stop this Homer. He is the real enemy."

"That's your assessment."

"Exactly, and I am the Mayor of New York City."

"Listen, don't call me and ask for help, then tell me how to do my job."

"What is it with you and Dirjke?"

"Nothing, it's simply a coincidence."

"Look, there is a terrorist whose agent is making additional and credible demands upon the safety of the citizens of Manhattan. In case you are not preoccupied with all the problems that I am dealing with, remember that because of the power outage, there are at least an extra 100,000 people in the city tonight. So, if you want to go on a treasure hunt with your old chum from college, it will be the last time you do anything in any official capacity. Do you understand me?"

"Got it," answered Sid. "I will report to you once I find this Homer."

Chapter 41

DECIPHER HEARTS OF OAK CODE
Thursday, August 14, 2003 11:50pm

At first it was difficult to decode the message contained within the hundreds of numbers written on the parchment they received from the priest at St. Mark's Church. Locating the page number, row number, and word number was a painstaking process. The message had to be decoded one letter at a time counting three different series of numbers.

Dirjke and Michael delegated the counting of rows and words to younger eyes. It took the kids about twenty minutes before Danny gasped, "Mortal – that is the last word hidden within the number sequence."

"That was not easy," announced Ana.

"I know, I think finding those letters gave me a headache," said Danny.

"Mr. Mayor, Professor, we finished decoding the message from St. Mark's Church," said Barry.

With the key to the Arnold Code deciphered, the message had been translated. Dirjke read the passage aloud to the room:

"Hearts of Oak, did you go down
alive into the homes of death? One visit
finishes all men but yourselves, twice mortal!"

"Hearts of Oak, again?" queried Danny.

"Looks like we are going in circles," said the Mayor.

"It must mean something else, but what?" asked Dirjke. "There has got to be a meaning to this that we are missing."

"Homer!" shouted Ana from across the room.

"What?" asked the others staring at the two-hundred-year-old piece of paper.

"The quote is from Homer's *The Odyssey*," finished Ana.

"I googled 'Hearts of Oak' along with a British soccer team, and the Homer quote was a search result."

A fearful look ran across Michael's face. "What is it?" asked Danny in the Mayor's direction.

"We did not tell you because you already had enough on your plate."

Ana then asked again, "What is it?"

"You three are agents of my office. You were given the information necessary to carry out your assignment. That is as far as this discussion needs to go. The situation is too important for hurt feelings. Now since you must know, the person who is claiming to have caused today's blackout identified himself as Homer."

"The son of a bitch gave you that name to test what you guys actually know," said Danny. Barry had moved himself to the corner of the room to focus on the words they had just decoded.

"And apparently, we failed the test," added Michael.

"We have a guy named Homer who claims to have caused today's blackout. Now, after finding a clue leading to a picture in St. Paul's Chapel and getting the incorporation documents for St. Mark's Church, we have a phrase from Homer's *The Odyssey*. However, that passage begins with the same three words we decoded at St. Paul's Chapel hours ago. We are going in a circle," said Ana.

"But we have to be on to something. We just have to connect the dots," reasoned Dirjke.

"What if we have not been collecting the clues in the correct order? I mean, we haven't found the Deed to Manhattan, but who is to say how close we are?" asked Michael.

"I don't know how close we are, but I just found the location for the next artifact," said Barry.

"Huh?" said Michael.

"I can't believe we did not think of it before. Hearts of Oak, that is genius."

"Barry, what do you mean?" asked Ana.

"Hearts of Oak is the name of the militia charged with the duty to protect Manhattan during the Revolutionary War, right? But little do people know that this included protecting the Deed itself. The phrase 'Hearts of Oak' is a reference to this passage in *The Odyssey*. We were just too obtuse to figure it out. The route to the Deed rests within the language contained in the Hearts of Oak passage. The phrase is the map to the clues we need to find the Deed."

Danny interrupted, "If Barry is right, then apparently Homer not only started the blackout, he started with knowledge of the Hearts of Oak phrase that has taken us nearly eight hours to find."

"How so?" asked Michael. Ana had re-read the Hearts of Oak passage and realized what Barry was talking about. "I get it, Barry. You're saying that Hamilton's grave was the first homes of death, which we already visited."

"So what's next?" asked Danny.

"Well, let's take a look at the language. Here's what I see," answered Barry, "'Alive into the homes of death? One visit finishes all men but yourselves, twice mortal.' I've got to say, I think we need to go to Hamilton's house," announced Barry.

"How so?" asked the Mayor pushing Barry and the issue further. "As Mayor, I need 'cause' to sanction this group's next field trip in Manhattan."

"I mean, Hearts of Oak, to begin with that quote, it is an obvious reference to the militia charged with protecting the island of Manhattan during the

167

Revolutionary War, right? We can agree on that," reasoned Barry, attempting to explain his logic.

"See where it says 'homes of death' it is plural and where it says 'twice mortal', I think it is saying there's a clue or something at Hamilton's home."

"The clues are contained within his home in this life and the next," added Ana. "Remember the characters in *The Odyssey* were polytheistic. The home, in this life and the next, had a more spiritual meaning in that era."

"It is our best lead," concluded Barry.

"Considering it's our only lead," added Danny in a nod of support for his new friend and co-worker.

"I have one question for you Barry. If this group actually had the Deed to Manhattan, why would they name themselves after a passage from *The Odyssey*? Hiding the answer in plain sight? No one with this type of document is this reckless," said Michael.

"Michael, the group's original name was The Corsicans. The Hearts of Oak represents the group's core members," answered Dirjke.

"They must have been a subset of the group that formed its leadership," said Danny.

"But, what evidence is there that Hearts of Oak ever had the Deed?" questioned Michael, moving past Barry's statement.

"The Hearts of Oak raided the battery at Fort Amsterdam a few months before the colonies declared their independence. We are banking on some pretty strong currency that, at this point, they got more than a cannon, which is what the official story would have us believe," answered Dirjke.

"Just to get this out of the way, where on Manhattan is Hamilton's house?"

"Harlem," answered Dirjke to his great-nephew. "Author of the Federalist Papers, First Secretary to the

Treasury, yet, he built a home in the rural portions of Manhattan at the turn of the eighteenth century."

"Exactly, Professor. You know Hamilton is known as the architect of this country's financial prowess, whereas Jefferson advocated for a farming society. Maybe these two men were actually similar," remarked Barry.

"I wouldn't go that far. Hamilton was born in the West Indies. He lived in this house for only two years," said Dirjke.

"But his life was cut short," insisted Barry. "Who is to say that?"

"Enough – back to the matter at hand," said Michael. "I can't believe that people actually devote time to learning and knowing these things. You two can argue and match facts with one another without end."

"There's only one problem with searching Hamilton's house," added Ana, trying to further the Mayor's transition.

"Only one problem?" answered Michael, showing who was in charge. Dirjke smiled to himself.

"Mayor, we would like to continue this assignment," pleaded Barry. It was the same formal tone Barry had begun to use when the Mayor first gave the youngsters their first assignment hours ago. "Sir, I believe that the job is not done yet. I think that we need to go to the Grange," continued Barry.

"The Grange?" queried Michael.

"We need to go to Hamilton's house in Harlem. The Grange was the term that Hamilton borrowed from his father's ancestral home in Scotland," added Dirjke. "He had quite a diverse background."

"It's a little past midnight and it has been one of the longest days of my life. Worse, it's not over. I will have to give another press conference later this morning and report on the blackout and potentially the whereabouts of the four-hundred-year-old Deed to Manhattan. Listen, your work is not done tonight…"

"What?" asked the group, almost in unison.

"You guys, and girl, are going to Harlem tonight. I want this Deed issue put to bed. What I do not want is my search team going to bed."

"Michael, with all due respect, Harlem on the night of the blackout. It could be dangerous," suggested Dirjke.

"Nonsense," countered Michael. "Looting and crime has been minimal. My sources tell me that the citizens of this island are treating this blackout as an excuse to have an August block party. Whatever terrorist simply thought that Manhattanites would simply tear each other apart without power has lost his bet. They underestimated the people of this city. You guys are here to find the Deed. The city is my job."

"How will we get up there?" asked Danny.

"An official city car; the Seal on the side doors may, as of yesterday, have the wrong year, but I know the engine works fine."

"But none of us drive," answered Barry. "We are each New Yorkers. I don't think that any of us would be comfortable driving during a blackout."

"The boy does have a point," admitted Dirjke. "I know I am not comfortable driving through Manhattan during the blackout. I mean, I haven't driven a car in nearly twenty years."

"I'll drive," declared Danny.

"You?" asked Michael.

"I'm from Maryland. I have my license. I'm used to driving through rolling hills on winding dark roads." It was the best Danny could muster, but Michael was not going to allow this to dissolve into an issue.

"Done," answered Michael, with a tone that ended this discussion. The intercom buzzed, "Mr. Mayor, you have a phone call."

"One moment, listen you all, don't do anything too stupid."

"We'll be okay," answered Dirjke.

"Go," answered Michael, as he sat behind his desk.

Chapter 42

DUROE LEVELS WITH MICHAEL
Friday, August 15, 2003 12:25

"Mayor, here," answered Michael. He left the phone on speaker.

"Mr. Mayor, we have a call from the power plant on 14th Street. They are saying that they will have the power running in six hours," stated the voice in an optimistic tone.

"I need to speak with whoever is in charge of the facility," replied Michael. Sam, the Mayor's assistant, transferred the phone call into his office in the windowless AT&T office building. Considering the event, this command center had all normal functions, if at a slower pace.

"You are a tough man to get a hold of. What else are you dealing with tonight besides the blackout?"

"You wouldn't believe it if I told you," answered Michael.

"This is Jack Duroe, Mr. Mayor. I am going to get right to the point. If the backup generators for the pumps servicing every subway and train tunnel leading into Manhattan don't begin running soon, all of Manhattan's tunnels will be flooded with water."

"The ripple effect from something like that is immeasurable for the economy and the entire Eastern Seaboard," said Michael.

"Yes, water on the electrified rail that powers the city's subways would cripple the entire metro area."

"Holy shit, you are right. Only the G subway line does not run through at least some portion of Manhattan. Replacing these lines could take weeks, if not months. The lost income to New York and the country would be in the trillions."

There was an awkward silence as Michael tried to catch up with the escalating circumstances surrounding the blackout. He felt like a chess piece under constant attack.

"So, in case you need another problem, if I don't get the power up to these generator pumps in at least some limited capacity, the subways and tunnels into the city are going to flood with water."

"Do you have a plan to get the generator pumps running?" asked Michael. "We have a terrorist counting on it."

"What do you mean?" asked Duroe.

"Without getting into details, I received a pointed threat that Manhattan was going to be flooded tonight. It looks like we have our answer. How do we get the pumps running?"

"It's going to take rewiring. The wires were cut. So there should be power running to the generators even during a blackout, because of a connection to backup battery generators."

"I need this fixed immediately," exclaimed Michael.

"I have an idea of how to do it, but I have to tell you, I am not confident," stated Duroe.

"This is your job," answered Michael. "Why can't you do your job?"

"There was a murder at the 14th Street Power Plant, hours before the blackout started," explained Duroe.

"How was the person killed?" asked Michael. "Maybe that will provide us with a lead. Bullets are traceable."

"With finesse," answered Duroe. "There was an electrified fence in the vicinity. Basically, someone held the live wire and simultaneously grabbed the victim who absorbed the end of the current. He was electrocuted. There is no trace of who did it. Or evidence to investigate. But I can guarantee you one thing, it was not a random act."

"I agree with you there," replied Michael. "My guess is that he was in charge of the generator pumps that you are trying to figure out."

"Yes," stated Duroe. "I will do my best."

"I don't want your best, I want what is good enough to keep the city functioning."

"I understand, but how could we have not seen this weakness in our infrastructure until today?"

"Now is not the time to discuss this," answered Michael.

"Basically, it's going to take me at least six more hours to figure out how to get the generator pumps running to keep the city's tunnels and subways from flooding."

"Will that save the city?" asked Michael.

"No, it's only a band aid. Eventually the power must return or the city will flood. New York's subway system will not survive without power returning at some point past twelve hours."

"All right, get on rewiring those pumps. Use materials from the other generators in the plant. The only generators that matter are the ones that operate the pumps and keep the subway tunnels from flooding."

"But, what about the fact that eventually the pumps will fail to keep up?"

"Again, I want you focused on returning the power to those generators. The power went out at 4:11pm, on Thursday. We have until 4:11am Friday morning to save this city. Now I know this is not the job you asked for, but this is the job you got. I am counting on you Mr. Duroe. Whether they know it or not, this whole city is counting on you. I need you working on this problem and me giving you a pep talk right now about what is riding on your skills is a waste of time. If you need something – you call me. Got it?"

"Yes, sir," answered Duroe with a military cadence. "I have been in combat. Pressure does one of two things to people."

Chapter 43

LATE NIGHT RUN TO HAMILTON GRANGE
Friday, August 15, 2003 1:01am

"So, tell me what is next on your plate," asked Michael of his search agents, after returning from his phone call with Duroe.

"What is it?" asked Dirjke. "Who did you just speak with?"

"A man from the power plant on 14th Street. We have figured out Homer's plan to flood the city."

"How?" asked Barry

"Someone sabotaged the backup generators that keep the city's subways from flooding. If we don't get the generators going within twelve hours of the blackout, the city will face an economic catastrophe that will ripple through the American economy. It could bring the United States to its knees without a shot fired."

"Commerce will cease if there are no trains running in New York," said Ana.

"Think the whole Eastern Seaboard," added Barry.

"What good are all those tanks, bombs, and fighter jets now? No one is going to invade the US – that's such a primitive mode of war. Our true enemies will attack us in new and evolving ways," said Danny.

"Now, I need the damn Deed to Manhattan, before all of this occurs. The only way to get our enemy to rise to the surface is to get the Deed," said Michael. "Let's get back to you all. Tell me again where you are headed next."

"Based on the language contained within the 'Hearts of Oak' passage, we need to go to Hamilton's house in Harlem," answered Barry.

"It's not quite that simple," said Dirjke.

Ana and Danny looked at each other with eyes that communicated 'it never is' – having spent two days with Barry and Dirjke.

"What are you talking about?" asked Barry. He was sure the note pointed to Hamilton's house.

"With all due respect, Professor Dirjke, I am an English major at Georgetown. The analysis of the passage, combined with the places we have already explored, point to Hamilton's house," added Ana.

"I agree with you. Analysis of the passage does point to Hamilton's house," said Dirjke.

"Then what are we talking about?" asked Michael.

"The location of Hamilton's house today is not the same location as it was when he died in 1804," began Dirjke.

"Go on," said Michael.

"The home was designed in the Federal style by John McComb Jr. The location was specifically chosen by Hamilton on a two hundred-foot elevation, with views of the Hudson River on the west and the Harlem and East rivers to the northeast," continued Dirjke.

"This sounds like a well-fortified location, especially for a man charged with protecting Manhattan," said Danny.

"That is amazing," added Ana. "Hamilton built a house on the top of a hill with a view of two rivers, which were protected by a branch of the same church where he is buried. 'Alive into the homes of death.'"

"Indeed," continued Dirjke. "However, when the grid plan of 1811 was laid over Manhattan and made its way up to northern Manhattan in the late 1890s, 143rd Street was designed to run right through the home. However, St. Luke's Episcopal Church – a branch of Trinity Church where Hamilton is buried – was planning to move uptown and bought the home for use as the site of their new church. At that time, the porches were removed and the house was lifted off its foundation and carried to a new site on Convent Avenue, near West 141st Street."

"Wait a minute," interrupted Michael. "Something doesn't make sense. Automobiles were not created until at least thirty years later. How do you move a house?"

"They were moved by horse power," answered Dirjke with a smile that said checkmate.

"Dirjke, what are you telling us?" questioned Michael.

"I am telling you that I am not sure which place to go. The original location of Hamilton's house, or where the house itself sits today in Manhattan."

"That is a puzzling question," pondered Barry.

"That is why he said it," retorted Ana.

"Well, they can't be that far from each other. I mean, how far can horses move a house?" asked Danny.

"True," answered Dirjke.

"Okay, just get to it. Enough analysis, I need action. If the power is not returned to the city, we are facing an economic crisis," stated Michael.

"It is ironic that Hamilton's creation, American finance, would be used to cripple the very country it had so thoroughly elevated. Meanwhile, Hamilton also had his hand in the Deed to Manhattan," noted Barry.

"Enough historical romance, Barry," said Michael. "I need action. New Yorkers are handling themselves admirably during this first post-9/11 crisis. That must be the message tomorrow, not that the Deed to the island is in jeopardy. Get me the Deed to Manhattan."

Chapter 44

SID GOES TO INSTITUTE
Friday, August 15, 2003 1:05am

It was just after one o'clock, when he arrived at the Ukrainian Institute. Sid stepped over the seat on his bicycle and locked it to a bench along Museum Mile. Sid could hear the breeze move through the canopy of leaves above him in Central Park. The cobblestone sidewalk surrounding the park looked as if it had been there for ages and could last another hundred years. Small groups of people were walking along 5th Avenue in and out of Central Park.

As he walked around outside and witnessed the pitch black darkness of New York City, Sid took a moment to look straight up at the sky.

"There haven't been this many stars over Manhattan in a long time," said Sid aloud to himself. He enjoyed the play on words he created, "Manhattan is home to the world's stars."

People of all ages and nationalities were enjoying this foray into the 1600s. There were groups of people sitting and still picnicking into the early morning.

Sid was pleased to see this result – a stark change from the 1970s. The people's will had either been stifled or satiated, but the result was the same – the State had quelled the people's will to riot or protest. It was a beautiful result in Sid's mind.

Sid arrived at the Institute on 5th Avenue. He crossed 5th Avenue and as he approached the front door, he walked on a few steps and approached the outside porch, which consisted of a stone enclave. He knocked on the door, knowing the buzzer would be silent.

Vlad was in a second floor room overlooking 5th Avenue. He watched Sid cross the street. Vlad made his way down the stairs and to the door.

He opened the door and said, "I've been expecting you."

Sid was surprised by Vlad's casual manner.

Sid also passed his first test with Vlad. Years earlier Vlad's father had one of the first primitive metal detector models. This model was undetectable except for the warning light which would light up as someone passed through the door's arch.

Sid saw lights on in the stairways of the former Stuyvesant mansion. Reading Sid's eyes, Vlad stated, "There is a generator in the basement."

"Do you know why I brought you here?" asked Vlad.

"I am not here to guess the answer to that question," answered Sid.

"The Bilderberg Group could use someone with your talents."

"What are you talking about?" Sid felt a ringing pain go down his back.

"Not all terrorist events are carried out by terrorists. Powerful people cause powerful events. They benefit from a 'crisis' whenever there is information or an object to be found. After today's results, your country's status as a sovereign power will be further diminished."

"I don't need a lesson in this subject," said Sid, as he cut off Vlad. He understood the implications of Vlad's statements.

"I know the careful balancing act that you are playing publicly, while privately making the document a part of the archives at their tomb on High Street."

"What are you talking about?"

"Tell me the story of an ambitious senator from Arizona who attempted to broker a deal with his fellow Republican, Vice-President George Herbert Walker Bush, for the return of Geronimo's skull to the native tribes in present-day Arizona. It was a futile attempt by this senator to entice a Bonesman to cross the line between duty and country."

"What's your angle?" asked Sid.

"What do you mean?" answered Vlad.

"You brought me here because you need me," responded Sid.

"Indeed, I do. A man with your talents should not be wasted. What have the past twenty years been like without a world power to act as a foil for your considerable talents? It is time for you to serve a higher power. Take your talents somewhere else. It's 2003 and we are in the post-9/11 world."

"What are you trying to tell me?" interrupted Sid.

"Sovereign states possess weaknesses that individual organizations do not. They can't be invaded by even the most powerful army." Sid knew this information.

"Think of it. A new challenge, a chance to serve an entity that is not held back by the population it is responsible for," began Vlad.

"The masses have their faults, but they can be manipulated. What are you getting at?"

"It was your country's intelligence failure that allowed it to happen. When the Institute moved to this location in the 1950s, we assumed the former residence of Augustus and Anne Stuyvesant, the last descendants of Peter Stuyvesant. The legend of the Deed to Manhattan may not be on the top of America's intelligence agenda, but I assure you other nations and groups are not behaving similarly."

"But why the Bilderberg Group?" asked Sid.

"With this task completed, we have been provided with 'a seat at the table' so to speak. Respectability and influence on the world stage," replied Vlad.

"We have had the means to cause the blackout. We have done it before. Remember the 1977 blackout. It took us three years from the date the Seal was oddly changed from 1664 to 1625, for no reason," said Vlad, his voice rising at the end of the statement.

"My guess is you didn't find much," said Sid, detecting Vlad's anger.

"No. We thought that someone in the City Council had found it in some archives by accident. But years of research yielded little result and the information collected during the blackout went nowhere. We were forced to recede into the darkness."

"I'll stop you right there," answered Sid.

"And you sold this Deed theory to whom, exactly?" asked Sid.

"They were intrigued by the idea. A technically 'nameless' group of the world's elite, if they were going to reveal themselves, could use the Deed to Manhattan, along with their combined supreme wealth and influence, to peaceably give them Manhattan. Real or symbolic, it would send a powerful signal."

"What do your people intend to do with the Deed?" asked Sid.

"Manhattan must return to its roots. New Amsterdam must be reborn," responded Vlad.

"What are you talking about?" asked Sid.

"It's time to once again separate Manhattan's commercial interests and value from sovereign rule. New Amsterdam was a company town run by the Dutch West India Company. It's time for a new entity, a modern entity, to act as trustees of this island. That is the clearest lesson from 9/11. The United States can no longer protect its most valuable asset – Manhattan."

"I will work with you, Vlad," responded Sid, who planned to deliver the Deed to Skull and Bones which was designed to avoid this doomsday scenario.

"Good, I was told that you would. This is a group of the world's elite that are seeking to split the Manhattan

Atom. Ownership of the island creates implicit control over all financial markets."

"What's in it for me?"

"Money. Firstly, I am sure that you have done well, but this is not government money. This is real money. From there, Sid, I will give you projects and the means to achieve great things. Your influence over the new war – the War on Terror – will increase. Your exploits are legendary in the few circles that they are even known. This is one of the few spheres of influence without all the bureaucratic nonsense."

"I will work with you," repeated the intelligence veteran.

"Good. Now we can get to business. The true secret of the Ukrainian Institute is that we found a number of Stuyvesant family crests. Each of them on the reverse side contained the numbers 12:25-27. After many years, we finally figured out what it referred to."

"What is it?" asked Sid.

"Over the years, I have learned the phrase by heart, ironically enough," said Vlad with a smile.

"What is the phrase?"

"The reference is to Book Twelve, lines 25-27 of Homer's *The Odyssey*, which reads:

'Hearts of Oak, did you go down
alive into the homes of death? One visit
finishes all men but yourselves, twice mortal!'"

"I'm still not sure. I mean, you pull the lights and then need help to find the Deed to Manhattan," teased Sid.

"If you think the hunt for the Deed to Manhattan is the only project being executed right now, you clearly don't have the vision to be a part of this," added Vlad. "There are operations on top of operations going on right now. This is a one-world operation against the United States. They can no longer be trusted with issues of global importance. With the way information travels now, governance of the world requires a board of directors, not politicians concerned with an election that is always less than two years away.

"Now, you can say 'yes' or 'no', but I tell you right now, if you don't take this offer you are as incorruptible as Gotham's Batman." His Russian accent provided extra emphasis on the final two words.

"What do you need me to do?" asked Sid.

"Well, the stakes are about to go up on our old mayor. He doesn't stand a chance. You are choosing the right side, the winning side."

"Tell me what you mean."

"Sid, I need you to get the next clue," stated Vlad.

Sid let out a laugh. "What if I say no? You have no one else in mind."

"Sid, you are being offered an opportunity. The group is taking a rather honest approach, because of your background. But if all this operation requires is a payoff to the right politician, so be it. Offering you this opportunity could result in a sustainable relationship, rather than a random plane crash forever silencing your story."

Sid knew there was only one answer. "Fine, I will accept your assignment. I will locate the Deed," answered Sid.

Chapter 45

DUROE GETS PUMPS GOING
Friday, August 15, 2003 2:00am

The room he was working in was a tin can from the outside. From the inside it held the generator pumps which continually pump water out of the city's subway tunnels. It was a sauna for Duroe in there, even at this hour of the night.

Duroe had sweat through his entire light blue shirt. Beads were dripping off his nose and chin and onto his work boots. He had shocked himself more times than he wanted to count over the past two hours in the old pump room near 14th Street.

He began to shake his hand and suck his fingers due to the latest jolt, when he announced, "I wish there was a less painful way to tell if the wire is live." He took his index and middle fingers from his right hand and wiped each side of his forehead to give his eyebrows a break from preventing the sweat from rolling into his already red eyes.

With that, he gave the switch a flip.

The pumps began to hum.

Duroe opened his cell phone and dialed the mayor's number.

Michael saw the call. He opened his cell phone and asked, "Please, give me good news."

"Sir, I have good news," stated Duroe. "Manhattan's subways and tunnels have been given a new lease on life."

"That is excellent, Duroe."

"Sir, we still need the power returned in the next four to six hours, or the subways will eventually flood. We are not entirely out of the woods yet. There is still an electrical infrastructure issue that must get resolved."

"I know it doesn't sound like much, but this is the first break we have had since this whole blackout started."

"Thanks, Mr. Mayor," said Duroe. "Helping this city gives me feelings of pride that this civil servant has not experienced since combat overseas."

Chapter 46

SID'S DISCOVERY OF MEANING OF HEARTS OF OAK

Friday, August 15, 2003 2:01am

Sid returned to his rooming house in Hell's Kitchen. The rooming house was a walk up red brick building with a fire escape along the facade of the building. There was a center staircase. He heard people having sex in three of the four rooms he passed. He waived his flashlight to guide the way, arrived at his door and unlocked it. He took his gun out of the holster in his leg.

Sid took two quick steps into the room. He shined his flashlight into the mirror and looked around. He was alone. He closed the door and began to get settled at the small desk against the wall in his room.

He spread out the artifacts he had collected throughout the day, including the Stuyvesant crests from the Institute. The stick, the note, and the crests were placed on the desk in his room. Sid took the mirror off the wall and reflected the light from his flashlight to compensate for the darkness in his room.

The stick had '1626' carved into it. The note stated:

11-25-1783

One Deed Left. I Pray Whereby you will find it.

7-11

He was struck by the poetry referenced in the numbers on the crest's back. He recited the words:

"Hearts of Oak, did you go down
alive into the homes of death? One visit
finishes all men but yourselves, twice mortal!"

"What if Hearts of Oak refers to a group?" Sid asked himself.

Sid flipped open his phone. He knew this person would be awake.

"Hoffson, here," announced the voice on the other line.

"It's Sid. Look, I have a strange question for you, but I know it is right in your wheelhouse."

"What if I said the words 'Hearts of Oak' to you? Does that have any meaning?" asked Sid.

"What is going on in New York tonight? I mean I know the lights are out, but a couple of hours ago I got a call from the Mayor telling me that the city is going to flood. Now, my best agent in the field is questioning me as to military trivia – and fundamental trivia at that. The 1st Battalion, 5th Field Artillery – the nation's oldest military unit – was formed from a New York Revolutionary War militia called the Hearts of Oak," continued Hoffson. "Truth be told, the five-pointed star in their coat of arms is the reason I am standing in a building called the Pentagon. There are fifty of them on the United States flag."

"Son of a bitch," said Sid.

"What is going on?" asked Hoffson.

"General, I have got to go. Everything in Manhattan is fine. Just following leads and such. Any word on the blackout?"

"Nothing, Sid. The President has already addressed the nation and labeled it a benign event, an infrastructure issue. We are simply concerned with getting the power back on."

"Hopefully Federal grants to infrastructure don't detract from the military budget," said Sid.

"That was the precise thing that Dwight Eisenhower, the former Supreme Commander of the

Allied-Forces and two-term president warned of in his Farewell Address to the nation on January 16, 1961."

"Yeah, I don't think we have to worry about that. We are going to push for greater funds to cope and stifle events exactly like this one. All right Hoffson, thanks for the trivia. I have to get going," said Sid.

"Going, where..." asked Hoffson, but Sid just flipped his phone shut.

Sid redirected his attention to *The Odyssey* quote. He recalled the remainder of the passages and had an idea. 'Alive into the homes of death.' What could Hamilton's grave have to do with this?

He located Hamilton's house on the map from the young entrepreneur. The house was in existence and on Manhattan. The Hamilton Deli on 116th and Amsterdam was the only other Hamilton location referenced on the map. Sid smiled at the young entrepreneur. He had sold them a spot on the map as an advertisement.

Sid had a plan, but it was going to be a very long bike ride from his room on 46th Street and 9th Avenue. It was about five miles to the 140s in Harlem.

Chapter 47

KIDS AND DIRJKE GO TO GRANGE
Friday, August 15, 2003 3:00am

The group drove from Lower Manhattan up the Harlem River Drive and made a left onto 145th Street in Harlem. The traffic along the West Side Highway was mild. The cars had allowed for an open lane of traffic for emergency vehicles. With a city car, the group used this land to their advantage.

They were each enjoying watching the community hanging out together outside. In seats, on blankets, and around cars, New Yorkers were enjoying the very early morning. Card games, cooking food, and listening to music were among the most popular activities.

"I have never been prouder to be a New Yorker," declared Ana.

"Yes, we are on a mission to save the island's sovereignty," answered Barry.

"It is reassuring to see people enjoying the very same island we are trying to protect," said Dirjke.

Danny was having no trouble maneuvering the car through this dark Manhattan night. Above 111th Street, the sidewalks were packed and the road was empty.

"We are doing this for them," said Barry. "Even though they are in the dark as to what is really going on."

People were sitting on lawn chairs. There were flashlights and radios everywhere. The car traveled eastbound on 145th Street. The hazard on the road was the people, not the small number of other cars.

"Look at all these jaywalkers," announced Danny.

"Ha," said Ana. "Who thought you were such a goody two shoes."

From the front seat Dirjke said, "If these people had any idea what was really going on..."

"I know, Unk, it is amazing," said Danny, looking over to his uncle for a second.

"They wouldn't believe it, if you told them," said Ana.

"How are we going to get into the house?" asked Barry.

"I think we are looking at breaking and entering," announced Ana, steering the conversation to the next obstacle. Dirjke was taken back.

"Really?" asked Dirjke, taken aback.

"Yeah, Unk. It seems like it is our only option. I mean we have to go 'into the homes of death'."

"All right, well that should be a last resort," announced Dirjke. "First thing we need to decide is where to park the car."

They found a spot on 145th Street and Broadway. Danny oriented himself and said, "Let's go this way."

"How do you know?" asked Barry.

"I checked the map at the building before we left," answered Danny.

"Look who is the early bird with the worm," smiled Ana.

"If anyone asks, you are students at City College, got it?" said Dirjke. City College, like all things New York, was ahead of its time. It was the first free public school of higher learning in the United States. The campus contains some of the best examples of gothic architecture in New York.

The group walked west on 145th Street to Amsterdam Avenue and then made a left turn and walked south toward 143rd Street.

Dirjke imagined what this area must have looked like in the 1620s and in the 1790s when Hamilton built The Grange. Hamilton referred to it as his 'sweet project' during the construction period.

Dirjke noticed the uphill walk as they proceeded to make another left and turned east onto 143rd Street. It was about thirty yards east of Amsterdam Avenue when Dirjke deduced where the home was originally located.

As Dirjke looked left, he could see the North River, now bearing the name, Hudson River. To the east, there was a large brick building that obstructed what Dirjke believed would have led to a clear view of the Harlem River to the east.

"Good thing you decided not to bury something, Hearts of Oak. The grid plan would have eviscerated any secret tunnel on Manhattan," said Dirjke into the night sky.

The kids moved ahead of Dirjke.

"All right, how are we going to do this?" asked Barry.

"What are we looking for?" asked Ana to Barry.

"Not sure."

"We have a disc, from his grave, right?" asked Danny.

"Well, I don't…" began Barry.

"I know. I have it…" said Ana. "It's a good thing girls always have a purse."

"Good, I think that disc has something to do with something," said Danny.

"But how are we going to execute a plan? I mean we burned a similar card yesterday at St. Paul's. I don't think we can count on a power outage as a reason to get access to an object we find potentially useful," worried Barry.

"True," admitted Danny. "We just need to continue to assess the situation. A solution will present itself."

The group made a left turn onto Convent Avenue in Harlem. At that instant, each person laid eyes on Hamilton's house for the first time. Even Dirjke with his extensive historical knowledge had never visited Hamilton's house, The Grange.

192

Hamilton protected the Deed to Manhattan – the guy on the ten dollar bill. The thought itself made Dirjke wonder how this story could hide in plain sight.

Hamilton's home was wedged between an old red brick building that looked like it was built in the 1970s and the backyard of St. Luke's Church. It was yellow with a white trim around the windows. There was a small front porch and a statue of Hamilton in the foreground that blocked the view of the house itself. The dark night concealed the worn down condition of the old home.

"Even in the midst of this blackout, this house could not look more dilapidated," announced Ana.

"Someone was under orders to keep this house and they must have known the secret, because otherwise they would have allowed the house to be destroyed," stated Danny.

"Good point," commented Dirjke, "but there is no evidence of any surviving Hearts of Oak members. Remember that. We are all we have got and all we can trust. All right, now is a good time for us to split up."

The idea caught the group off guard. "Barry and Danny, walk north up Convent Avenue and circle the block. Meet Ana and me in front of the house."

"What are you guys going to do?" asked Danny.

"Ana and I will check out the house from the front and meet the neighbors," said Dirjke.

"Okay, well let's get a move on," announced Ana, without any visible fear.

Chapter 48

DANNY AND BARRY ON HAMILTON TERRACE
Friday, August 15, 2003 3:31am

Danny and Barry continued south on Convent Avenue. The street had wide sidewalks and beautiful row houses on either side. These row houses were opulent country getaways in the 1900s.

Neither was thrilled about separating from the other two people, but they knew this was a job. They walked north on Convent Avenue and toward 144th Street. They made a right turn onto 144th Street and walked south on Hamilton Terrace toward St. Luke's Church.

It was an amazing sight – even in the dark. The old reddish stone building was worn down and appeared abandoned. There were unkempt shrubs and vines along the outside walls.

"What are we looking for?" asked Danny.

"I think we are looking for something involving the crest we found at Hamilton's grave," answered Barry. "The crest is a clue, but it may also be a key."

"Into the homes of death...twice mortal," repeated Danny, trying to work out the poem aloud.

"Yes," answered Barry. "There is a connection between the two places. The poem says so."

"We just have to figure it out," answered Danny.

They walked a couple of hundred feet to the rear of the house. They were at the bottom of a hill. Apart from a low wall and an iron gate, only a small grass field separated them from the back of the house.

"I think we should crouch behind this wall for a second and wait," announced Barry. "Turn off your flashlight, Danny."

As Danny turned his back against the wall, he crouched down like a catcher with his back against the wall. Danny was looking down the hill of 141ˢᵗ Street. He saw a figure that he recognized from his train ride into the city.

"There's Sid," said Danny, "No. Casually, turn your neck to the left, turn your eyes to the left and don't drastically move your head,"

"I have yet to see him," said Barry, knowing his weakness for being too eager. Barry observed a tall man in terrific shape. Sid was in dark dress pants and a collar shirt. "What do you think he's doing here?"

"He is not here for the tour," answered Danny, "but the real question is, why is he still going after the Deed? He should be handling the blackout."

"No, the real question is, how did he know to be here? This is not Lower Manhattan where the St. Paul's Chapel and Hamilton's grave are blocks apart. Apparently, someone else knows their New York City history."

"It doesn't add up," replied Danny. "This guy must be getting information from another source. But whatever it is, we need to be on our toes."

"I think we know enough. Let's meet with Dirjke and Ana and begin to formulate a plan."

"I agree," said Danny. The two proceeded up the steep hill on 141ˢᵗ Street and took a right onto Convent Avenue again. Danny was looking around for Sid, but he seemed to be lost among the groups of people in the neighborhood celebrating the blackout with barbecue grills, music, and general good cheer on a hot August night. They saw Dirjke and Ana and walked towards them.

"We already saw Sid. How are we going to get this done?" asked Barry to Ana and Dirjke.

Chapter 49

SID AT THE HAMILTON HOUSE
Friday, August 15, 2003 3:35am

Sid was walking west on 141st Street, uphill. He side-stepped two distinct groups of people along the way, the students at City College and the adults that lived in the neighborhood. Both groups were peaceably enjoying the night's activities and opportunities. As he arrived at the destination, Sid was surprised by the location and cramped quarters of the house.

There was a building on the north side that had windows that faced the house and were above the awning covering the front porch.

Sid noticed the groups of people milling around in front of the apartment building on Convent Avenue, adjacent to Hamilton's house. This was going to require some tact, but the blackout was the ace he needed to manipulate the situation.

First, the front door to the building was propped open with a rock, because the buzzer did not work with the power off. By counting the windows, he knew that he needed to go to the third floor. Sid walked into the building and, based on his outside observation, knew to proceed to the right edge of the building and used the stairs.

He made his way to Apartment 4G and knocked on the door. An African-American gentleman answered the door, only half awake.

"Marty Dirjke," he announced as he presented his military credentials to the man still rubbing his eyes. Sid put the ID back in his pocket before the man could read the name. "I am sorry to bother you and your family at this late hour, but I need to access your window along the side of the building."

"What for?" asked the gentleman in baggy basketball shorts and a ribbed white tank top.

"We have received threats to various locations in Manhattan by some crackpot. This includes Hamilton's house," stated Sid.

The hallway was completely dark. There was the buzz of people and music from the street, along with the charcoal smell of people grilling chicken and beef.

"Sir, I will not be in your apartment long. I just need to use your window to access the second floor of Hamilton's house."

"Why not use the front door?" asked the man.

"Because, I am trying to learn the identity of the eventual perpetrators. They can't know I'm in the house," he said. "Sir, with all due respect, I will be in and out of your way in no time."

"Do you have a warrant?" asked the gentlemen.

"For what?" asked Sid, "I am a Federal military employee. I don't need a warrant to enter Hamilton's house," answered Sid.

"No, a warrant to enter this house," repeated the gentleman. "No ticket, no laundry."

"Sir, this is an exigent circumstance. When, or how am I going to get a warrant in the middle of the night with the power out? Besides, by then, it will be too late," Sid pointed out.

"Is this really my problem?"

"It will be."

"Really, how?"

"The next time I am here, I will have a warrant, yes, but it won't be a search warrant. It will be an arrest warrant for your obstruction into my investigation. Am I communicating with you?"

"Yes," answered the gentleman in the doorway. "I don't want any trouble, but you must understand that I am not simply going to let someone into my home under these circumstances."

"I appreciate that," answered Sid, "but I have told you all my business and shown you my credentials. Now, I ask you again, are you going to give me access to your window, or are you going to be hauled into a court of law for your failure to grant me access to your apartment to protect a Federal Landmark during this city's first blackout since 9/11? I am not interested in your business, just your window."

At that moment, he heard a female voice ask, "Irvin, who is at the door?"

"No one," the man yelled back toward the interior of the apartment.

"Irvin, I think I have made it clear that I am not simply a 'no one'," answered Sid, with a devious smile.

"Okay, fine, we don't want any trouble. Come inside. Let me just try to explain this to my wife. Also, my daughter is asleep in the other room. Please don't wake her."

Sid had the rope he had bought at the bike shop hours ago. He planned to repel down the brick wall and onto the porch roof of the old house. Sid stood in the foyer and flashed his light around the apartment.

Irvin's wife approached Sid. She was more than happy to help and Sid thought that had she opened the door, the previous exchange with Irvin would have been largely unnecessary.

Sid extended a hand and saw an opportunity. "I am sure Irvin told you who I am – Marty Dirjke."

"I will be just a minute," said Sid. "Kindly untie the rope when I give the 'okay'."

"Sure thing," answered Irvin.

Sid tied the rope to a structural pole in the apartment and repelled his way onto the roof of Hamilton's porch. For an older man, Sid maintained uncanny strength in relation to his body to weight ratio. While much of the country and even the sports world had begun to focus on isolated strength movements over the past thirty years, Sid trained in the same manner that the Eastern Block Communist countries did during the 1960s. He employed a regiment that focused on body movements that included: pull-ups, push-ups, and the ability to perform the most basic gymnastic movements.

Sid recalled being in the weight room doing pull-ups, hand stands, and dips while hearing young men say, 'I am doing curls for the girls.' But, Sid thought, 'curls are for girls.' A man's strength is based on his ability to pull himself up.

He navigated down the wall with relative ease and found himself on the roof of Hamilton's porch. He opened the window whose alarm was inoperable due to the blackout. Sid crawled head first into the second floor of the home. With a simple wave from inside the house by Sid, the rope was untied. Sid pulled the slack line of the rope to himself and into the house.

He looked around the second floor. Sid waved his flashlight to get his bearings. It was a simple bedroom. There were twin beds and a children's desk in the corner. The walls were green and the floors made of solid wood. There was an old map of New York Harbor and the Long Island Sound on the wall. His purpose was two-fold: find whatever clue was left 'in the home of death' or hide and allow Dirjke and the kids to find it for him.

Chapter 50

CONFRONTATION AT HAMILTON'S HOUSE
Friday, August 15, 2003 3:40am

The group huddled at the front door of Hamilton's house. Without the power, it was a matter of picking the lock.

"There, I got it," said Danny.

"Good. Now can I get my hair pin back," replied Ana.

Dirjke was amazed at the ease with which Danny picked the lock of Hamilton's front door. "I will ask at another time where you learned that trick."

The walk into Hamilton's house was not what Dirjke imagined. "I never thought that I would be visiting Hamilton's house under these circumstances and with the purpose of finding the Deed to Manhattan," said Dirjke. The floor was a white tile with green walls. There was a classic Roman bust of Hamilton between two doorways.

Ana and Danny were in shock as they entered. "I feel like I am walking through a time machine."

"Look at these two parlor rooms – amazing," said Danny, waving his flashlight. The room had large windows on each side that were blocked by the adjacent structures. The walls were yellow. The furniture was accurate for the early 1800s.

"Including the lack of electricity, Ana, this is how the house would have appeared to Hamilton at the turn of the eighteenth century," informed Barry.

Barry was a step ahead of Danny and Ana. He walked to the fireplace in the dining room. Large and painted white, it was the centerpiece of the room.

"Ana, Danny, come here. Professor, look at this," announced Barry. "There is a circular disc about the same size and shape as the one we saw at Hamilton's grave."

"What do you think, Professor?" asked Barry. "We already inflicted damage onto Hamilton's grave. Are we going to do the same to a Federal Landmark, our hero's house?"

"The question is not if, it's how," stated Dirjke, with an approving smile in the dark New York night.

"I'll take care of that," said Ana. She walked to the dining room to retrieve two of the display knives on the table. "They are not the sharpest, but they will prove effective for the task."

"Can you believe what we are about to embark on," Dirjke said to the two boys.

"Unk, to state the obvious, this is insane. Why didn't you tell me that you were a treasure hunter in your spare time?" Dirjke just nodded his head in bewilderment at the situation.

"I know we are going to find the Deed to Manhattan. The homes of death – we did it!" said Barry.

"Not so fast. I have my doubts," replied Dirjke.

Seconds later, Ana walked toward the fireplace with the knives in her hand.

"I will do this. I am the only one with glasses to protect my eyes," said Dirjke. Ana handed the knives to Dirjke in the dark dining room of Hamilton's grange.

After a few minutes, Dirjke had managed to cut away at the layers of paint covering the disk. The paint was like chalk and he was able to pull it away from the old disk like string cheese. Eventually, he managed to free the disk from its old encasement.

"Here," he said, as he pulled the disk from the wall. Ana was the lucky recipient. The smell inside the hidden vault was musky and dank. But it was nothing like the odor from under Hamilton's grave. Dirjke flashed his light into the recess. "It looks like something is in here."

"Good, let's get the Deed and get out of here. This house is spooky at night," said Ana.

"I don't think the Deed is here," said Danny.

"Homes of death – it has to be here," returned Ana.

"Enough chatter," scolded Dirjke, as he reached into the recess. His thoughts were confirmed. "This can't be the Deed to Manhattan."

"Why?" asked Barry, before Dirjke had extracted the paper from its recess.

"The piece of paper seems too small. Also, it doesn't feel old enough."

Dirjke took the paper out of its resting place and gingerly opened it. The group crowded around Dirjke. Danny took the flashlight from Dirjke and pointed it at the old parchment.

"At least it is not a code," said Ana.

"Well, hold on a second. It's not a code with numbers, but it appears to be a coded message nonetheless," stated Dirjke. It took them each a few seconds to read the old script on the paper. Then Dirjke read it aloud, once he was sure of each word:

"The tunnel is preserved by my brethren,
And one more trip into the homes of death must begin."

Ana was the first to break the silence. "I know I have said this before, but I feel like we are going in circles."

"No, this is an interesting clue. We just have to parse it. Luckily, we have the best historians and a very able poetry expert," said Danny, with a small nod to Ana in the shadowy night.

"'Brethren' – who could that be?" asked Barry.

"I know the answer," announced Dirjke with a childish grin.

"You do?" asked Danny and Ana in unison.

"Like I said before, Hearts of Oak formed the core of the Corsicans, the actual name for the militia charged with the duty to protect Manhattan," stated Dirjke.

"So who else was in the core?" asked Danny.

"That is the million dollar question," answered Dirjke.

"I think it is worth a little more than that," answered Sid, as he walked down the stairs, gun in hand.

The boys, in their exuberance, both looked into each other's eyes and thought for a second about taking down the old man. But before the idea could make it fully across their minds, Dirjke shouted, "Relax boys, sometimes it is your turn to lose. Of course, Mr. Milliken here doesn't believe in that principle."

They were across the dining room table from Ana and Dirjke and close to the door Sid was entering through. They did not see his gun.

"This isn't really the time to antagonize me," warned Sid.

"What do you want? You already heard the poem that Professor Dirjke just read out loud. If you want the Deed, you have the same information we do," said Danny, trying to diffuse the situation.

"Only a fool settles for a level playing field. If you are not cheating, you are not trying, boy," answered Sid.

"Why are you doing this?" asked Barry.

"Simple. The arrogance that you dreamers have displayed in pursuit of the birth certificate of Manhattan is astounding. What makes you think you have a better plan for this Deed than I do?" asked Sid. "Obviously, the possibility that the document could find its way into the wrong hands concerns us all, but how do you plan to re-hide the Deed, if you even find it? Also, the chances of your group's secrecy being compromised are astronomical."

"Sid, you don't understand what it is like to be a New Yorker. This is a different issue for the people who live on Manhattan," answered Dirjke. "This group's loyalty is to the island."

"So what's your plan?" asked Ana.

"I will burn the document on sight," answered Sid. "There is no reason to bring about any type of discussion regarding the one western port that was *not* conquered by the brute force of war."

"Sid, think of what we would be doing. This document should be delivered to the Mayor and dealt with accordingly," argued Dirjke.

"Nonsense, power corrupts. Who can actually be trusted with such an important document? There has been a single story regarding the Deed since the 1850s. New York lasted nearly 225 years without questioning that Deed's existence and another 150 years thinking it did not exist. In this post-9/11 world, nothing can be left to chance," stated Sid.

"Think what you are saying. You are treating New Yorkers and the rest of the country as ignorant fools who need your protection," argued Danny.

"Exactly, there is nothing wrong with protecting the status quo. It is the easiest means to maintain power," stated Sid.

"Fine, if you want to maintain that status quo, then walk on. You already know what you need. But let me tell you this – we will beat you," said Barry. The comments evoked a slight laugh from Sid.

"I have what I need, but I do not have everything I want," stated Sid. "Thanks for the discs and the note."

"You keep doing this Marty, finding something and then handing it over to me. Thanks buddy."

"You still won't win," answered Dirjke.

"Really? Then that means I need an extra edge to push the scales in my favor. You know, under different circumstances and in different times, I would have killed you all and moved on, or at least taken one member with me. Tonight I am considering a different trade."

"What do you mean?" asked Barry.

"I mean my forearms are sore from repelling down the wall and I biked nearly ten miles in the August heat. How did you guys get all the way up here?" asked Sid. The room was silent. The kids knew enough to wait for Dirjke to respond. Dirjke knew where this was about to go. Sid only asks questions for one reason, precious information. Dirjke processed the alternative.

"Danny, give Sid the keys." Danny looked over at Barry and saw him lowering his center of gravity.

"There is an official New York City vehicle parked on 145th Street," added Dirjke.

Then, Danny tossed Sid the keys, but he let them fall to the ground at his feet. Sid looked at the young men, "You think I'm dumb enough to fall for that trick. C'mon fellas."

Barry was waiting for Sid to catch the toss from Danny. He was about to rush Sid and wrestle him to the ground.

"Now, each of you in a row and on these steps," ordered Sid. Sid tied the group to the stairs in the old house. In the process, he went through Ana's bag and found the disc.

"Give that back," shouted Ana.

"Wait, let me guess where you found it? Hamilton's grave."

The look on Dirjke's face gave away that Sid was correct. He looked at the group tied up and smiled as he looked back at the discs.

"Sid, think of what you are about to do," pleaded Dirjke.

"I have Marty. I am not going to allow the Deed to Manhattan to reach public discussion. It will be held in trust by the core of this nation's intelligence apparatus. I simply have different interests to you."

"You are wrong," stated Barry. "The pact citizens have with their leaders does not condone secret alliances

205

and cabals. America is a meritocracy. Only the best rise to the top."

Sid laughed. "Look at this idealist. You must be Dirjke's favorite student."

"Where do you go to college?"

"Harvard," hollered Barry.

"Marty, you've tried to tell me that I hang around the wrong crowd. Look at you," teased Sid.

"Shut up, Sid."

Sid looked in Barry's direction. "I have some advice for you. When the police book you in a few hours because you are tied up in Hamilton's house, ask for me. Like the Deed to Manhattan, no one will ever know about it."

"We would never count on you," answered Ana.

"Only time will tell, missy." Sid tossed Ana's purse onto the floor. "I'll probably hear from you before I see ya around," laughed Sid, as he left the old house.

Chapter 51

SID TO UKRANIAN INSTITUTE
Friday, August 15, 2003 3:50am
With an official car, Sid made record time. The vehicle, along with his military credentials, permitted him unlimited access to any location.

He was relaxed as he maneuvered through the dark Manhattan streets. He went east on 145th Street to Adam Clayton Powell Jr., Blvd., where he traveled south to Central Park North. At this early morning hour, Sid only saw the very drunk and the homeless along northern Manhattan's Seventh Avenue. Families like Irvin's were indoors.

He made a right at the intersection onto Park Avenue. The view Sid had as he maneuvered down this nearly empty street was something he never imagined. The buildings that lined this two-way avenue were as dark as the night sky. With the exception of his headlights and a few random people on the street, it was like driving into a cave. Sid sped down thirty blocks to 79th Street to the Ukrainian Institute. Dirjke and the good Samaritans were out of the game. Next was Vlad.

He was an enemy of the State.

Sid recited the poem from Hamilton's house to himself:

"The tunnel is preserved by my brethren,
And one more trip into the homes of death must begin."

Sid thought that it had something to do with the Institute. But there was another thing that he knew – the Institute possessed electricity.

Sid exited the car and walked toward the building. Sid casually opened the door and entered the Institute. From down the wide circular wood steps came Vlad. He was in his same blue pants and white short-sleeve button down shirt. He looked to a small light above the doorway that signaled that Sid did not have a gun or other large metal object.

"What have you found out?" asked Vlad.

"That is not how this works," answered Sid. "You have two choices. You can tell me what else you know about the Deed to Manhattan or you can tell me what you meant by flooding Manhattan."

The scenario put a smile across Vlad's face, as he arrived at the bottom step. "Why would I do that?" His eye twitched as he looked to Sid. His large nose was shiny with oil. Chest hair was protruding from above the top button of his shirt. Vlad remained at the base of the steps with one hand on the banister.

"You need the next clue. I have it," answered Sid. He was just passed the threshold of the doorway. "Yeah, I have cracked the code. And the signs point to this house, the last house of the last Stuyvesant ancestor. It is the reason your group purchased the house. Now, I don't care who you are working for. I need to know the secret this house has inside it."

"And you think I am going to tell you that?" asked Vlad.

"You have no choice, if you want the Deed. If you could do this without me, I wouldn't be here."

"When this house was remodeled we found these." Vlad then showed Sid the two crests with the markings on the reverse side.

The two crests were nearly identical in size to the crests he took from Hamilton's house.

"I want to talk about your latest threats to the Mayor. Flooding New York? How are you going to do that without any power? Don't tell me you are going to detonate a bomb underwater in the harbor or something," laughed Sid.

208

"Really, you can't figure it out. I am surprised that you cannot detect this city's ultimate weakness," answered Vlad with a smile.

Sid raised his gun with the confidence of a man who knew he was in charge. Vlad's eyes widened as he saw it. Sid was a few steps past the doorway and Vlad was about ten yards of burnt red carpet away.

"How did my metal detectors fail me?" asked Vlad aloud. His eyes were wide and his mouth was open in dismay.

Sid answered, "Carbon fiber. Now, Vlad, let's make a new compact."

"Wait, you can't kill me," stammered Vlad.

"Who said I was going to do that? But if I did, who is going to miss you? Do you expect people to come looking for you?"

Sid pulled the trigger. He did not miss. He hit Vlad where he wanted to – directly on the right kneecap. Sid walked over to Vlad who was lying on the carpet with his head on the first step. The wound started to flow blood. Vlad pressed his hand on his kneecap to ease the pain and stop the blood.

"I didn't want this to end this way," said Sid.

"Please, no," cried Vlad. Sid flashed a smile as he closed the distance between them.

Sid reached into his pocket with his free hand and took out another object. It was plastic, black, and smaller than a pack of cigarettes.

"What is that?" asked Vlad.

"You'll see in a second."

Sid hit Vlad with a taser gun to his shoulder to knock him out. "But unless you are the lead dog, the scenery never changes," finished Sid to himself. Vlad had passed out and was bleeding at the bottom of the steps.

Sid dragged Vlad up one flight of the stairs. He decided to power up his electronic devices. While they charged, he looked at the crests that Vlad had showed him. As in Hamilton's house, Sid looked to the large fireplace in the main room of the mansion for a clue. However, he had no such luck.

Chapter 52

SID TORTURES VLAD
Friday, August 15, 2003 4:02am

About fifteen minutes later, Sid returned to where Vlad was tied up. It was a large space that was used as a smoking room by the Institute's members. On certain shelves, out of reach, were bottles of vodka. The glass reflected against mirrors behind the bottles against the dim lights powering the room.

Sid had supplies in both hands. Vlad had awoken from the electrical shock. He was tied to the chair with ordinary telephone cords. The one pressed against his neck constricted his air and prevented him from using his strength to free his limbs.

"Now tell me how you plan to flood the city," demanded Sid.

"At last, your true colors, your CIA roots come through. You think you are going to torture the information out of me," whispered Vlad's raspy voice.

Sid walked over to the fireplace. He struck a match and threw it into the prepared fire. "There is imminent danger to mass populations. I bet even this country's most liberal senator would support me doing whatever is necessary to learn what I need to know." He put the poker into the fire to heat the end of it.

Sid took a dish rag and the screwdriver out of his back pocket. "Thanks for the supplies. Now let's get this bullet out of your kneecap," stated Sid.

"No," pleaded Vlad.

"Yes," answered Sid. "I can't have you dying on me. Not until you tell me what I need to know. Now, how do you plan to flood the city?"

"Don't put words in my mouth – I said Manhattan," said Vlad. "Although there are subway tunnels in the outer boroughs, none have the extensive underground network that Manhattan does."

"Don't fence with me," replied Sid. He knelt down on one knee so that he was eye to eye with the man tied up in the desk chair. Sid raised the screwdriver over Vlad's left knee and locked eyes with Vlad. There were two seconds of silence. Then Vlad let out a loud scream as the screwdriver dug into his gunshot wound.

"Too bad this is not a Phillips head screwdriver. I would have an easier time getting rid of the bullet."

"Please, stop," implored Vlad.

"Can't right now, this is the only evidence that could prove who actually shot you." Vlad screamed as Sid did his best to inflict pain.

"You know there is always a fine line between torturing someone for accurate information, or what you simply want to hear. That is the trick."

"Please, please stop," screamed Vlad.

"Ah, there it is," stated Sid. "Can you hear the metal screwdriver tapping sound on the metal bullet?"

"You can't stop it. It is already happening," whimpered Vlad.

"If you are so sure, then tell me how you plan to flood the city?"

"Your reign as a lone superpower is over. The rest of the world is finished engaging in ground wars with you. Newer, more subtle attacks are necessary."

"See, now you are adding insult to injury," replied Sid. "So allow me to use another cliché." Sid took a grinder out of his other pocket.

"Recognize it?" asked Sid with a smile. "Now flooding Manhattan?" Scared with anger, Vlad spit at Sid's face.

"Okay," said Sid as he wiped the warm liquid from his face. He rubbed it on Vlad's shirt. He then turned the grinder and put salt on the wound. It was a basic kitchen model with a twist grinder at the top. The canister was filled with more than enough rock salt to do the job. After about fifteen minutes, the pain was all Vlad could handle.

Vlad vomited over his left shoulder as Sid alternated between digging a screwdriver into the wound and grinding salt onto the screwdriver and into the wound. Sid knew from training that a person's tolerance from a time perspective was a little over twenty minutes.

Eventually, he pried the bullet out of Vlad's knee. Sid wiped his fingers and the bullet off with the rag he brought into the room. Vlad was out of breath and sweating from the pain.

Of course, fifteen minutes was just enough time to heat up the poker resting in the fireplace. "All right Vlad, how are you planning to flood the city?" asked Sid.

"Manhattan," answered Vlad. "I don't know."

"What do you mean, 'you don't know?'" asked Sid.

"My contact was just concerned with how long the power was going to be out."

Sid took the poker out of the fire.

"No," said Vlad, as his eyes widened with the view of the orange tip of the poker.

"What did he ask?" demanded Sid.

"All he wanted to know was how long the power was going to be out," quivered Vlad. "Wait. What are you going to do with that?"

"We are not done talking yet. Don't make me repeat myself. What did he ask?"

"He, he wanted to know if the power would be out for more than twelve hours," answered Vlad. "Now, please don't burn me with that poker."

"Burn you. I am not going to do that. I am going to cauterize your wound. Maybe there is more you can tell me. Don't worry, I will take my time." Sid placed the poker into the wound. Vlad let out a huge scream.

"Now, tell me how this guy intends to flood Manhattan."

"I told you. I don't know."

"Why would you have agreed to this? He must have alluded to something," continued Sid.

"We had a simple bargain, in exchange for offing some stoolie at an electrical power station."

"What did you get?" asked Sid.

"He told me to seek you out during the blackout, but then you landed right in my lap."

"How is that working out for you right now?" asked Sid.

"Ha, what's it like to know that Manhattan is going to flood? Or wait, not knowing what that actually means."

Sid slapped him in the face. Looking into Vlad's eyes, he slapped him five more times. He gave Vlad a ten-second reprieve.

"The only other thing I remember him saying was that no one was going to die because of the flood. I am not a monster."

"Huh," asked Sid more confused than ever. "Why do it?"

"I don't know," answered Vlad. Sid applied the poker to Vlad's knee and crudely cauterized the wound. Vlad's torso heaved up and down as Sid crudely closed the wound. With the bullet removed and the bleeding stopped, Vlad was as good as new as far as Sid cared.

"What do you want?" asked Vlad still tied up. He had pissed his pants while Sid cauterized the wound.

"How does your friend intend to flood Manhattan?" asked Sid.

"I don't know."

"C'mon."

"You don't want to know what I have planned next to get this information out of you. There are two things you are going to tell me. Your life depends on it. Now what is the plan to flood the city and who is your contact?"

"I don't know," answered Vlad.

"You must know something."

"I just know it is by omission."

'Omission? What do you mean?"

"That is what he called it."

"How do you flood the city by omission? Is it a bomb in the ocean or something akin to a gigantic tidal wave? How else could someone move the necessary amount of water?"

"That is all I know," pleaded Vlad. Sid had tortured people before. The goal as the interrogator is to walk that fine line between pain and fear.

"How many people is your friend planning to kill?" asked Sid.

"You are naïve enough to think that I am doing this to kill people I don't know and don't care about? This country's weakness was exposed on 9/11, but it is not mass murder. Remember, both planes hit the towers before 9:30am. The point was not to kill people. The world has stopped trying to kill your civilians, or beat your military. The world is aiming to beat the United States financially. China and India – they are your newest rivals. Not a bunch of religious extremists, but that is not what buys tanks," said Vlad. "I know the United States' bulging military and covert budgets. Lots of good it's doing now."

"Is that really all you know?" asked Sid.

"Yes, I am not a monster. The people I work with are not monsters, either. This is a new era and a new war has been created to supplement and augment the land wars and religious wars that have plagued mankind for centuries. This century will know economic wars."

"Why did you give the Mayor that time frame?" asked Sid.

"I don't know," answered Vlad.

Sid needed to privately assess the information before going any further. He decided to take a few minutes to compose himself. "I'll be back," said Sid, as he walked out of the room.

Sid walked into Vlad's office at the Institute. He knew what he needed. There was no way to coordinate the flood of the city without it. Sid found the phone under a few papers. He took it and walked back into the room with Vlad tied up.

"When is your contact set to call you again?" asked Sid.

Vlad was too tired and too scared to resist Sid's questions. "What time is it?" asked Vlad.

Sid looked at his watch and said, "It's 4:05am."

"He will be calling any minute."

*   *   *

Vlad's phone began to ring. Sid opened it up and put the phone to Vlad's ear. Next to his temple was the gun. Vlad spoke first. "The twelve hours have passed."

"Indeed, the people and the leaders of this city don't even know of their biggest threat. This just proves the point that Manhattan is ready for a different type of leadership," stated Zeke.

Vlad was not sure what to say. Sid hadn't given him any instructions.

"Let them know that their subways have been flooded. The economic damage will be in the billions. We still want the Deed to Manhattan," said Zeke.

"Why would they still give that to us?" asked Vlad.

"If they don't provide us with the Deed to Manhattan, you will go public with the information that city and Federal officials within held information from the people. While threats were made to flood Manhattan, its officials made no attempt to evacuate the island or part with a mere historical artifact in exchange for their lives. My group will alert the masses to their new protector. They will embrace our governance with a rousing applause. The next peaceful transfer of power in Manhattan will be complete."

Sid had heard enough. He took the phone away from Vlad's ear. Vlad turned his head and met eyes with Sid. It was the last image that went through Vlad's mind, before the bullet.

Sid pulled the trigger. The bullet hit him just above his right eye socket. His lungs heaved up and down and his fingers were still tense despite him being brain dead. It took about five more seconds for the life to drain from Vlad. Sid raised the phone to his ear.

Zeke, on the other end of the line was startled by the sound.

"Looks like someone is not abiding by our arrangement."

"Don't be so naïve. Your strict adherence to those rules and customs of Skull and Bones is from a bygone era."

"No, we are a secret group. Our loyalty is to our country and the government when it furthers our purpose, Zeke. Your plan to flood the city goes too far."

"The fact that you can't figure out Manhattan's true weakness during the blackout is proof that, two years following 9/11, Americans no longer have the ingenuity to compete in this new century."

"What are you talking about?" asked Sid.

"Eventually, emerging markets and countries will beat you economically and non-sovereign entities will beat you militarily."

"You?" asked Sid. "Where is your loyalty?"

"Are you listening to me? Nothing is too far in the pursuit of power. It is the force I now represent that you should fear. Your work is no longer significant."

"We'll see about that," answered Sid.

"You are nothing more than a pawn. My plan is minutes away from fruition."

Chapter 53

KIDS AND DIRJKE TIED UP IN HAMILTON'S HOUSE

Friday, August 15, 2003 3:57am

The group found themselves trapped inside Hamilton's house. The sounds and smells outside were quieting down. It was pitch dark in Hamilton's house. In a row, their wrists were tied to the banisters of the steps leading to the second floor. Their feet were strung together at the ankles.

"This sucks," announced Danny. "I can't believe the shit shape we are in."

"At least we are alive. I thought that crazy old spy was going to shoot us," replied Barry.

"Spies only kill traitors, because they can't be trusted by anyone. They are dangerous to the entire paradigm. We are loyal to our beliefs. Sid respects that," analyzed Danny.

"Great, that is reassuring," replied Ana.

"Aside from that, Sid is kicking our ass," finished Danny. "We are trapped in Hamilton's home in Harlem during a blackout and having lost the two crests that we found in our previous homes of death visit. And Manhattan is going to flood."

"Relax," said Dirjke to everyone. "Let's just think for a second. What do we need to do and what do we anticipate happening?" Dirjke was employing the Socratic Method as they were sitting on the steps in Hamilton's house.

"Clearly, we need to get out of here," stated Ana.

"We have to figure out where Sid is headed and then formulate our own idea as to whose homes of death we must enter," said Barry.

"Precisely, Barry, but we have got to get out of the immediate situation first. We can't afford to be on the sideline, in some police precinct, having lost our car to our adversary during the blackout," replied Ana. "It might take us hours and add permanent stains on all our records."

"Right, that is what he is counting on – that we are a bunch of amateurs. That is why we have to get out of here before we get caught," added Danny.

"Where do we go? What do we look for?" asked Ana.

"I think we need to go to my office," said Dirjke. "Who knows when this blackout is going to end and it has the best hardcopy books in the city."

"Plus, if the power does go back on, your office will have Internet access," added Barry. "I am happy to look through old history books, but I am a master at obtaining information on the Internet, especially in a targeted source circumstance."

"It's actually not that far from here on the Upper West Side," said Dirjke. "The only problem is that we have to walk."

"Let's worry about that when the time comes," replied Ana.

"How are we going to get out of this without breaking the banisters on the stairs?" asked Barry.

"I am not sure that we could do it, if we tried," stated Danny.

Dirjke asked, "What do you make of the language we found, Ana?"

"Not entirely sure and I know I have said this before, but it feels like we are no closer than before. Once again, 'we have to go alive into the homes of death.' This feels like a circle, Professor."

"I do not entirely know the meaning of the poem but there were two words that caught my attention: brethren and tunnel," Dirjke said.

"How so?" asked Ana.

"The New York militia's true name was the Corsicans. The Hearts of Oak was the group that formed the militia's core, but even with my knowledge, I do not know who the other individuals were. I need my books."

"The reference to a tunnel was equally perplexing," added Barry.

"I know the likelihood that it was still in existence today seems remote," answered Dirjke. "The New York City grid plan of 1811 would have destroyed any tunnel through the rock that comprises Manhattan. Further, the tunnel system within the subways made the chances of a viable tunnel through Manhattan even less likely."

"Sounds like Manhattan's bedrock is Swiss cheese," finished Ana.

"We have to hurry," stated Ana toward Barry and Danny. "We don't want to be here when the lights go on. We will be locked inside because the alarm system will reactivate." The squirming by the group was not getting them anywhere.

Danny called out, "Enough of this." With his hands tied to the banister, he was sitting on the step with his feet tied together. He stopped trying to use his arms to break the polls that held the up handrail along the steps. Instead, he put his feet against the wall in an attempt to push through the polls holding up the handrail.

"No," said Dirjke. "Danny don't press your feet against that wall. This house is too old and you will just put two holes in the wall."

"Wedge your feet into the bottom of the wall where it meets the step," said Ana.

"That is not the statement that I expected to hear," said Dirjke.

"Okay," replied Danny. Without hesitation and with one big push, he dislodged the poll and spilled head over heels onto the floor.

"Are you okay?" asked Dirjke.

"Nice work," said Ana.

"I'm okay," gasped Danny, as he shook the cobwebs away and gained his bearings.

"Well, get us free!" demanded Barry.

"Calm down, Barry," replied Danny. "Just let me get these knots undone," as he worked the knot around Dirjke's wrist. After a few minutes, Dirjke was free. Those two worked to untie Barry and Ana. Dirjke was first to untie Barry.

Danny looked at him and asked, "How did you do that so fast?"

"I recognized the knot. You need to go fishing more," replied Dirjke. Dirjke then untied Ana and the group was free.

"Let's move," said Ana.

"But where?" asked Barry.

"It really doesn't matter. We just can't afford to be caught here when, or if, the power returns."

"She's right. Let's go. I have an idea," said Dirjke. "City College is a few blocks away. Let's go there. I have little doubt that the students who are enjoying the pre-fall semester orientation activities are out having fun and partying, even at this late hour."

"We'll be able to hide in plain sight," noted Barry.

"The real challenge is getting to your office while the power is still out," added Danny.

Danny opened the front door of Hamilton's house and announced, "Let's go." As the group exited the house, each person looked out to Convent Avenue to assess the situation. The power was still out in New York City, but the streets were near empty. Garbage containers were overflowing. The area outside Hamilton's house was deserted.

With Dirjke leading the way, the group turned south on Convent Avenue towards City College. Then in the dark of night, a figure approached them. Irvin was still in his ribbed shirt and basketball shorts.

"Stop right there." Irvin heeded Sid's words of patriotism, or vigilante justice. He was standing between them and the street. His arm was outstretched and he had a gun turned sideways at Dirjke.

Dirjke looked to Danny – telling him not to do anything stupid or sudden with the squint of his eyes. Barry as well did not know how to react. Ana was downright scared.

"What do you want?" asked Dirjke, with his hands up.

"I was told you would be looking in that house. I watched from my window," said Irvin. "You guys are going to jail. I am going to see to it."

"Wait? You don't know what you are doing," began Ana.

"Yes, I do. A gentleman with military credentials told me that you would be coming by."

"And what did he tell you about us?" asked Danny, trying to figure a way around the heightening tension in the situation. "We are innocent."

"He told me that a group of people would be coming out of Hamilton's house," stated Irvin.

"That's it? What else did he tell you? And what would he have needed you for?" asked Dirjke.

"I live in the apartment that overlooks the house," replied Irvin.

"So, you gave him access," stated Barry.

"We are not who you think we are," said Ana.

"Think about it," added Danny. "What was 'your friend' doing here, if he wasn't trying to catch us? Let me tell you – he was a tall slender man with a beard."

"Yeah," replied Irvin. "He told me that his name was Marty Dirjke."

The news hit the group like a punch. Dirjke fumbled for his wallet. Danny exclaimed, "That's his name," as Danny pointed to his uncle.

"Huh?" asked Irvin.

"You have been had. Sid Milliken, the person we are after, gave you Dirjke's name. It is such a simple and effective idea," said Barry.

"The only thing is, Sid thought you would be going to the authorities, not attempting instant justice during a blackout," added Ana. "Think about it. You get the police and this epiphany moment never occurs."

"Under these circumstances, there would be no reasoning with the NYPD," said Barry.

"Look, here is my license." Dirjke then presented his New York State identification to Irvin. He waived his flashlight onto the card.

"Looks like you are right," answered Irvin.

At that moment, the lights along the road in nearly every window lit up.

The deafening noise of TVs, stereos, alarm clocks, and lights was startling. Everyone looked around amazed and half scared by the immediate sounds.

"Do you have a car?" asked Barry. "See, we need to get to an office on the Upper West Side. The power is back on, but the subways are probably not yet running, we need to get on the roads before everyone else does."

"Sure, I have a small compact car. It's from the nineties, but I don't care when other people hit my bumper," said Irvin. "I'll drive you to wherever you need to go."

"Great, let's get a move on," said Dirjke.

224

Chapter 54

SID TELLS MAYOR WHAT HE KNOWS
Friday, August 15, 2003 4:32am

The Mayor had taken the past twenty minutes to refresh himself for the new day. He was only awake about thirty minutes earlier than a typical workday. Of course, that usually includes a night's sleep. He was in a private bathroom splashing water on his face after shaving. He looked at his reflection for a second to gauge if he looked as tired as he felt. His phone rang as he toweled off his face. He flipped it open and put it to his ear.

"Mr. Mayor. I have a few things to tell you," announced Sid, "in this late night and very early morning phone call." He still was in the Ukrainian Institute, eliminating any evidence connecting him to Vlad's death.

"What do you mean?" asked Michael.

"I figured out how Homer intends to flood the city," said Sid.

"So have I," answered Michael. "The generators are being worked on as we speak."

"What generators?"

"The plan was to allow the subways and tunnels to fill up with water during the blackout. Once the third rail is compromised by water, travel stops."

"My information was that twelve hours was the tipping point," said Sid.

"Sort of, assuming the generator pumps that continually keep water out of the subway tunnels never kicked on. After twelve hours it would not have mattered – they would never catch up in time to save the subway tunnel system of over 700 miles. But we got the generator pumps working around 2am. That bought us some more time. Then thank goodness, power was returned city-wide at precisely 4:12am."

"Do you know what this city would have been like without a running subway?" asked Sid rhetorically. "This is an economic terrorist event: the Deed to Manhattan or New York comes to a standstill."

"I already know this," replied Michael. "Sid you are late in your reporting and intelligence. I am out of patience with you."

"Excuse me?"

"Listen, your work here is done, understood? Mr. Milliken, you will be at my 3:00pm press conference."

"Are you telling me my job?" asked Sid. He was in a room within the Institute. He was tying up the loose ends before Vlad's demise was revealed to the press and investigated by law enforcement.

"No, I am telling you your mandate within this theater. You arrived in Manhattan to combat a terrorist attack, not to intercede in an internal historical investigation. Who did you torture as part of your investigation?" asked the Mayor. "I know your tactics by this point. I don't need or want Federal entanglements over the Deed to Manhattan."

"Mr. Mayor, I am a member of the military, Office of Internal Security. When you get authority that trumps that card, you let me know."

"So, I will see you at the press conference at three?" asked Michael. "I know that I am going to have a busy day tomorrow. A press conference late in the afternoon will be my will be my last opportunity to comment on the recent events before the weekend newspapers."

"I can understand that. I have to laugh at the way politicians and public figures attempt to sculpt the stories around them."

"Sid, it might be nice if you were there to make some comments on the events," asked Michael. "According to Hoffson, you are the sole military presence on the island."

"I guess I have a job to do then."

"Good, I was expecting some resistance from you."

"No problem, Mr. Mayor. I will be there," answered Sid.

"Okay. I will see you at three o'clock."

"You got it," answered Sid.

Chapter 55

IRVIN, KIDS, AND DIRJKE GO TO OFFICE
Friday, August 15, 2003 5:01am

"Here you go gang," announced Irvin, as he turned onto 77th Street and West End Avenue. It was right in front of Collegiate School Church. It was an ornate church that was built in the 1890s with a Flemish design. The tan yellow sides framed the stained glass windows along the perimeter.

They each exited the vehicle. "I've enjoyed meeting you all. Danny, you should definitely take a look at City College."

"Thanks, Irvin."

"But I just have one question. Why were you all in Hamilton's house during the blackout?"

"I think it is better that you don't know," replied Barry.

"Trust me, the young man is correct and thank you, again Irvin," added Dirjke.

"It was my pleasure. It is the least I could do considering I nearly shot you uptown," answered Irvin, slouching and bringing his shoulders to his ears.

"All behind us now," answered Dirjke.

"You teach here?" asked Irvin.

"Thirty years," answered Dirjke.

"Long time in one place. I'm a city employee. I can relate."

"Well, you know."

"No, I don't."

"I will tell you about it sometime," said Dirjke with a smile.

"You know my daughter gets nearly straight As in her classes at P.S. 123, but I find that they don't have nearly the standardized preparation for the ACT and SATs."

228

"Know what? Call the school after Labor Day and ask for me," said Dirjke. The two men looked into each other's eyes and knew they had an understanding.

"Yeah, thanks Irvin," added Ana, as she ran a few steps behind the boys into the school.

The group rushed up the stairs to Office 42. Dirjke's many books along with Internet access made the place a historical bat cave. Barry moved to Dirjke's dinosaur of a computer. Ana was behind him.

"Who has any ideas as to the next 'homes of death' that we are to enter?" asked Danny from the window in Dirjke's office. "Which AM radio station should we listen to?"

"Smart," complimented Ana.

"Just turn it on. It's on the station we need."

"*Brethren* – he must be talking about someone, but who?" asked Ana in the direction of Dirjke and Barry.

"Hearts of Oak meant the core of the militia," stated Barry thinking out loud. Dirjke was looking through one of the many books on his shelves.

"Nicholas Fish and Robert Troup," said Dirjke, as he entered his office. "They are the other members of the Hearts of Oak. Let's think in that direction."

"Robert Troup was Hamilton's roommate at King's College," said Barry.

"Just call the place Columbia," said Ana.

"You are annoyed that I call JFK International Airport, Ildewild, simply because it is the historical name of the airfield."

"That's not the point," answered Ana.

"If the Tri-Borough Bridge ever gets renamed, I guarantee that you will still continue to call it by the old name from habit."

"Enough, Barry you are not even old enough to remember when Idlewild was renamed. Ana beats you on this one," said Danny.

"But Troup did some more notable things than simply being Hamilton's college roommate. Troup presided over a large land grab between New York State and Massachusetts," stated Barry, getting back to the point.

"Maybe he got his experience dealing with the Deed to Manhattan," added Danny.

"Based on what I am finding, it looks like Troup is buried somewhere in Brooklyn," continued Barry.

"But he was moved there sometime in the 1870s, as he was originally buried on Manhattan," added Dirjke.

"It doesn't seem like the right avenue to go down. The answer, when correct, should jump out at us," said Ana.

"Let's focus on Nicholas Fish," began Dirjke.

"Why is that?" asked Danny.

"Well, for one, he is buried on Manhattan, but that is not the only reason. Does anyone know Nicholas Fish's son's name?" asked Dirjke with a smile on his face.

"Professor, you know we have no idea," replied Ana.

"Hamilton," stated Barry. "I just found it on the Internet. Nicholas Fish named his son Hamilton Fish."

Danny and Ana turned their heads toward Dirjke, with astonishment in their eyes. Dirjke nodded, signaling that Barry was right.

Ana then recited the poem they found at Hamilton's house:

"The tunnel is preserved by my brethren,
And one more trip into the homes of death must begin."

"I think we are closer than we think," continued Dirjke. "Nicholas Fish lived in a house on Stuyvesant Street, which is approximately two hundred yards from his grave at St. Mark's on the Bowery."

"Is that the same St. Mark's Church we were at yesterday evening?" asked Danny.

"Yup," said Dirjke.

"Into the homes of death," reminded Dirjke.

"Uh guys, I think there's something you should see," said Barry in a nervous tone.

"Oh no," said Ana. She began to read aloud from over Barry's shoulder with her soft hands resting on his shoulders. His heart began to pound for additional reasons, as his favorite girl read him history.

"At 21 Stuyvesant Street there is what is known as the Stuyvesant Fish House which was built in 1803 by Petrus Stuyvesant, the great-great grandson of Peter Stuyvesant, the last Dutch West India Company's Governor of Manhattan. Petrus gave the house to his daughter, Elizabeth, as a wedding present when she married Nicholas Fish, a Revolutionary war hero and political ally of Alexander Hamilton..." an astonished Ana let her voice trail off.

"That is amazing," stated Danny. "You mean there is a nexus between Peter Stuyvesant, the man who surrendered Manhattan in 1664 to the British, and the Hearts of Oak, the militia responsible for protecting the island during the Revolutionary War."

"That is amazing," repeated Ana. "This could be the 'home of death' we are looking for. Unreal, I mean the Seal of the City was changed from 1664 to 1625, which is a year before the purchase of the island."

"We need to figure out a way to get in there," said Barry looking to Ana and Danny.

"No, what we need to do is think this through and come up with a plan. Not just an idea to get to the next square. As we get closer to actually obtaining the Deed, at some point we are going to actually have to best Sid, or we are not going to win. This history stuff is amazing and more than anything I ever dreamed through my career's worth of research. But our job is not only to find the Deed to Manhattan. Our job is to do it before Sid."

"It's not how you start, but how you finish," stated Danny.

"My coach says that all the time," added Ana. She was looking over Barry's shoulder as she waited for the Internet to load.

"Tunnel is the word that gets me," mused Danny, breaking the silence that developed while the group researched the next step. He was pacing back and forth. "As we discussed regarding Hamilton's house, any tunnel in Manhattan was likely to be destroyed by subways, basement excavations, and the Manhattan grid plan of 1811."

"Well, Stuyvesant Street is pretty far downtown. But Manhattan was developed from the Battery and Fort Amsterdam, north. Professor is it possible that these streets we are talking about are close enough to the East Village to have already been in place before the grid plan was laid over the island?" asked Ana.

"That's unlikely," said Barry. "It's called St. Mark's on the Bowery, because 'Bowery' is the Dutch word for 'farm.' So the land would be nothing but pasture. St. Mark's Church was not even built until 1795, when the first cornerstone was laid. The formal street itself would be around that time as well."

"Thanks, Professor..." said Ana in a mildly annoyed tone to Barry. Yet, the remark got Dirjke's mind firing. He dropped the two books onto his desk. The loud sound caught the attention of the others. Dirjke looked left then right and reached for a small book wedged into place.

"Unfortunately, I think Barry is right. Stuyvesant Street straddles 2nd and 3rd avenues near 10th Street. It appears to be within the grid plan," said Danny.

"Just as I thought," exclaimed Dirjke, he was standing next to one of his overstuffed bookshelves. He had two open books on top of each other in his right hand.

"What's that?" asked Danny.

"Danny, Barry, you are not looking at the plan closely enough," said Dirjke.

"What map are you looking at?" asked Danny, but Dirjke turned toward him to reveal nothing but prose in a book.

"Look closer at Stuyvesant Street. You'll figure it out."

Danny looked back at the screen. "Stuyvesant Street cuts through 9th and 10th Street between 2nd and 3rd Avenue."

"Exactly, there is only one street that was exempted from the New York City grid plan. Are you ready for this?" asked Dirjke with the exuberance of a teacher during a perfect lesson.

"Yes," answered the group all at once.

"Stuyvesant Street in Manhattan was the only street exempted from the grid plan."

"Huh?" asked Barry.

"It was never changed in the plans. In fact, it says here that Stuyvesant Street is the only street that runs due west and east on the entire island," said Dirjke, as he pointed to the book in his hand.

"So there could be an undisturbed tunnel, leading to the homes of death, under the only street exempted from the Manhattan grid plan of 1811," mused Ana.

"Precisely," answered Dirjke. Barry had begun looking at the contemporary version of 21 Stuyvesant Street.

"You are not going to believe this," said Barry.

"Why? Is this another Federal Landmark that we are going to have to break into?" asked Danny.

233

"What celebrity now lives in this house?" asked Ana.

"It is now the official home of the President of Cooper Union," replied Barry.

"We were supposed to take a look around there, Unk."

"Cooper Union is dedicated to the belief that the highest education should be 'Free as Air and Water.' For over a hundred and fifty years the institution has admitted every one of its students based on a merit-based full-tuition scholarship," stated Barry.

"Hold on Barry. Let me hear this story on the radio." Dirjke furrowed his brow, slouched and put his hands on his hips as he looked at the radio.

"Despite New York's admirable handling of the blackout, there was a murder at the Ukrainian Institute on Museum Mile. Federal Authorities are already on the scene..." screeched out of the radio in a garbled tone.

"Did you hear that?"

"Hear what?" asked Danny.

"The Ukrainian Institute," stated Dirjke.

"Why is that so interesting?" asked Danny.

"Well, the report also said that Federal Authorities were on the scene. That likely includes Sid," said Dirjke.

"Under the cloak of the blackout and a suspicious death, he constantly has a reason to be nearby and search for the Deed," added Ana.

"Not that – the address is unusual. Almost scary," said Dirjke.

"How so?" asked Barry, "I know Museum Mile on 5th Avenue better than most. I had no idea the Ukrainian Institute was even there."

"You don't know everything, Barry," replied Ana.

"The Ukrainian Institute was the home of the last surviving descendant of the Stuyvesant family, the last Dutch Governor of Manhattan," added Dirjke.

"Are you kidding me? What you are saying Unk, is that through the course of the blackout there was a murder at the home that was occupied by the last living descendant of Peter Stuyvesant," surmised Danny.

"And his great-great grandson built the house we were just discussing?" asked Danny.

"Indeed," said Dirjke.

"Well the loose ends are certainly tightening around this situation," stated Ana.

"Which is why we need to be as careful as ever. It doesn't matter what the score is along the way, the final score is the only one that matters. We need that lead," insisted Dirjke.

At that moment, he got a call from the Mayor. After a few 'ahs' and 'okays' he hung up the phone. The rest of the room waited for what Dirjke had to say.

"I have got to see the Mayor to explain what happened at Hamilton's house last night. You guys keep working. Report to me about your ideas. You know what we need to do next."

Chapter 56

SID WAKES UP AS THE POWER RETURNS
Friday, August 15, 2003 6:09am

It was early Friday morning. Sid had had about ninety minutes of rest. "Quick power nap," thought Sid. He liked the pun, because power was what he chased all his adult life. After a shower and search around the Institute for new clothes, Sid was in a corner room on one of the higher floors of the mansion.

New day, same plan – dominate the competition. On top of his secret mission, there was the premium for his work, under the guise of Federal Power. He would obtain the Deed. He turned his attention to his recharged electronic devices, a small laptop computer, and his cell phone.

The sun had just risen above the eastern skyline in New York. Sid looked out at 5th Avenue, from a corner window from the Ukrainian Institute. He needed to know where Dirjke and the kids were.

If they were in the hands of the authorities, he would bargain for their release without a mark on their record. He was waiting until 9 o'clock and the shift change before he would make any inquiries. If they had gotten free, they were likely en route to the next location. Sid recited the poem found at Hamilton's house:

"The tunnel is preserved by my brethren,
And one more trip into the homes of death must begin."

Sid had no idea how to find the other members of a militia that died out nearly two hundred years ago. "This information is not kept in books," thought Sid. From the window, he saw people walking their dogs and leaving for runs in Central Park. Cars were returning to 5th Avenue.

"At least I have these four discs," thought Sid. He rubbed his thumbs on the relief to try to determine what the image depicted.

Further confrontation was unavoidable. However, this early morning he would be preoccupied with providing the cover story necessary to explain away a random murder at the Ukrainian Institute.

Sid had a job to do. No one did it better.

Chapter 57

DUROE AND MICHAEL TALK
Friday, August 15, 2003 6:45 am

Michael was calling to personally thank Duroe for his efforts during the blackout. Duroe answered the phone in his front pocket. He was sitting in the break room with a black coffee and a stale muffin. His skin was a deep tan with blonde hair. His graying facial hair showed how long it had been since his shift started. Duroe's light blue shirt was still wet under his armpits and around his neck.

"Jack, Michael here. I just wanted to call and personally thank you for your work. You went beyond the call of duty in returning the generator pumps to power by 2:12am."

"Thank you, Mr. Mayor. I served on some special forces. It turned into a valuable asset, as a civil servant during this crisis."

"Military, huh? What unit?" asked Michael. He was not terribly interested in the response. It was just a means to keep the conversation going until he could invite Jack Duroe to his press conference at 3:00pm. Michael was squeezing a stress ball with the City seal on it in his office at City Hall.

"1st Battalion, 5th Field Artillery," stated Duroe. "I was on a mission in 2000 to Kuwait. We were part of a special task force."

"Really, that is amazing," said Michael with childlike exuberance.

The comment caught Duroe off guard. "No one likes military combat, but as a professional army, the United States military operates with a businesslike approach. It's not that amazing. The secret is not letting anyone know how scared you really are," answered Duroe.

"I can relate to that. I am the Mayor that maneuvered this city through potentially the biggest economic crisis I can imagine. But I was talking about the unit you are a part of. Jack, I want you to come to my press conference at 3:00pm."

"Mr. Mayor, I'm really not the public speaking type."

"Nonsense, I want you there. You won't have to speak. Just smile when I say your name. Besides, I want to hear about what it is like to be a part of the army's oldest military unit. It is the militia unit that raided the Battery months before the Declaration of Independence."

"What do you mean?" asked Duroe.

Michael felt like Dirjke for a second. "I can't believe I am telling you historical facts that you had no idea existed."

"What are you talking about, Mr. Mayor."

"Just bring your fatigues. I want to see the uniform. If I am right, the unit's logo will provide the answer." Duroe shook his head in dismay. "Mr. Mayor, you want me to come to the press conference in my fatigues?"

"No, I just want you there. That is an order. Dress comfortably, but bring your fatigues in a bag."

"Ahh, okay" replied Duroe. "That still doesn't make any more sense to me, but at least I will not be sweating in my military gear on a hot August New York afternoon."

"Come to City Hall. I will leave your name with security."

"Will do," answered Duroe.

Chapter 58

DIRJKE AND MAYOR
Friday, August 15, 2003 7:05 am

With the power returned to New York City, Michael was in his office at City Hall. He was preparing his remarks for this afternoon. He was enjoying the air-conditioning that he kept extra low. He was tired, but comfortable in business casual attire.

"The focus must be on New Yorkers and how we handled this event."

"Okay," said Sam. "I know exactly where to go with the rhetoric on this point. But with city services not yet running at full capacity, how do we present that to the public?"

Michael answered, "Take the day off. Last night was a panic averted by the sheer will of the people of this great city. How does that sound?"

Michael turned his head and saw Dirjke walking toward his office. He finished, "Sam, that is enough for now. Beef up the areas we discussed and have it ready for my 3 o'clock presser."

"But Mr. Mayor, we have not gone over street parking rules, garbage, any of the other governmental services we provide to New Yorkers. Not to mention terrorism."

"I'm about to deal with that now," answered Michael under his breath. "Sam, you have been at this job since I was sworn in. You are leaving me in six months to work on the campaign of some senator from Illinois. Surely you can handle this task."

"Okay," answered Sam.

Michael looked over at Dirjke standing in the doorway. He was not impressed. Dirjke was wearing the same clothes as he had worn for their meeting nearly 24 hours ago. His hair was tattered. The look on his face was one of exhaustion.

"You look terrible," said Michael. "Now then, tell me what happened last night." In an annoyed tone, he added, "I expected you to be back hours ago."

"There was little we could do. Sid is pursuing the Deed. He tied us to the banisters in Hamilton's house and took the disc we found at Hamilton's grave," said Dirjke.

"What do you mean?" asked Michael.

"We were right about our homes of death theory. We found another note and an identical disc to the one in Hamilton's house."

"So what did Sid do?"

"He somehow figured out that Hamilton's house was the location of the next clue. Then he took the discs and the note we found."

"Why is he doing this? There is no way I will allow the Federal Government to have possession of the Deed to Manhattan."

"He is saying that pursuant to his office at the Pentagon, obtaining the Deed is a matter of national security and he intends to burn it on sight to maintain a false story generated by President Van Buren in 1849," replied Dirjke.

"What evidence is there for that?" asked Michael. "Sid was probably giving you disinformation to push you down the wrong path."

"I doubt it. There is folklore around Yale that Skull and Bones robbed Van Buren's grave. He wants the Deed for Skull and Bones, not to protect the Federal interests of the nation."

At that moment, Dirjke saw the memo on Michael's desk about a murder at the Ukrainian Institute.

"This is the next thing we need to discuss. I heard this report on the radio while I was at Collegiate School earlier this morning." Dirjke pointed to the piece of paper.

"I got the report a few minutes before it went public. It's crazy, Marty. This city handled the blackout so well. Now, we have this random event that besmirches all of the kindness displayed by every other New Yorker."

"Mr. Mayor, a murder at the Ukrainian Institute is no random event."

"Why is that?"

"Don't you see? Sid killed whoever was there, thinking it might be the next 'home of death' referred to in the Hearts of Oak passage."

"This is going to be a diplomatic nightmare. I have got to get on this right away," said Michael.

"Exactly, but I will handle it," replied Dirjke

"You will handle it?" queried Michael. "I need information as to this guy's potential enemies and things of that nature. This is a police matter."

"No, it's not. The Ukrainian Institute is the last home of the last surviving member of the Stuyvesant family. I think it's connected to the Deed to Manhattan," stated Dirjke.

"You really think the two events are connected?"

"Yes."

"All right. Well get yourself and your crackerjack kids onto it," ordered Michael. "Where are they anyway?"

"They are going to the Stuyvesant Fish House on Stuyvesant Street near Cooper Union."

"Why is that?" asked Michael.

"Our 'into the homes of death' theory from the Hearts of Oak passage was spot on. We found a Hamilton crest identical to the one from Hamilton's grave. It was above the fireplace in his house. Really amazing – and behind the crest was a poem."

"So what is on Stuyvesant Street?"

"One of the other core members of the Hearts of Oak was Nicholas Fish. And his son married the great-great granddaughter of Peter Stuyvesant."

"Stuyvesant, that is the name you mentioned as the prior owners of the Ukrainian Institute building," said Michael.

"Precisely, but I think we are looking in a better location, because guess what the couple named their son?"

"Just tell me, old friend! You are not in a classroom," said Michael.

"Hamilton Fish," replied Dirjke.

"For real?" asked Michael.

"Yes," answered Dirjke, "but that can be argued as random. The truth of the matter is that Stuyvesant Street is the only street exempted from the New York grid plan. It runs due east and west, not the approximately 30 degree angle that typical New York streets have on Manhattan."

"So the street is old. Is it really so amazing?" asked Michael. "I don't want you on some foolish chase for coincidences at this point."

"Michael, if the street is that old, it's possible that there is an undisturbed tunnel," explained Dirjke.

Michael cut him off, "But where could it lead?"

"To Nicholas Fish's grave at St. Mark's Church on the Bowery. It is a couple hundred yards from the house. Based on the Homer poem, that is the final homes of death that we need."

"Nicholas Fish's grave," repeated Michael.

"Yes, he is buried at St. Mark's Church a few hundred yards from the house."

"St. Mark's – that's the place where the priest gave you that parchment with all the numbers and we used the dictionary to decode it," said Michael.

"Right. It was an Arnold Cipher decoded with Entick's Dictionary. It gave us the entire Hearts of Oak passage from Homer's *Odyssey*. I mean, encoding a map within the name of your militia and a Greek epic poem."

"So the kids are checking the Stuyvesant Fish House in the East Village?" asked Michael.

"And we have a murder at the location of another Stuyvesant house. However, we have one thing Sid doesn't have the ability to do – the ability to be in two places," answered Dirjke.

"And one other thing, I have the ability to manipulate Sid's maneuvers. He will be present at my 3 o'clock press conference. Do with that information what you must," said Michael.

"What is it?" He knew the look on Dirjke's face.

"At some point we are going to have to out think Sid, if we are going to save the Deed to Manhattan."

"Dirjke, you know as well as anyone that we only need to have the lead at the end," answered Michael. "Get it done."

Chapter 59

KIDS FIGURE OUT HOW TO GET INTO FISH HOUSE

Friday, August 15, 2003 7:15am

Following Dirjke's departure for City Hall, the kids got to work. Danny was exhausted, but knew that he needed to focus on the job.

"I need to refresh my mind. I am going to the showers," said Danny.

"You know, the shower is the best place to think. The hot water and steam take the dust particles out of the air. Except for going outside immediately after a heavy rain, it is the freshest air you can breathe," added Barry.

Danny just shook his head. "Barry, I bet if I asked you the time, you would tell me how the clock works."

"Thanks for the compliment," answered Barry.

"I need a shower too. Actually we all do, if we are going to fit in and hide in plain sight now that the power is on," stated Ana. "Smelling good and being dressed in clean clothes should help. I am going to 72nd Street to get us some new clothes. I will pick up some clean shirts for you boys."

"Girls, they will think of any reason to shop," teased Barry.

"I don't comment on a female's propensity for shopping," finished Danny.

"Don't worry, they have nearly everything including accessories," smiled Ana. "You boys look like nothing but mannequins in my mind right now."

"Ana, I know you would have thought of this, but make sure you get Barry and me different shirts and I could use some new socks," said Danny.

"Sure thing," replied Ana. "I got you boys covered."

"Okay, that's fine, thanks," answered Barry, but he was moving to his own expertise. "I found a United States Department of Interior Registry Application for the house. It has an amazingly detailed description. I am going to try and sketch out the layout. I will shower after you Danny," said Barry, with his nose pressed to the computer screen.

"All right, everyone handle your business, but be ready to leave here at 8:15," said Ana. Danny proceeded to the locker room. They walked out of Dirjke's office together.

"You know that is amazing, you growing up in Manhattan and your father going to Columbia. I want to go to Columbia too. They have a superb fencing program."

The two were shoulder to shoulder as they walked down the hall. Danny put his hand on Ana's back. She looked at him and smiled.

"For real, you know my father was a fencer at Columbia."

"Did you know that Columbia has won more national titles in fencing than any other team since fencing became a NCAA sport," stated Danny. "Thirteen titles to be exact," he said, as he slid his hand to her shoulder and gently pulled her toward him.

"I have heard all those stories from my father. You know my parents met at Columbia. My father always said that because Barnard is across the street, the male to female ratio is nearly three to one in favor of the boys. You're good-looking, you might do well with those odds." She looked up at him.

"I can't argue with your logic," answered Danny, as he stepped in front of Ana. Her nose hit him just below his Adam's apple. He moved to kiss her.

She grabbed his face and moved her head out of the line of fire.

"Hold on, there. C'mon, you are a high school senior. Forget it. I'm flattered, but for real?"

Danny smiled as she let go of the gentle but forceful grip she had on his cheeks.

"I guess I am only surprised that you didn't make a move sooner."

"Alone on Wall Street was not the best time, with my uncle negotiating old scores with spies."

"I like your confidence, Danny, no doubt about that. But I have to go shopping."

Danny put out his fist and settled for a knuckle tap.

*   *   *

Eventually, the group reconvened in Dirjke's office. Barry printed out the ten-page document and left it for the others while he showered and changed clothes. Ana went third. Her hair was wet and in a ponytail.

"What do we think, Barry?" asked Danny.

"We have the Stuyvesant Fish House on Stuyvesant Street."

"We have to be more discrete now that we no longer have the cover of darkness. I have a few ideas," said Ana.

"What ideas do you have?' asked Danny.

"According to the Cooper Union website, there are orientation activities for students, including an open house at the President's home," announced Ana.

"That's amazing," said Barry.

"Barry, you know I am in the amazing business," Ana said, relishing the latest find of the moment.

"Unreal," agreed Danny. "The row house was only attached on the westside." Danny was reading from the National Registry of Historic Places – Inventory Nomination Form to the group.

"Why does that matter?" asked Ana.

"Because it allows for a tunnel to St. Mark's Church, which is where Nicholas Fish, a member of the

Hearts of Oak, is buried," answered Barry. "I am amazed. The idea that Manhattan's militia during the Revolutionary War and the army's oldest unit protected the Deed to Manhattan was beyond even my wildest historical theories only two days ago."

"So you're telling me that unlike Hamilton, whose grave and home are miles apart, the distance between Nicholas Fish's house and his grave is a couple hundred yards," asked Danny.

"Yup," answered Barry. "And the architect is unknown – amazing, simply amazing. I mean did F. Phillip Geraci know what he actually owned? Why did Cathy Alexander from Nashville, Tennessee fill out this form?"

"Enough, let's focus on the job the Mayor gave us to do. We're not trying to develop a documentary," said Ana. "I have to believe that we are getting close."

"But, Barry the woman's last name is 'Alexander'?" teased Danny in a sarcastic tone.

Barry caught his new friend's tone and slight smile. For the first time, Barry laughed to himself about his own singular historical focus.

"When is the orientation activity at Cooper Union?" asked Danny, as he turned toward Ana.

"9:00am. We should have plenty of time to get there. I say we spend some more of this cash we have and take a cab."

Chapter 60

KIDS GO TO STUYVESANT HOUSE
Friday, August 15, 2003 8:30am

"Okay, here will be fine," answered Danny. The yellow cab stopped on 8th Street and Broadway. The group walked east on 8th Street to Third Avenue. NYU students were walking in all directions. Cars were moving smoothly through the intersection. There was a salty smell to the morning air.

The group made a left toward the crooked little street within the rigid New York City street grid – Stuyvesant Street. It is an iconic street that demonstrates New York architecture from a bygone era. Vintage Gotham.

The group approached the southwest end of Stuyvesant Street. There were red brick row houses along the northern side of the street.

"I would venture a guess that the house with the maroon and gold balloons out front is the Cooper Union President's house," stated Danny.

"All right, I think we need to be realistic here. The idea that the three of us are all going to get into the house is silly," said Ana. "I will take care of this."

"You," answered Danny. "That's a bold proposition, even for you."

"Yup," answered Ana.

"How are you going to do that?" asked Barry.

"It will depend on the defense, or the security offered at the event. But if our names are not on any lists, it would likely be because of yesterday's blackout," said Ana.

"How do you know the event is going on there?" asked Danny.

"I went to the Cooper Union website and looked up their new student orientation activities."

"It's a question and answer session with the President of Cooper Union," added Barry. "I read that too."

"I should go to the event," said Danny. "I actually have some real life questions for the President of Cooper Union."

"Me three," added Barry, determined not to be left out.

"Fine," answered Ana, "but I do the talking, got it?" The boys nodded in agreement.

They each walked toward the house at 21 Stuyvesant Street. Trees swaying in the breeze lined the street. Many of the row house along the street had facades that were engulfed in ivy. The brown and reddish row houses each had a flight of steps that led to the front door, ten feet above street level.

At the front stoop of their destination, they were met by a preppy young student behind a folding table with a maroon tablecloth. Yellow balloons were taped to the four corners of the table. Ana and the boys approached the table and she said, "Hello there, Edwin," having noticed the boy's name tag.

"Well hello," answered the young man in a southern accent. Ana's ears perked up. She took a course last year that focused on the hundreds of dialects and accents, titled *Dialects of the English Language*.

"Let me guess, Texas. I'm thinking Austin."

"Hook'em horns."

"Too bad, I am a Sooner fan. Is this the morning question and answer session with the Cooper Union President?"

"It sure is," answered Edwin, as he looked up from that laptop computer screen on the table. The printed list on the table flapped in the breeze.

"What are they saying about yesterday's blackout?" asked Ana. "Lucky we can even have this activity. Fortunately the power is back on."

Barry and Danny stood behind Ana with their hands in their pockets.

"Not that much, really. With the power out, there was no means to report anything. It appears that Cooper Union suffered no ill effects from the event."

"Well we are here for the Q&A with the president," stated Ana.

"You're in the right place," replied Edwin. "Now if I can just get your names to cross them off the list."

Ana sharpened up and said, "See that is the thing. We signed up yesterday right as the blackout occurred."

She used the recent events as a shield and a sword. The only difference between her and Sid was her incorruptibility. From Sid's perspective, he was no less incorruptible.

"So you are not on the list?" asked Edwin.

"No, probably not, but check, please," answered Ana, with the realization that this was going to take more than her nice smile.

"Well, how long until the program starts? Maybe we can fill in for the people that are sleeping in after what was probably a late night last night."

"I don't know. What if they show up late?"

"If they show up late, too bad. Didn't I tell you this already? I'm a Sooner's fan. You know why they are called the Sooners?"

"C'mon, they are called Sooners because they got to the land first," answered Edwin. "That doesn't make'm bigger or better than the University of Texas."

"Fine, but it proves my point here, that if you are late, you lose."

"Okay then, you and your friends write your names here. If they are not here when the program starts, I will give you a 'sooner' discount this one time."

"Thanks, Edwin," smiled Ana.

Chapter 61

SCENE AT INSTITUTE
Friday, August 15, 2003 10:01am

There was press lined up and down 5th Avenue. They had been given complete access by the new person in charge of the Institute following the murder. Although there was a gunshot wound to the leg, which was primitively repaired, the death appeared to be a bizarre suicide. Vlad was dead in a chair.

Sid was walking freely within the building. He was standing at the top of the circular stairway in the mansion looking at the people milling around.

Then he noticed Dirjke on his way up the second level of steps and looking around like a child at his favorite museum. Shock went through Sid's mind and body. Irvin failed in his assumed job of snitching Dirjke's name to the authorities.

The ability to maneuver the situation was the constant challenge, as a man who pushed things to the limit. By definition he would not stop until he met resistance.

"Marty Dirjke just doesn't seem to get the hint," mumbled Sid.

Dirjke felt differently this time. He wanted to confront his old nemesis.

"Fancy seeing you here," said Dirjke, as they met on the steps of the third staircase, Sid going down and Dirjke up.

"Not fancy at all, just doing my job," he responded. The two men moved so their backs were against the railing of the wooden stairs. A gold ornate chandelier was parallel to their heads.

"It must be a lot of work, creating the same crime scene you are investigating," said Dirjke.

"What basis do you have to make that allegation?" asked Sid.

"Look around. This has all the hallmarks of your work," answered Dirjke. "A break-in without anything stolen, or better yet nothing appearing stolen."

"The real question is if these people even knew how powerful they were," stated Sid. He was looking up for clues or instances where the four crests he had could lead into the homes of death. "I am perplexed by the demise of this Dutch-American family, a brother and sister that carry out their last days living together in the same house. Even more strange was that Augustus Stuyvesant rarely left the house after his sister's passing."

"Was that the result of a forbidden love between the two siblings, or his failure to handle the family name and responsibility? More interesting is that you must either think you have not found what you need, or you are simply lost," added Dirjke. "Why else would you be here?"

"Keep guessing?" answered Sid. "You do understand that you are not going to beat me. You have been little more than my puppet for years and that is not going to change."

"That is what you think," answered Dirjke. "Why do this? The Mayor had no choice but to employ your services. Of course, it took blackmail based on the fact that the Mayor and I knew you took the stick, and because Hoffson said you were in the area. Mere coincidence? You have lost complete focus. You are using the military to sanction your clandestine affairs."

"You and I just disagree as to the facts. Who is the only person with actual authority in this setting? Imagine a proceeding to explain your actions, based on whose authority?" said Sid.

Dirjke stared back at his old friend. He caught Dirjke's hesitation and said, "Yeah, go ahead – try to out me as a Bonesman. See what that does for you when you are the person looking for the Deed to Manhattan during a blackout. Think about your future, Marty."

"But the Mayor knows the truth. He knows you're after the Deed."

"No, he thinks I am after the Deed, because you told him that. Meanwhile, it's a baseless allegation. I have helped end this city's blackout and a potential economic catastrophe. You and your group continually got in my way."

"Those may have been the facts, but that is not the truth," answered Dirjke. "Sid, this has gone on long enough. So I started as a pledge, but decided not to join."

"It matters because those actions mock the seriousness of our organization. You remember the question you were asked: 'Skull and Bones accept or reject', not want to try out."

"C'mon, surely someone has been rejected by membership – during the pledge process?" asked Dirjke.

"Nope," answered Sid. "We do our research ahead of time. You embarrassed that research."

"And for that you have made me a lifelong enemy."

"Not true," stated Sid. "I have in some ways protected you. Who do you think has advocated for your life all this time? Do some research into the Skull and Bones members who did not live long enough to comb gray hair, Marty. Without me, you would be on that list."

"No, that's just how you see things, from your twisted perspective," interrupted Dirjke. "I will beat you this time. You are out of your element and I am adapting to yours. You will prove to be no match." He turned to face Sid along the steps.

"Bold words," answered Sid. "I will hold judgment until I see your ability to act." Sid stepped back, up a step, and achieved the high ground.

"I will see you at the Mayor's press conference."

"I will be there, bells and whistles," smiled Sid, as he stepped back again.

Dirjke responded in kind, "Good seeing you ole chum." A small smile developed on Dirjke's face as his back turned to Sid. He had learned what he needed.

Chapter 62

KIDS IN STUYVESANT HOUSE – COOPER UNION
Friday, August 15, 2003 10:15am

The kids were standing outside 21 Stuyvesant Street, waiting to go inside the house. The red-brown bricks were weathered and worn. Two large windows framed with green shutters were on the first floor. The house itself was shorter than the adjacent houses it was sandwiched between.

The home possessed more of a Federal design than a Dutch one. It was also more a modest row house than a mansion. But no matter what, it had been an amazing wedding gift to a daughter and her husband.

Two figures appeared outside the home. "Hello. As you probably know, I am John McCormick and this is my wife, Helen." John was a middle-aged man with a medium build and a reddish-pink face complimented with green eyes and light brown hair. His wife had white skin and a big smile with a thin frame.

"Hello," responded the group.

"Good to see you all," said John. "Well, come inside. We have set up some chairs in the living room on the first floor for some questions and answers. You all must have a lot of questions about your next four years."

Barry, Danny, and Ana each walked into the house with their eyes wide open and looked left and right. They seemed like first-years, because they were so eager.

The first floor consisted of a double reception room that the family used as a living room on the west side of the building and a dining room and kitchen to the east side of the building. The walls were decorated with various art paintings.

In the west room, there was a circle of seats for the group to converse with John and Helen. There was a wall in the living room devoted to the children's accomplishments.

An off-white area rug covered all but a one-foot perimeter around the walls.

Barry, as the last person to enter the house, looked left and right and asked, "Can I use your bathroom. My contact lens fell out."

"Sure," answered Helen. "Better yet, use the one upstairs, my daughter wears contact lenses too."

"Thank you, Mrs. McCormick," replied Barry.

Barry walked up the stairs.

Ana and Danny sat next to each other. Ana noticed that, similar to Hamilton's house, this room also possessed a fireplace. However, she did not detect any hidden crests. The walls were painted a lemon yellow with white trim around a stone fireplace. There were fake logs and flowers occupying the space.

Barry looked around on the second and third floors of the home, but he did not observe anything hiding in plain sight. Each bedroom was impeccably decorated and clean. It was clear that the McCormick family was ready for the upcoming school year.

He walked down the steps and noticed an arch that he did not see as he entered the building. It was reflecting the light from the window over the entrance to the home. He saw two circular crevices.

He got to the last step and rotated one hundred and eighty degrees. He saw a circular indentation that looked to have the same circumference and diameter as the crests Sid took from them at Hamilton's house.

Barry recalled the National Registry of Historic Places – Inventory Nomination Form and the mention of a 'semielliptical transverse' over the stairway.

Ana noticed his awkward maneuver and could only shake her head. Meanwhile, Danny was asking some legitimate questions and posing as a first year student.

"And that is why you should choose a field that balances your interests with your aptitude. It is your future career and profession. It must be considered paramount from this day forward," stated Mrs. McCormick.

At that moment, another student raised their hand and questioned Mr. McCormick, "What about the requirements for graduation and the required curriculum?"

Barry walked in the room. He sat down at the only open chair. His back was to the stairs he just descended. His eyes met Ana's and he gave her a nod. She attempted to inconspicuously look at her wristwatch. The plan was to wait out the remaining time for the question and answer session.

Seconds later, Edwin entered the home with two New York Police Officers. The group had a plan for this contingency.

Edwin and the officers maneuvered to the McCormicks, who were the greatest distance from the door. The group looked with anticipation toward each other.

They followed Ana's advice: once every adversary was further away from the front door than each of them – run.

Chapter 63

CHASE TO CITY HALL
Friday, August 15, 2003 10:30am

The group raced down the iron steps at 21 Stuyvesant Street. Danny was in the lead. Ana and Barry followed their blocker. Danny was focused on anticipating the next open lane. They sprinted to Third Avenue and looked for the Astor Place 6 train downtown.

"I can't believe it. Edwin looked me up and ratted me out."

"You did lie about everything you said," answered Danny.

"I told him I was a Sooner fan, Texas people."

"So you are really an Oklahoma Sooners fan because their rival is the University of Texas?"

"Not just that, they were rivals of the University of Miami in the 80s. That's Barry's favorite team."

"Miami's the sixth borough," gasped Barry.

"You two can disagree over anything. C'mon, green line," shouted Danny.

"Only tourists call it that," answered Ana.

"Is now really the time to crack a joke?" asked Barry.

"Pay attention. Does everyone know where their Metrocard is?' asked Ana.

"Metrocard?" questioned Danny.

"Don't worry. I bought a sixty dollar card when I got those awesome threads for you boys. I will pass it back," replied Ana.

"Just remember to focus when you swipe the card. The three of us can't afford to get stuck at the turnstile," added Barry.

"Like a baton in a track meet," said Danny.

"Just remember to lead with the black strip facing you and your right thumb on the 'M'," added Barry. Just as they stepped down the last flight of steps onto the platform, a 6 train came barreling into the station.

"My father's favorite line about the subway was that 'true faith is the belief that a subway car was approaching your station.'"

"Looks like our faith in our city, Ana, has been rewarded," followed Barry. As they got to the bottom of the steps, they could feel the air in front of the oncoming train, as well as the rush of sound as the train passed them on the platform and came to a stop. They stepped into the second car of the train.

"That was one lucky run," panted Ana.

The train was packed. They were nose to nose with each other and everyone else in the subway car.

"I hate this train. This is the only line that runs on the East Side. The train spends forever on the platform as people push in and out of it. Sometimes it takes three tries for the doors to close," groaned Ana.

"How are we going to ever get out of this?" asked Barry.

"Relax, we just need to think," answered Danny.

The group was now in the third car of the train. The officers managed to get into the last car and were proceeding through the crowded subway train. It was the only thing buying the group time or anonymity.

Before they knew it, the train was about to stop at Spring Street. Danny had counted the seconds that the train doors were open at the earlier station – Bleeker Street. The group continued to press forward trying to stay ahead of the NYPD.

"How many stops until we get to City Hall?" asked Danny.

"Two more," answered Barry in a frantic tone.

"Let's keep moving forward on the train. Maybe we will get to the platform at Brooklyn Bridge/City Hall before we get to the front of the train," said Ana.

After the walk through the fifth car, they could feel the train slow down as they were thrown forward. "This is not going to work. We are going to get to the front of the train before we get to Canal Street Station," said Barry.

"How do you know?" asked Danny.

"I have been counting the cars. We are near car seven. A typical train only has ten cars."

"Ha, as if we need another problem," stated Ana.

"What side does the train platform at the next stop?"

"The left," answered Barry and Ana at once.

"Okay, I have a plan. Stand still," ordered Danny.

"What? You must be crazy," answered Barry.

"No. Haven't you ever seen *Top Gun*? Just like Maverick. We have to draw them in and then slam on the brakes and let them fly by," explained Danny.

"We can't just get off at Canal and walk. We won't get safely to the Mayor's office," reminded Ana. "There is no way we can get a mile through downtown without getting picked up by police."

"No doubt the police have broadcast our descriptions via radio," said Barry.

"No, we just need more cars to run through. Follow me."

"What are you thinking?" asked Ana.

"We need to get to the front of this car," repeated Danny.

"Just so you know, the next car is the front car. Mind letting us in on what you are thinking?" asked Barry.

"We need to stand at the front of this car until we see them in the same car as us. When we get to the next car, I want you two to run to the middle doors on the left side of the train. I will be in front of the doors immediately upon entering that front car," said Danny, taking control.

"Great coach, you told us the formation, now how about the play?" demanded Ana.

"All right, when the doors open at Canal, get on the platform and run back two cars. We'll start this race all over again in the other direction."

"Brilliant," announced Ana, sarcastically.

"Why are you going to be at the door closest to the officers when they enter the front car?" asked Barry.

"Because, with three of us there we are sitting ducks. This way, at best they will only get me," stated Danny. "Based on my count from Bleeker and Spring Street, we have approximately ten seconds before the ding dong signaling that the doors are closing," said Danny.

"You are going to be fine," said Ana, reassuringly. "Just make sure you time your move to the front car as we are about to stop."

"Thanks Ana," answered Danny. "Now go…"

Barry said, "You know, if things do not go well, we are not going to see you for at least the rest of the day."

"Don't forget about me while I am processed by the NYPD."

"Danny, you know I must admit it is a risk that you don't need to take. You don't need to risk your future over this."

"Don't assume I will lose. Just do your job and be ready." Barry gave Danny a fist pound as he moved forward up the train.

Barry and Ana side-stepped and 'pardoned me' and 'excused me' to the precise location necessary to step onto the platform. They hugged against the small space between them and the door.

The green line, as tourists called it, was the busiest subway line in Manhattan. While the West Side had the A/C train and the 1/9 and 2/3 express, the 4/5/6 were the only subway lines that ran along the East Side of Manhattan.

Years ago, it made the East Side exclusive; now it only made it a painful commute. In this area of Manhattan, the city's youngest, newest dwellers, fresh from college with their finance degrees, crowded into apartments at night and meat market bars on the weekend.

The train began to leave Canal Street Station on its way to Brooklyn Bridge. Danny steadied his nerves. He noticed the two officers proceeding into the back of the car he was in and they were gaining fast.

"These guys are gaining and maybe a little too fast," thought Danny.

Brooklyn Bridge is the last stop on the 6 line. Most of the passengers had cleared out. There was only one stop left on the subway line. It was not something Danny considered when he explained his plan to Ana and Barry. But he had an idea.

Danny stepped toward the door that leads from one car to the next. Unlike New Yorkers, Danny had never stood between moving subway cars before. The attached subway cars created an unsteady platform to walk on. On the sides was a chain link guard, black with soot from traveling through the city's over seven hundred miles of subway track.

Danny opened the sliding door at the front of the car he was riding in. He stepped both feet onto the space between the two cars and let the door slam shut. He kept the handle in the locked position with his right hand. As the officers moved forward, Danny locked eyes with the two men through the window. Danny knew he had hooked the fish. His only problem was that he was the bait.

Danny could feel the train slow down as he was jerked forward toward the front car of the train. A few seconds later, he saw the white tiles that marked the beginning of the City Hall/Brooklyn Bridge subway station. He decided that after five more seconds of holding the door closed, he would make a run for it.

Danny shifted his eyes to the left. He saw the yellow strip signaling that the front car had just hit the beginning of the platform.

The train car made a final jerk backwards. The results were mixed. The officers were taken off balance by the jerk forward. The kids were prepared. Danny stepped into the front car, anticipating that the doors would open within two seconds.

Then the doors parted.

The three kids scurried out of the subway car and onto the platform. Barry and Ana easily ran out of the middle door and onto the platform. Barry started running back two cars to reverse the chase. As Barry made his way into the train, he looked back at Ana and saw that she was looking behind her to find Danny.

"What are you doing? Get on this train," demanded Barry.

"No wait. I want to see if Danny is all right," replied Ana. She remained with one foot on the platform and one in the train car. Her butt was blocking the door from even attempting to close.

There were not enough people entering and exiting the train to force the doors open and shut a second time.

"That is not how this works. He is doing his job. We must do ours. Otherwise the whole plan breaks down," answered Barry.

Danny timed his exit from the rear door of the train and onto the platform. The lead officers were caught off guard as Danny stepped off the train. They were ten to twenty feet behind Danny.

He was about to pass the train doors that Barry and Ana were standing in front of, but the officers were so focused on Danny that Ana and Barry went unnoticed.

Danny was running along the opposite side of the platform from the train. He took a path that required him to hurdle a bench in the middle of the platform. New York's finest would have to take an alternate route, if only because of all the equipment they carried in addition to a bullet-proof vest.

It was enough to give him a lead when he went to jump back on the train. As soon as the officer passed them, Ana yelled down the platform, "On two."

As he passed her, he noticed that she was holding the subway doors open, in the event that they closed before Danny had a chance to reenter the train.

Barry figured out Ana's reasoning and jumped into action. He held the door opposite to Ana open.

The level of fear that ran through Danny was something he had never felt before. He heard the first ding dong and knew he had to act. He began to angle toward the 6 train car doors, running the hypotenuse of the triangle toward the subway doors he intended to dive towards.

He used the wooden bench in the middle of the platform as a step to jump forward and as a blocker for the older and less agile police officers. He got to the yellow strip signaling the edge of the platform at Canal. The door slid open and he rolled in left shoulder first and onto his backside. Ana was looking to her right and saw Danny sit up on the train, through the window one car in front of them.

The officers were not ready for Danny's decision to reenter the train. They were caught on the platform as the doors closed a second time. Barry and Ana smiled as they saw the officers stranded on the platform shaking their heads. They ran to the next car to meet up with Danny.

"That was intense," panted Danny. "That was not a competition; that was for real."

"Good thing we have Dan Marino here calling the audible, or I would be calling your parents," as he patted Ana on the back.

"My parents?" asked Ana.

"They are the closest lawyers I know," said Danny with a smile, as he caught his wind. Ana smiled back, "Not that close. They are in Europe. Ironically enough, Amsterdam, I think."

"You are going to have a lot to tell them," replied Danny.

"The plan worked better than anticipated and the officers were left on the Canal Street Station platform," said Ana.

"We have to get into City Hall," announced Barry.

"Agreed," said Danny.

They walked to the south end of the platform at Brooklyn Bridge/City Hall. As the group got above ground at Chambers Street and Centre Street, they looked around for a landmark to establish which direction they were facing.

"Barry, isn't that the statue of the guy who died before all the electoral votes were counted?" asked Ana.

"Don't forget, he founded the *New York Tribune*," teased Danny with a smile toward Barry. Barry was so happy they listened to him. His chest puffed up with air. He nodded in silent agreement. The path behind City Hall was shaded. There were tables for games of chess being utilized by everyone, from college students to can collectors.

As they approached City Hall, the security guard who knew what the inside of a gym looked like, blocked their path. It was the same security guard that questioned Dirjke a few days earlier.

He stepped in front of them and put his arm out to clothesline anyone that dared try to pass him. He was leery of two sweating young men and a young woman, whose face was flushed.

"Where do you three think you are going?" announced the silhouette that looked like the outline of the Incredible Hulk with the sun behind his shoulders.

"We need to see the Mayor," stated Barry. The guard was not impressed and placed his hands on his belt.

"So do a lot of people. There was a blackout yesterday. Do you think I am going to make a call to the Mayor's office, because some kids want to see him? You must be nuts. I could lose my job for something so ridiculous."

"Would you just call Marjorie, the Mayor's secretary, and tell her that the kids from yesterday are here. She will know who we are," said Danny. "Be reasonable."

The guard laughed with his hands resting on his equipment belt.

"First of all, your savior, Marjorie, is not here today. So you're back to square one."

"Sir, with all due respect, we are here to see the Mayor. You have to alert someone to our request," insisted Ana.

"Have to? Who do you think you are Missy," answered the security guard, getting annoyed with these kids.

"Hearts of Oak," countered Danny.

"Huh?"

"Call the Mayor and tell him the Hearts of Oak is here," repeated Danny.

"That sounds more ridiculous that just telling him that three kids are here to see him."

"It's your choice. Tell the Mayor whatever, you want: 'three kids are here' or 'Hearts of Oak is here.' But please, this is an emergency," pleaded Danny.

"Fine." The guard reached for the telephone and dialed the Mayor's office. He looked at the kids as he smiled and said, "Hearts of Oak is here for the Mayor."

The three kids stood in anticipation. Danny was wringing his neck with his left hand. Ana had her arms crossed tightly over her chest. Barry was chewing his fingernails.

"It will be a minute or two before the Mayor gets the message and it gets relayed back outside here," stated the security guard.

A few minutes later, the security guard said, "Okay," and hung up the phone.

"And?" asked Ana.

"Hearts of Oak, the Mayor wants to see you immediately."

"Told you," said Danny.

"Take it easy, boy. All I need is a reason to detain you."

Barry tried to cool the situation. "All right, now everybody here is just doing their job. Let's just go inside."

Chapter 64

DIRJKE AND KIDS MEET AT CITY HALL
Friday, August 15, 2003 11:14am
The group was escorted into the Mayor's office by Sam, the staffer leaving to work with an Illinois senator. It carried out Sam's exit strategy for leaving New York: make it here and then make it anywhere – else.

"Where is the Mayor?" asked Barry.

"He is dealing with some issues surrounding the blackout," answered Sam. "You guys must be important, or at least trustworthy. He never allows people into his office without him being here."

The comment stroked Barry's ego, "Well, what can I say?"

"Nothing," answered Ana, cutting off any conversation. "Thank you. Please tell the Mayor we are here."

Sam left the room.

"First things first, we need to discuss what we found at the Fish Stuyvesant House," announced Danny.

"I agree. What did you notice before we had to run?" asked Ana.

"Above the stairway were two recesses which looked similar to the diameter and circumference of the discs that we found along our trips 'into the homes of death,'" began Barry.

"You mean the discs that Sid took from us in the early morning at Hamilton's house?" asked Danny.

"Yeah, those," responded Barry.

"Oh boy," said Ana, sarcastically. "This is going to be easy."

"Easy? Stealing from Sid is probably like robbing a bank," said Danny.

"No, I mean telling the Mayor that we lost the keys to the location of the Deed to Manhattan," replied Ana.

"That's not our biggest problem," worried Danny.

"What is then?" asked Barry.

"We only have until he figures out what 'door' those discs open. A few days ago I thought that would give us substantial time. But that has turned out not to be true."

"Speaking of knowledge of the city, where is Dirjke?" asked Ana.

At that moment, the Mayor walked into his office with Dirjke right behind him. His business casual attire made him more comfortable, but did not hide the signs of fatigue around his eyes.

Danny was relieved to see his uncle. So was Ana. Barry was glad to have this city's valedictorian of its history here to help them once again. Michael made his way behind his desk.

Before Michael and Dirjke arrived, Danny took the chair in front of Michael's desk. When they came in, Danny stood up and gave his uncle the seat. Danny relegated himself to the sofa in Michael's office, similar to last night at St. Mark's.

"All right, kids. Since you were the ones that came here with a cloud of dust and confusion surrounding you, you go first, Hearts of Oak," said Michael.

"Hearts of Oak?" asked Dirjke.

"Yeah, apparently, now if you need the Mayor's attention, you just tell him Hearts of Oak," stated Michael with a smile that let the room know he was not annoyed.

"We found it," said Barry with his big brown eyes wide open.

"Found what?" asked Dirjke.

"What my colleague is saying is that we found a circular indentation in the Fish Stuyvesant house near the Bowery," added Danny.

"Really?" asked Dirjke.

"Yes really," repeated Ana.

"So that means, what we lost at Hamilton's house is the…" stated Dirjke.

"Exactly," said Barry, Ana, and Danny all at once.

"I know that look. It is the same look you had during math tests and the opposite look you had during any social studies exams," said Michael.

"Remember the disc that Barry took when we were at Hamilton's grave?" asked Dirjke.

"Yeah," nodded Michael, waiting for the full explanation.

"We found an identical crest at Hamilton's house in Harlem. Behind it we found the poem, but Sid took both crests before he tied us up."

"And what about the poem?" asked Michael.

"We have the poem memorized," replied Dirjke, trying to sound confident.

But before Michael could take any solace in that statement, Barry blurted out, "But Sid also knows the language in the poem."

"Can it really be that big of a threat to us?" asked Michael.

"Not sure," answered Dirjke.

"His knowledge of where we have been, coupled with the clues we've found, makes him formidable and let's not forget, the man is relentless," said Dirjke.

"Poetry?" asked Ana.

"Yeah, Sid majored in poetry at Yale," said Dirjke. "It's only a matter of time before he figures this out."

"Kind of like the guy who gets a Rubik's Cube brand new, makes one turn of the cube, turns it back to where he found it, and pats himself on the back for solving the cube," stated Danny.

"All right," answered Michael. "We have our work in front of us. But I have a plan."

"What plan do you have old friend?" asked Dirjke. "There is no way that the Mayor could move through the city without attracting attention."

"Well, it is not exactly a plan, but more of a set-up," said Michael.

"With all due respect, Mayor, what do you mean?" asked Ana.

"I have a press conference at 3 o'clock. I have invited Sid, because of his role in the blackout. He has agreed to be the military face of the Federal Government's response to the blackout. Since today is Friday, it will be my last chance to speak before the weekend newspapers go to press."

"What else?" asked Barry.

"That's it," answered Michael.

"I am telling you where Sid will be in approximately four hours. Do with it what you will. I can't know and, more importantly, I don't want to know. What I have to know is that the Deed is safe. And by safe I mean either in my hot little hands, or tucked away wherever this Hearts of Oak put it last."

"Got it, Michael," said Dirjke. "I know where Sid is hiding the discs. He has a gray and black backpack."

"I remember that pack too, from Hamilton's house," added Danny.

"Good," answered Dirjke. "That will save me a lot of explaining as to what this thing looks like. We need an identical one."

"Ana, you want to go shopping with me?" asked Danny.

"Sure, I know the style and brand. Consider it done, Professor." Ana went to the nearest computer in the office, narrowing down the stores that might have this particular bag. It was a girl's dream job. "The key is not finding who is selling the bag. The key is who is open the morning after the blackout," added Ana.

272

Barry began to feel left out, but before his thoughts could devolve any further, Michael said, "Barry, I want you to come with me."

"For real?" asked Barry in disbelief.

"Yeah, you need to know the scheduling of the press conference, before you can figure out how you are going to switch bags, or do whatever, um, you are going to accomplish."

"Dirjke, I will invite the President of Cooper Union and his wife to attend the presser."

"Is that really going to help?" asked Dirjke.

"Do you have any other way to get into the house and get them out of the house?" asked Michael.

"Hell," admitted Dirjke. "I haven't been to my apartment since you called me days ago."

Chapter 65

MAYOR'S PRESS REPORT
Friday, August 15, 2003 3:13pm

At the north end of Washington Square Park, a group of reporters were seated and standing in a small semi-circle. On a platform of about five feet, the Mayor stood at the podium with blue felt and the Seal of New York City in bronze on the front. The back edge of the platform alternated with city, state, and federal flags. There were over two dozen politicians and city employees crowded onto the small platform.

The Mayor's statements praised the coordination between city and Federal responses. He showered accolades onto the city's swelled population, rightfully, not politically. "I learned something that politicians find out only after they have been sworn into office – we are only as powerful as the peoples' capacity to change and improve government services."

The sun was shining brightly. He was in the shadow of Washington Square Arch, modeled after the Arc de Triomphe in Paris.

He was dressed in business casual attire. Michael chose to wear navy blue pants and a white polo shirt with the City seal stitched on the left.

"I am fortunate because I am mayor of the best city in the world. And the people make New York the best city in the world. This had been proven in New York's past and once again during this blackout. The manner and resilience of New York and its citizens was special. Special places are composed of extraordinary people and New York does not settle for second best – at anything."

Minutes earlier, Sid had stood up at the precise moment he was supposed to.

In the background, the Mayor commended the coordination of efforts between City, State, and Federal responsibilities. He returned to his seat and looked for his bag. It was there, but he noticed that it had been rustled since he stood up to stand next to the Mayor to receive his praise.

Sid opened his wireless device and looked at the red tracking dot on the screen for the location of his bag. He removed himself from the stage area of the press conference.

Sid had learned to use his unavoidable public appearances as a credit, to establish who he was in intelligence circles. Sid was amazed at the number of intelligence agents in some of the most iconic photographs of the past fifty years.

The Mayor's statements ended a few minutes later. As the Mayor retreated to his seat and another politician stepped up to the podium, Sid used that commotion to take the three steps down the small stage. He walked to Waverly Place and 5th Avenue. The row houses that faced Washington Square Park were a gorgeous red brick, with large windows and iron gates.

He got into a cab and ordered, "Take me to Broadway and 3rd, no 4th Street."

"That is less than a half a mile, sir."

"Just do it. I may need you to drive further from there."

"You got it."

The cabby stepped on the gas. Sid was pulled back against the seat as the car jetted forward. Then Sid leaned forward to be sure the gun he kept at his ankle was loaded.

Chapter 66

BACK TO STUYVESANT STREET
Friday, August 15, 2003 3:30pm

The kids sprinted from Washington Square Park to Stuyvesant Street. There was moderate traffic on the sidewalk and roads. The kids weaved between these obstacles on Waverly Place to Broadway and then Astor Place.

"How much time do you think we have?" asked Barry.

"Before Sid figures out what we did? Not long," answered Danny.

"Now, are we sure that the house is clear?" asked Ana.

"That is what Dirjke is doing," responded Barry.

"We are going to be fine," stated Danny. "I have confidence."

"Based on what I saw, there is a space for two discs. I know, I saw them. What comes from there, I don't know," said Barry.

"Yes, you do Barry – 'into the homes of death' 'twice mortal.' We are going to Nicholas Fish's grave at St. Mark's Church on the Bowery," said Ana.

"Yes, the real question is, what are we going to find when we get there?" added Danny. The group ran across the disjointed intersection of Astor Place and Third Avenue.

"Sooner or later it is going to be the Deed to Manhattan," responded Barry. "We are coming up on Stuyvesant Street."

They slowed down as they arrived within sight of the doorstep, where Dirjke stood in front of the old building. The house appeared ordinary. The red brick and the two windows protruding from the roof made it look more like a building in Boston rather than New York.

276

"Hey, guys, did you get what we need?"

"Yes," answered Danny, with his chest mildly heaving.

"All right, we'll see if this works," said Barry.

Barry was alongside the metal detector, when the Cooper Union President placed his wallet into the plastic bin to enter City Hall. As Mr. and Mrs. McCormick placed their keys in the Tupperware before going through the metal detector, Barry looked for the keys the couple had in common. Then he pressed that key into the three pieces of gum that he was chewing on.

The day after the blackout, the sensors were at their most sensitive. The McCormicks submitted to a wand search after walking through the traditional metal detector. Danny used his wood and metal shop skills to replicate a key from the gum impression.

Michael had access to every room in City Hall. In the eighteen months he had been in office, he had silently rekeyed the entire building. Homeland security starts with home, thought Michael.

"At least we are not breaking and entering," said Dirjke.

"No, this is more like burglary," replied Danny, "but we are going to be fine."

Dirjke inserted the freshly made key. He turned the lock and it worked.

"You know, between Barry pressing the key with his bubble gum and Danny, your shop skills to replicate the keys, I don't want to seem like I condone this behavior."

"Unk now is not the time for this. We've got to get the Deed to Manhattan."

"You're right. Let's go," said Dirjke.

The group walked into the house. The chairs were still aligned as they were before the kids rushed out.

"I wonder what they discussed after we dashed out?" wondered Ana.

"Yeah, I was just about to ask about the core program within Cooper Union."

"I knew we would get to visit Cooper Union one way or another. Never thought it would be the President's house..." as Dirjke let his voice trail off and shook his head at the circumstances.

"Apparently, they dropped what they were doing to accept the Mayor's invitation," stated Ana.

"I dropped what I was doing to see the Mayor two days ago. Who thought it would lead to this?"

"I know – this is amazing," said Ana. "But we need to win. Analysis can come later." She had one chair under each arm and was bringing them to the transverse in the doorway as they walked in.

"Professor Dirjke, I think you should do the honors," said Ana.

"All right, just hold the chairs Danny. This old man cannot afford to fall on his head." Dirjke stepped up onto the chairs and looked at the crevice.

"All right, which set of discs should we try first?" asked Danny.

"We are in the house where the couple named their son Hamilton," said Barry.

"With all due respect, there are only three combinations. Let's start with the Hamilton crests and work from there," said Danny. "We don't need a historical exchange."

"Yeah, here you go." Ana handed Dirjke the Hamilton crests.

He placed the first and then the second discs into position. There was a tight fit that let him know they were in the right space.

"Now what?" asked Dirjke, as he looked toward the kids.

"Maybe turn the discs, with your hands," suggested Ana.

"Huh?" asked Dirjke.

"Yeah, turn them clockwise," said Danny.

With a couple of twists of the discs, the group heard a sound. A strange rumble from inside the old house, then there was a scraping sound of the stones sliding against each other.

"Look," said Barry. From under the fireplace, the stone was sliding back. "Keep going. Keep going Professor," exclaimed Barry. He and Danny rushed over to the fireplace.

"Hey," said Dirjke.

"Don't worry. I am holding the chairs," said Ana.

"Thanks Ana," replied Dirjke, relieved to still be safe. He turned his hands faster to reveal the tunnel from within the fireplace.

"That should do it," said Danny. Barry and Danny's hands were black with soot from removing some of the items in and around the fireplace.

"All right," said Dirjke. "Let's go into the homes of death, Hearts of Oak."

"One visit finishes all men, but we are twice mortal," stated Barry.

"Truer words, never spoken," added Ana.

"The path is alive. The Deed to Manhattan is hidden within the name of the Hearts of Oak, which provides the map hidden with the Homer quotation," added Barry.

"Exactly, if this is not a modern day odyssey, I don't know what is," finished Danny.

"Enough talk, let's go…" concluded Dirjke.

Chapter 67

GO TO GRAVE
Friday, August 15, 2003 4:04pm

Dirjke and the kids made their way down the steps that led from the base of the fireplace. It was nearly as steep as a ladder and was a rectangle just wider than an adult's shoulders. The black rocks sparkled against the flashlights in everyone's hand. It smelled like musky salty air.

"The design of these steps is really amazing," said Danny.

"Yeah, we saw an identical design when Dirjke and I went to Hamilton's grave."

"Wow." Ana's green eyes were the size of quarters. The ledge of each step jetted out just enough to step on. It was nearly as steep as a ladder – an engineering hybrid of the two concepts.

"Look at the rock – its Manhattan Schist. See the sparkle; that's how you can tell," stated Dirjke. These blocks were in a random rectangular setting, similar to the earth wall surrounding Trinity Church. The color here was a dark gray, rather than the reddish brick surrounding Hamilton's grave.

Dirjke led the way down the steps. Barry followed, then Ana. Last was Danny. Always thinking ahead, he asked, "Should I push back the rocks that covered this hidden passage?"

"Smart, Danny, cut off our only means of exiting?" snapped Ana.

"True," answered Danny. He took a deep breath to focus his mind and calm his nerves. He was tired, but he knew everyone else was too.

"I am awestruck at how this could hide in plain sight for so long. We are under the only street exempted from the New York grid plan," said Dirjke.

"Not even Hamilton's house was exempted from the rigid rectangles that form Manhattan's street grid," added Barry.

"Can you imagine how long it must have been since someone was down here!" said Dirjke.

The tunnel was dark. But after the recent days' events, it went unnoticed by the group and was not commented on.

"Unreal," said Danny.

"No, this is real," replied Dirjke.

The passageway they were walking through was narrow. The clearance was just at six feet and just wide enough for their shoulders to pass along the sides. Each of them waived their flashlights in all directions. It was over one hundred degrees in the tunnel.

Manhattan Schist lines many of the city's sidewalks. It is distinctive because of its highly reflective crystals.

They kept moving forward at a faster than walking pace. Spider webs lined the passage way along with the feces of small rodents who had previously scurried in and out of this tunnel. The ground was slightly slick from moss and the humid air.

They got to the end of the passage. There was a large square stone designating a tomb and 'home of death' they were looking for.

"What we are looking for is on the other side of this," stated Barry.

"Thanks for the obvious," said Ana.

"How are we going to get past it? That is the question," mused Danny. Dirjke rubbed the two hundred years of dirt and salty air out of the recesses made for the remaining two crests.

"Twice mortal. I think it is time to put these Stuyvesant crests into the recesses," said Ana.

"I agree, but... nothing," said Dirjke. His slight hesitation went unnoticed by the group.

Ana was digging through the bag for the other crests. She handed them to Danny. He arranged them into their places. "Unk, perhaps you should do the honors again. At least you are not standing on some wobbly chairs."

"Yes, thanks, Danny. I cannot believe what we've been through these past few days. What started out as a weekend trip to look at New York City colleges has led to this."

Dirjke crouched down into a baseball catcher's position. He placed the crests into the recesses and heard a click at the moment he pushed on both of them simultaneously.

He looked up at the youngsters and smiled with anticipation.

"The moment of truth," announced Dirjke.

He turned the crests within their recesses. The steel plate between the two crests moved to the side with the loud shrill of metal sliding on stone.

The kids aimed their flashlights into the space. "It looks like the small side of a coffin," said Barry.

They each moved closer to the opening. Inside was the worst smell the group had ever encountered.

"At least we know what Nicholas Fish's dead body smells like," said Barry.

"There are only two things that smell like fish and one of them is not Fish," said Ana.

Dirjke remained silent.

"Let me get through here," said Danny. "I am the strongest person in the group." He reached into the hole and grabbed a metal handle that *schreeecked* as he turned the hinge.

"Don't use all your strength at once. You will just break the coffin. Then we'll have to crawl into the hole to get the contents of the coffin," said Dirjke.

Ana nodded her head in Danny's direction with a smile. Danny reached in with both arms and his head and tugged the old coffin toward him. As he pulled back further, Dirjke and Barry each took a side of the coffin. Like reverse pallbearers, they placed the coffin on the ground.

They each waved their flashlights over the coffin.

"Let's get this open," said Barry.

"What a place to hide a treasured object," said Danny.

"I know – amazing," added Ana.

The group opened the lid on the coffin and looked inside. Dirjke was confused by what he was looking at.

Ana was not fazed by the sight of bones remaining inside a green jacket and pants. She had been interested in medicine before deciding to focus on English. She reached into the coffin and turned open the jacket of the dead body. Danny was looking around the edges of the coffin.

Barry was looking through the pockets on the clothes of the dead body, as well. Then he stated, "This is the part where we are supposed to find a piece of paper that says Deed to Manhattan on the top."

Dirjke was perplexed but still, while the kids rummaged through the coffin.

"I don't see anything," said Ana exasperated.

"Me neither," stated Barry. "But there's something else. Something is not right," as Barry took his head out of the old coffin to gain some perspective. "Not to sound like Ana, but his clothes are not right."

"Huh?" asked Ana.

"These clothes are not from the 1800s," stated Danny, as he caught onto Barry's statement.

"We are in the homes of death within the Hearts of Oak. We went into Nicholas Fish's House and took a tunnel to his grave. He was a member of the Hearts of Oak, like Hamilton. The Hearts of Oak passage tells us to be here. Moreover, the poem in Hamilton's house points to this location. This is the only street in the whole city exempted from the Manhattan grid plan. It has to be here," exclaimed Barry.

Dirjke was just staring into the open box in complete silence, until he said, "Sid is close by. We need a way out."

"Why is there nothing in here?" asked Barry.

Dirjke looked inside the coffin and saw a wooden stick that was about twice the length of the stick found three days ago on the original Manhattan shoreline. It had a slight taper and a silver inlay into the design. That made it the best weapon available.

Chapter 68

SID ARRIVES AT STUYVESANT FISH HOUSE
Friday, August 15, 2003 4:15pm

The cab stopped at Astor Place. Sid was at the intersection of Third Avenue and the beginning of Stuyvesant Street. The intersection of the roads created a natural pedestrian gathering place. However, all that filled the natural plaza was a cube sculpture that could rotate with enough people pushing in one direction.

"Told you, you could have walked faster," stated the cabbie.

"Don't worry, you did fine. My friends have an errand to do before I meet them."

"Whatever, $6.50, sir."

Sid complied and paid the man. He exited the vehicle, closed the door, and got his bearings. Sid walked from Third Avenue to the west end of Stuyvesant Street. Businesses were recovering from the blackout and New Yorkers were running errands in all directions.

He was watching his screen pinpoint the location of Stuyvesant Street. It followed the movement of the bag. He knew how to interpret the data he saw. However, oddly, it appeared as though the group was walking along Stuyvesant Street. Sid expected the dot to be in a single location.

Sid arrived at the western edge of Stuyvesant Street. He looked at 21 Stuyvesant Street and then looked for Dirjke and the kids.

Sid walked up Stuyvesant Street toward St. Mark's Church. There was still no sign of Dirjke and the kids. Eventually, Sid was standing precisely where his radio device told him. He looked around confused for just a second. Then he looked down at his feet.

Having noticed how much time the red dot on his screen spent at a certain location. Sid raced back to 21 Stuyvesant Street.

Sid rushed into the house. He looked around for something out of place. His eyes then caught on to the two crests above the staircase.

"The crests are keys," answered Sid aloud. "What does it open?"

Sid looked around the open area near the fireplace. There were white folding chairs in a semi-circle around the fireplace. The house's fireplace was very similar to Hamilton's house.

"So simple, so beautiful," said Sid aloud. "The Hearts of Oak passage from *The Odyssey* is the coded message leading to the Deed to Manhattan. The passage is the map. I can't believe the odyssey you put me through, one of the best of my career, Alexander Hamilton."

Hamilton became Sid's favorite Founding Father, not that he had ever asked himself the question before.

"Dirjke and the kids must be accessing a grave," said Sid aloud, as he looked around the room. Then he saw the stone that was moved away at the base of the fireplace.

A smile washed over his face. He rubbed his right hand on the left side of his beard. It was a nervous habit that Sid did not display often.

He walked down the steps in front of the fireplace. He stood as still as he possibly could. Then he slowed his breathing to as little as possible. With his senses sharpened, Sid could hear the faintest echoes of people talking farther down the tunnel.

Chapter 69

CONFRONTATION WITH SID IN TUNNEL
Friday, August 15, 2003 4:20pm

"At last we meet again," declaimed Sid, about 45 seconds after Ana's statement that she could not see anything. His shoes were covered in the muck that lined the bottom of the tunnel. He had a flashlight in his hand. He was standing at the entrance to the chamber room where the coffin was lying on the floor.

"It has been about twelve hours since our meeting in Harlem at Hamilton's house." Sid was about ten feet from the coffin, with Dirjke closest to him and the kids behind Dirjke.

"But we were here first," answered Barry.

"Yeah, we also had to take back the things you took from us at Hamilton's house," added Danny.

"So technically speaking we beat you twice," finished Ana.

"And from my perspective, you haven't beaten me even once," retorted Sid. "You guys merely took the bait that I set for you. Now you are trapped with no other options."

"Sid, this is it. We are here at this grave. 'Into the homes of death' as the Hearts of Oak passage from *The Odyssey* directs us here. But there is no Deed. No Birth Certificate of Manhattan. No proof that this island was had by commerce instead of the brute force of war," said Dirjke.

"Nonsense, there has to be something more. This can't be all for nothing."

"Sid, these could have been tunnels used to smuggle slaves into freedom," said Barry. "New York State banned slavery in 1827. Or smuggle goods. It isn't like New York hasn't spent most of its history as a port town."

"Don't try and cloud the facts boy. That is my job. Dirjke, you know where to go next, don't you?"

"Sid, I don't know where to go next. I told you that."

"Marty, don't make me force your hand," as Sid let Marty see the gun on his ankle.

"Sid, I don't have any new information," Dirjke had the tapered wooden weapon tucked into the back of his pants.

"That won't help you," answered Sid. "Don't you realize that I tied you up in Hamilton's house so that I could follow you to the final location; this location. Since I caught up with you all in the middle of night, whether you knew it or not, you have been my pawns. And I am prepared to do what is necessary."

"You intend to give the Deed to Skull and Bones. Bonesmen raided Van Buren's grave decades ago in upstate New York in search of the Deed. You would complete this quest," said Dirjke. "Your public façade of burning the document to protect Federal interests isn't going to fool anyone."

Sid laughed. "Do you really think you can win that battle? Good luck. Remember when Kennedy gave his speech on secret societies?"

"If you think I am going to let your organization, your world, steal this document, you are dead wrong. This chapter in the quest for the Deed to Manhattan may be a stalemate, but you will not win."

"Marty, you have no chance. Face it. Give me the next clue." Sid took the gun from his holster.

"Don't Sid," cautioned Dirjke, reading the thoughts on Sid's mind. Sid fired his gun in the direction of Danny. He dove out of the way with all his speed.

At that moment, Dirjke reached for his weapon took a swing at Sid with the tapered stick he had found in the coffin. Sid did not know that Dirjke had a weapon.

The stick connected with Sid's torso and the bullet headed for Danny ricocheted against the wall. Danny was terrified. Ana was paralyzed with fear. The sound was deafening in the small tunnel. Barry did not waste a second after Dirjke's swing and rushed Sid.

Barry tackled the old man with everything he had. Sid tried to step backwards, but Barry kept marching forward, with his feet and back straight, until Sid fell onto his butt. Barry was using the technique learned from a wrestling chapter taught during his physical education class at Collegiate in ninth grade.

Sid furiously punched Barry in the head, as he stepped backward. It did not slow Barry down, as he locked his hands around Sid's hips.

Dirjke took another swipe at Sid and hit him with all he had using his ancient baseball bat. Sid let out a large yell as the stick made contact with his rib cage. Barry crawled up Sid's torso and now had his knees under Sid's armpits. He began to rain fists onto the old man's head.

Danny rushed and got the gun that had gone onto the floor of the tunnel.

"Enough," yelled Danny, in Barry's direction. But Barry was not done with this old man.

"No, it is you who doesn't understand. This is America – we were all at one time visitors. No one permanent cabal holds the strings of power. This country is a meritocracy. Secrecy is by its nature repugnant to society."

"Enough," said Ana, as she stepped closer to Barry.

Dirjke had the tapered piece of wood cocked right at his shoulder, not too differently from the way Derek Jeter looks when he is waiting for the first pitch of an at bat.

"You can back off for a second, Barry," said Dirjke. "Danny's got his gun and one false move from Mr. Milliken here and I will literally detach his head from his body. Also, I think he's learned enough history for one day."

Barry had never won a fight before. And this was more important than any playground argument that he had ever had and lost.

His legs from the knees down were black with disgusting muck; his socks and shoes looked no different. He was still breathing heavily due to the adrenaline running through him. He was sweating like a beast in the muggy underground tunnel.

Then he looked at Sid and said, "Told you we would beat you."

"He's right, Sid. You tried to separate and divide this group. In essence, use the numbers within the group against itself," rationalized Dirjke.

"For now," countered Sid.

"Your little misguided quest for the Deed is finished. Tell your comrades at Skull and Bones that you have failed," said Dirjke, as he gently tapped his tapered bat into his right hand.

"All right, let's get to the surface," said Ana. "I don't think we need to worry about being caught since we are the heroes that nabbed the criminal."

"That is only your point of view. Today weakened this country. There is still no Deed, despite the fact that by Monday everyone will know that it exists in a location unknown. The money spent countering these new treasure hunters by the City and Federal governments will be a new expense the government doesn't need, not to mention the military implications."

"And 'ye shall know the truth, and the truth shall set you free," teased Barry. "Isn't that the phrase all intelligence agents see on their way into CIA Headquarters in Langley, Virginia?"

"Not bad," answered Sid. "You have hope for a Harvard lad."

"John 8:21-32," replied Barry.

"The truth alone has consequences. That is why 'light and truth' are necessary to shape the masses," answered Sid.

"Don't in this moment of truth, retreat to your old college's motto," said Dirjke.

"Every time I walk by the phrase at CIA Headquarters, I am reminded of Harvard's motto 'Truth' and Yale's motto 'Light and Truth.'"

"So what?" asked Barry.

"From that point of view, it always made me smile. It's proof that Yale is better than Harvard. Graduates from Yale, including portions within this country's intelligence apparatus, sculpted the truth and it does set us free."

"Say what you want, Sid. This is the only time that I was ever happy that Harvard beat Yale."

As Danny and Barry maneuvered Sid to his feet, his back and ass were filthy with a muddy oil-like substance. His right eye was blood shot and his left arm held his right side where Dirjke had hit him with all his might.

Chapter 70

MICHAEL MAKES THE CALL
Friday, August 15, 2003 4:35pm

"Where are you located?" asked Michael from the comfort of his chair in City Hall. He was seated behind his desk and comfortable, because he was not wearing a suit on an August Friday. He tossed his city stress ball in his hand.

"Exactly where you told me to be," answered the voice on the other end of the line. "I am in front of St. Mark's Church." The church possessed a magnificent steeple with a clock at the top.

"Have you seen the targets yet?"

"No."

"When you do, swarm. This has gone on long enough. I want this ended."

"We will apprehend the individuals," said Duroe.

"I know that. But it is how you apprehend them that counts. I want them scared shitless and very much alive. This is all going to end."

"Copy, Mr. Mayor."

Chapter 71

GET ABOVE GROUND
Friday, August 15, 2003 4:40pm

"All right we are going to the surface," said Dirjke. A new calm crossed his mind now that Sid was under control. Dirjke motioned to the group that they would be going back from where they came.

"Back the way we came," answered Sid. "C'mon, Marty, you know there is another way out of this tunnel. No one finishes a tunnel that doesn't have at least two exits. It is a safety measure at the least and a means of escape in case you found what you are looking for."

"But we didn't find what we are looking for you crazy old man," yelled Danny.

"He is right. We can't just walk out the front door of 21 Stuyvesant Street," said Dirjke. "There must be another way," answered Ana.

Barry was already looking around and said, "Look, over there. There I can feel the slightest bit of cool breeze from inside the empty crypt."

"I think we found our other way out," said Sid.

"I'm going to the surface first," said Dirjke.

"No problem. I can't wait to shoot this turkey," replied Danny. Sid made his way onto the ladder and pulled himself to the next rung. Within a series of grabs his elbows reached the Manhattan surface. Dirjke reached a hand out to an old college friend. Sid took it and got his knee onto the surface.

Danny looked at Barry and Ana. "It looks like this treasure hunt is over."

"Yeah, pretty stunning, I wonder if we ever did get close to the Deed to Manhattan," added Barry.

"You know. I am glad I met you guys. See you above ground."

Danny clicked the safety and put the gun on his hip held in place by his belt.

"Careful on the way up," advised Ana, as she watched his feet slither into the crypt. She turned to Barry and flashed the light against the side wall to avoid blinding his eyes. He was already shining his light against the wall that held the crypt.

"You know, Barry, thanks."

"For what?"

"For the date you took me on. My life has not been the same since we went to the Mayor's meet and greet downtown. My eyes are open now."

"What do you mean?" asked Barry.

"This history stuff, your passion, it's real." She stepped toward him. "This made me realize what kind of person you are."

"And what kind of person is that?" asked Barry, his blood pulsing in a whole new manner.

"You are a man who doesn't back down from right and wrong, no matter the odds," as she moved her face toward his.

"Thanks," he said, as he took a step toward her.

"Good," answered Ana, as she kissed Barry. His hands brought her close to his hips, while they engaged in a passionate embrace. After about eight seconds, Barry stole second base with his left hand. Ana's right hand was holding the flashlight.

"Hurry up down there," called down Danny, who had Sid's gun.

Dirjke looked around. He had his weapon of choice. He stayed within arm's length of Sid.

"Relax, Marty, I'm not going anywhere."

They were in the cemetery at St. Mark's Church. It was nearly covered in cement and bricks. A black iron fence quartered off the cemetery from the sidewalk.

Then Dirjke saw the grave he was looking for, the proper homes of death. It was next to the church. A small bronze plaque told the name of the coffin the group had rummaged through.

Barry got to the surface, still pulsing with excitement.

Ana was alone in the tunnel, she whispered, "God, give me strength. This life is going to be a stranger journey than I ever imagined." Then in a loud voice she announced, "I'm on my way."

Barry arrived on Manhattan's surface a new man. Ana was about ten seconds behind him. The group had crawled through a storm drain hole in the cemetery.

From three different angles, three men approached the group. One was in military fatigues; the others looked like civilian soldiers. "I think we are in some kind of trouble," said Danny.

"Trouble?" asked Dirjke.

"Yeah, Unk, there are three people each with guns approaching us."

"Well, it looks like you will be some use for us Sid," said Dirjke. "I suggest you use your credentials and get us out of this mess."

"Yeah, they are probably just wondering why a group of people are exiting from a storm drain," added Barry.

"Sid, it can't be hard for you to think up a lie – or maybe they even work for you," said Danny.

"Freeze," commanded the stocky man in the military fatigues, as soon as he was close enough that he did not need to raise his voice.

"Sir, I am Sid Milliken," Sid replied, taking out his wallet. It was sopping wet and covered in dirt and grime. Sid's appearance was disheveled and his face was beginning to swell.

"What part of 'freeze' don't you understand?" shouted the man. He whispered into the microphone on his shoulder, "Targets immobilized, bring it around."

"Who do you think you are?"

"It doesn't matter who I am," stated the stoic figure. The careful choice of this man's words was not lost on Ana. She looked at the patch on the arm of the uniform.

"Sid, you know you surprise me. The real question was who this man represents. We are all servants to Kings."

"Take it easy young lady," answered Sid.

Danny looked the man's military camouflage up and down. Then he noticed the patch on the man's shoulder. There was a portion of the logo that looked familiar.

"The first thing I should tell you is that if you run, I will shoot you down."

"Got it," said Dirjke for the group. About ten seconds later, before the silence of having a gun pointed at you could get any more awkward, a van pulled up.

"In the vehicle," commanded the stocky man. The van had no windows and was bullet proof.

"Who are you?" asked Dirjke.

The man looked back and did not answer.

"Where are you taking us?" asked Dirjke.

No response.

While they were in the van, Dirjke's eyes locked on Danny's. At that moment, Danny made a motion with his left hand against his right shoulder. His index finger and thumb were connected in the universal 'okay' formation.

This secret message had mixed results on Barry and Ana. Ana looked back and smiled.

Barry, agreeing with Danny that they would be 'okay', made the same symbol back at him seconds later. Danny smiled and just shook his head. He was reminded of the fractured version of the story that Dirjke told with his dry sense of humor: you can lead a horse to water, but it takes a strong man to drown him.

Chapter 72

TAKEN TO MAYOR'S OFFICE
Friday, August 15, 2003 5:00pm

The kids, Dirjke, and Sid were taken into the back entrance of City Hall. The officials working in the building stopped and looked up as the group was escorted at gun point toward the Blue Room.

It was the largest press meeting space in the building. The room was painted light blue with white trim around the windows, which adorned curtains with gold lining to compliment the oil paintings on the walls.

Michael walked inside. The three men remained with their hands on their guns.

"Frisk him," said Michael, pointing to Sid.

"But wait, who are these people?" asked Sid.

"1st Battalion, 5th Field Artillery," said Michael.

"Ha," announced Barry, as he figured it out.

"Huh, well I am Sid Milliken. I work…"

"I know exactly, who you are," said Duroe.

"Perhaps, you will know them by their alternate name – the Hearts of Oak," said Dirjke in an authoritative teacher tone to his old adversary.

"Can't you tell from the patch on his arm?" asked Danny.

"Yeah, doesn't the tree in the crest remind you of anything? You know, I thought you were more intelligent," teased Ana.

"Great, Hearts of Oak, you are finally here," said Sid. But the man continued to move toward him with his gun pointed at Sid's chest.

"Wait… You can't. I'm…" said Sid.

"I don't care who you are. You are coming with us." Duroe escorted Sid out of the room.

Chapter 73

DIRJKE, SID, MAYOR, AND KIDS
Friday, August 15, 2003 5:15pm

"What just happened?" asked Dirjke, still standing in the Blue Room at City Hall.

"The Mayor of New York always has a card up his sleeve. That's what makes him the Mayor of New York. I could give you some story about a hidden book that was passed down from Mayor Jimmy Walker to me. But that's not the truth. Sometimes, you have to tell people who they are. That way they can help you."

"What do you mean?" asked Barry.

"Do you think that I haven't been listening to you and Dirjke for the past two days? Duroe helped restore power to the generators that continually prevent the subways from flooding. While I was on the phone with him, he told me that he was a part of the 1st Battalion, 5th Field Artillery. So I asked if they would assist."

"I hope you didn't tell them about the Deed," said Dirjke.

"You haven't found the Deed. Why would I do that?" answered Michael. "They are not Hearts of Oak," with a motion to the kids. They each looked at one another and smiled.

"I told Duroe that they were this island's first militia, which from a certain point of view supersedes their duty as the oldest regiment in the US Army – their genesis was on this island before the Declaration of Independence was signed. They raided the battery at the tip of Manhattan months before the colonies declared independence. I said I needed his help because of the blackout. He asked how they could help with no other questions asked."

"Wow, Mr. Mayor, impressive," exclaimed Ana.

"Thanks, this thing had gone on long enough. I mean, it was just a matter of time before someone got hurt, or even killed. I was willing to allow you guys to get to the last 'homes of death,' because I knew that none of you, and even Sid, would have stopped. Now, with that last avenue exhausted, we can all go home and leave this legend to rest."

"Not if I am correct," started Dirjke. He waived a small tapered piece of wood.

"Huh?" asked the whole group at once.

"Professor, we were all there. There was nothing in the last tomb of death. No Deed, no clue – nothing but clothes and bones."

"But when were those clothes from?" asked Dirjke.

"The 1600s," guessed Ana.

"Are you saying that we didn't go to Nicholas Fish's grave?" asked Barry.

"Exactly," said Dirjke.

"So now that the Mayor has gotten Sid off our tail, let's go back to the cemetery at St. Mark's and find Nicholas Fish's grave," said Danny in an intrepid fashion.

"Don't assume we went to the wrong grave," cautioned Dirjke. "Remember some really smart people including Hamilton and Washington planned this path to the Deed to Manhattan."

"Well, if we didn't go into the homes of death of the Hearts of Oak, where did we go?" asked Ana.

"I think we went to Peter Stuyvesant's homes of death. The clothes are from that era. But more importantly, Peter Stuyvesant had a peg leg and we found this tapered stick," said Dirjke. "The cemetery rests on Peter Stuyvesant's bowery, or farm. Peter Stuyvesant is buried within the grounds."

"But so what?" asked Danny.

"Peter Stuyvesant is the person who surrendered the island called New Amsterdam to the British who renamed it New York," said Dirjke.

"Surrendered, what do you mean? All this time we have been talking about who purchased the island," said Ana. "I am not sure I understand how you are phrasing things."

"He was the last man from the original company to likely have had possession of the document," replied Barry.

"Wait, I am lost," said Danny. "Whose grave did we go to?"

"Peter Stuyvesant's. He had a peg leg. In fact, Peter Stuyvesant had a peg leg with silver lining inlaid within the wood. He was known as Old Silver Leg," said Dirjke.

"You mean we opened the grave of Peter Stuyvesant?" asked Danny.

"Yes!" answered Dirjke.

"How can you know that?" asked Michael. Dirjke held up the tapered wooden stick he had been carrying for the past hour. "If you can't lie, it is better to just remain silent."

"And I am the politician," added Michael, mocking Dirjke's statement.

"Stuyvesant was missing the lower portion of his right leg," continued Barry. "In 1644, he led a battle at St. Martin and was hit by a cannon ball."

"And from that time forward, he used a peg leg to walk around wherever he went," stated Danny. "It's the perfect place to keep an important document."

"I think I agree with you," stated Michael. "We are going to need to split the wood open."

"Just how we started this," answered Dirjke.

"How far we've come from Wednesday morning when you scored open the stick with your eyeglasses. However, this job is going to require tools. We can't damage whatever may be inside during the process."

"Okay, here's how we are going to do this," said Michael. "Danny, there is a tool kit in Room 322."

"Ana, there is a first aid kit on the lower floor in Room 212."

"Okay," said Ana in an unsure tone.

"If we are dealing with the Deed to Manhattan, we at least need latex gloves," finished Michael.

Dirjke was standing there looking at Peter Stuyvesant's peg leg with a childlike grin on his face. His brown puppy-dog eyes let everyone know that he was in complete heaven right now.

"What about me?" asked Barry.

"I'm not so sure. I mean we have tools to open the casing and gloves to work with the document," said Michael.

Before Barry could let all the air out of his lungs, Dirjke said, "Can you bring a computer in here. We need to use the Internets."

"Marty, for God's sake, Internet is already plural. Now, Barry go to my office and get my laptop," ordered Michael.

"Yes, sir," replied Barry. Barry dashed out of the office to his destination. Michael and Dirjke were alone.

"So old friend," asked Michael, "what are we going to do?"

"First, we see who gets the island. Then we decide what to do next," replied Dirjke.

"Who?" asked Michael. "Damn, that's right."

"Exactly," replied Dirjke.

"Is there any reason that we need a computer?" asked Michael.

"Yeah, Peter Stuyvesant saw and read the Deed to Manhattan, unlike the Hearts of Oak who must have only found its location. One other thing must be true: Peter Stuyvesant negotiated the surrender of Manhattan as the only one with knowledge of who actually held title to the island."

"Two days ago, I would have been skeptical there would be any connection, but now I guess let's wait and see," finished Michael.

Chapter 74

DIRJKE REVEALS DEED AND TELLS ALL
Friday, August 15, 2003 6:05pm
Within ten minutes, each of the kids returned with their assigned items.

"All right, let's get to business," began Michael.

Dirjke was in the process of pulling off the silver tip on Peter Stuyvesant's peg leg. The object was pressed between his knees. His right hand was twisting the battered silver cap. After about twenty seconds, he got it free.

"Let's see if anything will slide out like a poster roll." He held the peg leg above his head and looked into the hole.

"I doubt it, Marty. The taper on the piece of wood makes it impossible to fall out."

Danny had pliers, a screwdriver, and a small hammer. He was waiting for Dirjke's experiment to finish.

"Who is going to split this open?" asked Dirjke.

"Unk, I had two semesters of shop class. I got this."

Michael shrugged his shoulders in Dirjke's direction.

Danny used a wedge and a hammer and tapped at the top of the peg where it met with Peter Stuyvesant just below the knee. "Now be careful, Danny," said Ana.

"Yeah, the piece of wood is already over three hundred years old."

"Don't worry," answered Danny. He continued to split open the wood casing along its length, toward the narrower end of the primitive prosthetic.

Dirjke took that object and broke it open like a loaf of bread. A rolled up piece of parchment revealed itself inside the old peg leg.

Ana moved a table close by from under the window adjacent to the mayor's podium in the Blue Room. Dirjke placed the peg onto the table. The group crowded around.

"See, how much older that paper looks than the parchment we came across over the past couple nights."

"Marty, I think it is your turn," said Michael. Ana handed Dirjke the gloves. He snapped them onto his hands. Dirjke then unwrapped and placed the document on the table. The paper was a light brown color. It was drafted in an ornate script with ink that was almost as clear today as the day it was drafted.

"This is glorious," said Danny.

"Not until we read it," said Michael. Ana placed the laptop at the other end of the table, as she waited for it to load.

"You don't really think this is written in English, do you?" asked Ana.

"I'm sure Dirjke here knows enough Dutch to translate the document," said Michael.

"Negative," said Dirjke, as he lowered his head.

"Okay, what's our next best option?" asked Danny.

"We get a dictionary and translate it word by word," said Ana. "How many other times have we translated a code one symbol at a time during this journey?"

"Ana, translating the Deed with a Dutch dictionary amounts to a really challenging task. We don't know the alphabet. There has to be a better way," answered Dirjke.

"Wait, a minute," interrupted Barry. "If Peter Stuyvesant had the Deed and no one knew it, he would have protected it in the Articles of Capitulation. We can use that document as a key."

"What?" asked the group.

"The Articles of Capitulation is the document that peaceably transferred the island of Manhattan from the Dutch to the English. It is the 'Second Deed to Manhattan' so to speak."

"I must admit that I am impressed with your analysis. At this point, it's safe to say that Peter Stuyvesant would have sought to protect the Deed, even during the surrender of the island," said Dirjke.

"So what does the Deed to Manhattan have to do with the Articles of Capitulation?" asked Ana.

"Any deed only has two important words: who has it and who it goes to. We know one. We can translate the other word from the Dutch contained in the Articles of Capitulation, the 1664 surrender of Manhattan."

"Barry might be right," suggested Danny. "Look at these two prominent words toward the bottom of the page. We should translate them first."

"They look like the names or signatures of the parties to the agreement," added Ana.

"Right, look, one of the names on the Deed is 'Lenape,'" exclaimed Dirjke. "It's spelled phonetically."

"What is the other word?" asked Michael.

Danny was searching the Internet for a PDF version of the Articles of Capitulation to decipher the one Dutch word on the page that determines who received the island.

"Don't worry. It doesn't say Dutch West India Company. I can read that in Dutch," said Dirjke.

Dirjke, Michael, Danny, Barry, and Ana each reviewed the Articles of Capitulation against the English translation.

Danny placed the Dutch and English version side by side on the computer screen so that everybody could review it all at once. There was silence for about forty seconds as each person read as furiously as possible through the Dutch version for the symbols they found on the old parchment from 1626.

"Got it!" exclaimed Dirjke.

"Where?" asked Danny.

"Read Article 4 aloud," said Dirjke. Danny began:

306

"If any inhabitant have a mind to remove himself he shall have a year and six weeks from this day to remove himself, wife, children, servants, goods, and to dispose of his lands here."

"'Inhabitant' is the word identical to the first source document – the Deed to Manhattan," said Dirjke. "I can't believe that statement would ever leave my lips."

"Manhattan was sold to the inhabitants?" asked Michael "What does that mean?"

"Yeah, wasn't that the Lenape Indians?" asked Ana.

But before Dirjke could explain further, Barry exclaimed, "Wow! The Dutch West India Company was true to form."

"Huh?" asked Ana.

"You are saying that the Dutch West India Company bought shares in the island of Manhattan," stated Dirjke, finishing Barry's thoughts.

"Exactly, they only bought a right to trade here. They merely exchanged a right to do business here. They bought a right to inhabit the island – for trade and commerce," explained Barry.

"Kind of like every other person who has ever inhabited this island, for even one night on vacation, or business," added Ana.

"It is beautiful," said Dirjke with a wide grin on his face.

"Unk, it is cool, maybe even interesting, but it is not beautiful," said Danny.

"But it is. Manhattan belongs to the people who inhabit it. We are the ones responsible for this island's success. Manhattan – New York – goes only where we take it," stated Dirjke.

"Are you angling to be my next speech writer?" teased Michael.

"He's right. Think how well the inhabitants of Manhattan handled the blackout. Even the commuters who were stuck here for the night. The overnight population must have swelled, but crime did not, a credit to Manhattan's inhabitants," added Barry.

"See, Barry is trying to become your next speech writer," laughed Ana.

"So the island itself was the first 'stock exchange,'" added Michael.

"Amazing," said Dirjke. "The root of New York's tolerance rests in the right to inhabit the island negotiated alongside the Lenape Indians."

"Marty, I have a few questions," announced Michael.

"How did you get to Peter Stuyvesant's grave?"

"That is the secret to the path of the Hearts of Oak," said Barry, not letting Dirjke speak.

"Huh?" asked Danny. "I am just so thrilled we won."

"The path of the Hearts of Oak leads to the 'home of death', but not the one you'd think. Instead of going to Nicholas Fish's grave, the tunnel under the only street exempted from the grid plan of 1811 leads to Peter Stuyvesant's grave."

"Then why did Peter Stuyvesant last have the Deed to Manhattan?" quizzed Danny.

"For the reason that he was the last employee of the Dutch West India Company to work on the island, that's why," said Dirjke.

Ana spoke up. "I'm a little confused. What does this have to do with the Revolutionary War? I thought we spent the past three days chasing clues left behind by Washington and the Hearts of Oak."

"True," answered Dirjke. "See, as I said days ago, there was a militia that raided the battery at the tip of Manhattan months before we declared our independence in

July 1776. Apparently they learned its location. Our first clue, 'I pray whereby you will find it' applies to not only Washington on Evacuation Day, but to Peter Stuyvesant and the Deed to Manhattan – with Stuyvesant buried under a Church."

"You can't get more literal than that. You mean that small battle before the fourth of July decided the fate of the island?" asked Danny.

"More than that," said Barry. "It is the basis of this country's independence. In this document rests the current sovereign nation known as the United States of America," announced Barry, as he pointed to the piece of paper with enthusiasm. "The British attempted to burn New York to the ground in the hope that if they could not have the Deed, no one would."

"Yes. And from within this militia, known as the Corsicans, the Hearts of Oak formed."

"They couldn't have chosen a better name," stated Michael.

"For real," said Danny. "I mean, naming your group after a passage from *The Odyssey*, which is really a coded map that leads to the Deed to Manhattan."

"No one ever called Washington and Hamilton fools," said Ana.

"Amazing," announced Michael. "So in 1783, we ended the British's formal occupation of Manhattan since…when," asked Michael.

"1664," said Dirjke.

"That is the original date on the Seal of New York," replied Michael.

"Washington and Hamilton created a map that was hidden within *The Odyssey* quote. Amazing," added Barry.

"Apparently the reference was on the back of the Stuyvesant crests originally contained within the Stuyvesant mansion on 5th Ave, now the Ukrainian Institute. The Hearts of Oak passage was all that stood between someone and the Deed to Manhattan. The path of the Hearts of Oak was contained within that passage. All it took was someone intrepid enough to make it happen," added Dirjke.

"Professor, you know if we had run your pencil over the other side of the Hamilton crest, we might have uncovered the same code."

"Yeah, I bet the salty mucky air had an effect," said Danny.

"Think how close we were the first time we went to St. Mark's," lamented Ana.

"Very true," answered Dirjke.

"Who changed the seal to 1625?" asked Barry.

"I'm not sure," answered Dirjke. "It doesn't really matter. Apparently, people have pursued the Deed for centuries. It just proves that someone knew enough to know that the purchase of Manhattan was the fault line of the island. That the Seal was changed to 1625, one year before the date of the actual purchase, says enough. I will leave historical analysis of this issue to the conspiracy theorists."

The last part caught Barry by surprise. He was thinking about how he was going to look into the City Council records to review the votes.

Ana recognized the look on Barry's face. "Don't worry, Barry. When you uncover this arcane information, I will listen with a new perspective."

Michael shook his head and put his index finger and his thumb on his temples.

"What now old friend?" asked Dirjke.

"Yeah, Mr. Mayor, the good guys won," said Barry looking around at the room.

"Now the good guys have to be modest in victory. Understood? I don't want you to have a few drinks at some Harvard bar and start bragging about your adventures. That goes for all of you."

"Understood," agreed Barry, Danny, and Ana.

"What is your plan for the Deed?" asked Dirjke.

"I am not sure. The way I see it, if the Dutch West India Company bought the island for the inhabitants, the people who live on the island are the people who own the island."

"In a way that has always been the case," said Ana. "My father used to tell me in the early nineties that 'the only reason New York has a crime and grime problem is because New Yorkers tolerate it.'"

"Precisely, the inhabitants of the island hold its destiny," stated Michael. "I don't intend to release it to the public, for now, but I will consider the idea further."

"I am sure that is the best idea," answered Dirjke.

"Listen to yourself, Unk," said Danny. "How can you, of all people, argue against the disclosure of this document – the birth certificate of Manhattan?"

"Call me when you need the document re-hidden," replied Dirjke.

"Re-hidden? Is that even a word?" asked Ana.

"Opportunities will present themselves," said Michael. "I am not closing the door on the idea. And I want you kids to truly know the debt this city owes you, despite the fact that they will never know what you did or accomplished."

"Really, is that what's in it for us?" asked Danny.

"Danny," warned Dirjke.

"C'mon Unk, you saved the city. We followed along and helped and no one is ever going to know it."

"That has nothing to do with it. The journey is the reward. We followed the path of the Hearts of Oak, a coded and hidden message that led us to the Deed to Manhattan. Imagine the larger world that you are a part of now that you found it."

"Yeah, it was really amazing, Professor. You are the best tour guide I ever had," added Ana.

"Mr. Mayor, do you think that I could maybe send you my resume? I would like to help out around here during the December and January break."

"You can't even wait until the summer to get back here!" Barry's goody-goody ways annoyed Ana.

"Sure," said Michael with a smile. "How else are we going to find a way to hide this damn thing?"

"Between now and then, if I should expire suddenly..."

"Or if you are hit by a bolt of lightning..." interrupted Danny.

"We will do what Hearts of Oaks does," said Dirjke for the group. "You are going to be fine."

"Where are you going to keep it?" asked Barry.

Dirjke interrupted, "Hopefully we don't have to find that out."

"But if need be, I am sure you could figure it out," concluded Michael.

"I have to admit, I am ready to go to my own home, finally." It was a reference to where Dirjke thought Michael would keep the Deed. "A permanent place will present itself," concluded Dirjke.

Ana's cell phone began to ring. "My parents...I forgot that they got back from their yearly European vacation today with my younger brother. Looks like my evening is taken care of."

"What do you have planned, Barry?" asked Danny. "I am ready to hit the New York town. I feel like I own it."

"I'm not sure. A few of my friends who go to Columbia are having a get-together on the Upper West Side. It's not too far from Dirjke's apartment. I am too amped up to rest now."

"Me too, yes. I am ready to see more of the town."

"You guys have too much energy. I am going home. Going to steep some tea and watch the news, or at least what they tell us the news is. Now that this is over, I can actually think about how tired I am."

"Can you believe what we accomplished since Wednesday?" asked Ana.

"I know," said Danny.

"Looks like we are all headed uptown," announced Dirjke.

"Might I suggest the subway," said Michael.

"Are you thinking what I think you're thinking?" responded Dirjke. "I might have enough energy for this one last field trip."

"What is it?" asked Ana.

"The location is the stuff of popular legend," answered Dirjke.

Chapter 75

SID EXITS
Friday August 15, 2003 7:00pm
Sid recognized the subway station. Hell's Kitchen. Four blocks from his rooming house. The World Wide Plaza building was above this station, 50th Street on the C/E line. The site was once the location of Madison Square Garden.

The present building at this location was capped with a pyramid that imitates the pyramid on the back of a one dollar bill. One of the Pentagon's most trusted law firms worked inside. Sid was escorted to an anonymous room inside this firm's leased space. The view from the windows on two sides of the room provided a near 180 degree view of midtown. The walls were lined with a dark mahogany wood and classic legal books that the attorneys in the firm had stopped using years ago.

"Seems like you've had one hell of a trip to New York," remarked Hoffson, as he swiveled his chair to reveal his face.

"You would not believe it. There was a terrorist event that must never reach public discourse. The blackout was a trigger to expose this country's weak infrastructure. We were minutes away from an economic terrorist event."

"What are you talking about?" asked Hoffson.

"The point of the blackout was to get the people out of the subways and tunnels. The attack was to our system of commerce – commuting to work. The intent was to cripple the New York Transit System and hopefully all trains from Long Island, Connecticut, and New Jersey, if they got lucky."

"What about the bad actors who caused this event?" asked Hoffson.

"I killed one of them. One of them remains in society," stated Sid.

"We have got to find this man," said Hoffson.

"Relax," replied Sid. "Let me do my job. The best enemies never have to reveal themselves during the crime. He failed that test. I will find him and as soon as I do, he will be our newest asset."

"The Deed to Manhattan?" asked Hoffson.

"I don't know what you are talking about," said Sid.

"The Mayor told me you negotiated with an artifact. If I am not wrong, that was the whole reason you left the Pentagon for New York. That press release about some stick found during the excavation of the new South Ferry Subway Terminal."

"General, my ability to place myself within the theater is my talent. It is why I hold my post," responded Sid. "Here is the artifact from the press release that caused all of this. I had a hunch it would cause a furor and boy was I right."

"I am not so sure that is the truest interpretation of the facts," said Hoffson.

"It will all be in my report," said Sid. "May I go General?"

"Sid Milliken, I am going to have my eyes on you. I want your report in two weeks."

"You will get it," answered Sid.

"You'll live to fight another day."

"General, you will get my report, analyze my actions. You will see I did nothing wrong."

"I will consider the source when I read it."

"Don't ever question my integrity or loyalty to my office. Look at the results."

"Fair point Sid. Dismissed."

Chapter 76

DIRJKE AND KIDS EXIT
Friday August 15, 2003 7:30pm

Dirjke was staring at the paper lying on the table with his left hand covering his mouth. His hair was tattered and his clothes were muddy, but as his wire glasses hung halfway down his nose, he nearly refused to blink.

"I am only gonna let you look at it for a few more minutes," said Michael. Barry was on the other end of the table with his hand on his hips and his nose about ten inches from the document.

"I do have one cool thing to show you kids," said Michael. "Danny, it is the closest thing I can offer as a reward for saving the Deed to Manhattan."

"What is it?" asked the group.

"There is a private exit from this building to the old City Hall Subway Station, that's what," said Michael.

"Amazing," said Ana. "It's where the 6 train turns around."

"The station has most of the original interior. It has a classic look. It is also the most private way to enter and exit City Hall. I take the subway most weekdays to work. I just stay on one stop farther than every other transit rider."

"I heard, Mr. Mayor, that some tourists stay on the 6 train at Brooklyn Bridge Station to see the transit system's most iconic subway station," said Barry.

"I am following you kids one stop and then I am going to catch a cab," said Dirjke.

"Never too tired for a historical field trip," added Michael. "We need a little more time to bask in our accomplishment." Michael put his arm over Dirjke's shoulder.

"Indeed," answered Dirjke. "I will never ignore one of your emails ever again."

"Okay let's close this up," said Michael, as he pointed to the Deed to Manhattan.

Dirjke and Barry lifted the paper off the table. Dirjke carefully rolled up the parchment. He placed it back into the alcove of Stuyvesant's peg leg. Michael reached in and united the two pieces of wood.

"Now, put the cap on it," said Michael. Dirjke picked up the silver cap and blew into it. Then he placed the cap back on the end.

"There, that should do it for now," said Michael. He placed the object under his arm. "Let's get out of here."

The group walked out of the Blue Room with Michael in the rear.

Chapter 77

A NEW HEARTS OF OAK IS FORMED

Sunday, June 7, 2008 12:00pm

It was a gray day in New York and a day that passed without substantial press coverage. The only recognized political figure was a United States representative from the fifteenth district in Harlem. The kids were standing on the hill on 141st Street on the corner of St. Nicholas Avenue.

"Can you guys believe we are here right now?" asked Ana. She was a few years older, but in the same great shape.

"Hamilton's house is being moved to St. Nicholas Park on the edge of City College. It was city land, but a Federal Landmark for the National Parks Service and administered by the United States Department of the Interior," said Barry.

"Do you think the Mayor is here?" asked Danny.

"No, I know for a fact he is not," answered Barry.

"It was very thoughtful of him to extend this information regarding the movement of Hamilton's house to a third location," added Ana.

"True. It has been nearly five years since our odyssey," said Danny.

"The Federal Government supplied the funds, at least according to the signs around Hamilton's house," said Barry.

"But that is not the true result," retorted Ana.

"Anyway, the home is freed from its confines between a church and a red brick building from the 1970s."

"I feel like I am looking at the past," said Danny.

"Well, I am thinking about the past," said Ana in an annoyed tone. A lot can happen in five years. The group's lives had changed in ways they had not imagined since August 2003. The group had had their ups and downs since

2003, but each was doing well in their own way. They knew that this day was not about them.

It was also for all purposes a whisper on the day's news. A whimsical story to be dismissed soon after it was heard.

Only one man could make that happen. But Sid was not on their minds.

"Calm down every one," said Barry. "This scene is magical. Hamilton's house is being moved again."

"Let's just enjoy the moment. We have all been through a lot. Think about where you were almost five years ago," finished Danny.

"Amazing," added Ana.

"Where is Dirjke?" asked Barry.

"He is up close for the placement of the house in its newest location. You can imagine what this day means to him," said Danny.

"I bet. I mean I did not expect the invitation, but I received it from the Mayor, a personal call, no less," said Ana.

"Me too," added Danny.

The group looked on as Hamilton's house was maneuvered into position. Horses were not being used this time.

"This patch of Manhattan is still within the acreage of Hamilton's original estate," informed Barry.

Danny laughed to himself. "Look at the irony of what is occurring before our eyes. I bet you and my uncle never thought something like this was possible."

Barry shook his head and smiled at the accident of history he was a part of. "You know, they basically dismantled the house to move it. Imagine if that note was found by someone else."

"Very true," agreed Ana.

A few seconds later, they saw Dirjke walking in their direction. "Can you believe it?" asked Dirjke, as he got within ear shot of the young adults.

It was a question to which he already knew the answer.

ABOUT THE AUTHOR:

Jeffrey Rubinstein grew up in North Miami Beach, Florida. He obtained a degree in history from Columbia University in the City of New York. Currently, he practices civil litigation. He has resided on Manhattan since 1996 and in Hell's Kitchen since 2000.

ACKNOWLEDGEMENTS:

Most importantly, *Evacuation Day & The Lost Deed to Manhattan* is dedicated to my Mother and Father. Their guidance and support is a continual source of strength. I am forever grateful to both of you in vastly different, but equally important ways. To my Brother, Andrea, and Landon, thanks for your tolerance. To Sandy, the one with the most Rubinstein years among us. I cannot leave out the impact of others – not with us today – Marty, Bob, and Dottie. My only regret is that you will not read *Evacuation Day*.

Next, I must mention the friends who I bombarded with this endeavor. Thank you for listening. My Aces. Alyssa, the first person not named Rubinstein to read *Evacuation Day*. Kenul, what can I say? Derrick, you heard my rants more than anyone in 4N. Thank you. Lucy, for being you. Joelle Chase-Bartfield. Ella Aiken. Sarah Litt. Nadine. Max Litt. Donna Azoulay. Kirl Francis. Ed Haynes.

Professionally, I must thank PoppTech, the cover by Graphicz X Designs, and editing by Gary Smailes and Sarah Ridley of BubbleCow.

I must thank the United States Institute of Heraldry and the Army Trademark Licensing Program for the use of the images of the Coat of Arms and Insignia for the 1st Battalion 5th Field Artillery.

Evacuation Day & The Lost Deed to Manhattan, owes itself to the contributions of these people and many others.

16863386R00172

Made in the USA
Charleston, SC
14 January 2013